BOY'S
POND

BOY'S POND

A Novel

Warren J. Stucki

SUNSTONE PRESS
SANTA FE

Sunstone books may be purchased for educational, business, or sales promotional use. For information please write: Special Markets Department, Sunstone Press, P.O. Box 2321, Santa Fe, New Mexico 87504-2321.

Library of Congress Cataloging-in-Publication Data:

Stucki, Warren J., 1946–
    Boy's pond: a novel / by Warren J. Stucki.
        p.cm
    ISBN: 978-0-86534-976-6
        1. Nuclear weapons—Testing—Health aspects—Fiction.
        2. Radiation victims—Fiction.
    I. Title.

PS3619. T84 B69 2001
813'.6—dc21   2001034472

Published in  SUNSTONE PRESS
Post Office Box 2321
Santa Fe, NM 87504-2321 / USA
(505) 988-4418 / *orders only* (800) 243-5644
FAX (505) 988-1025
www.sunstonepress.com

This book is dedicated to:

The hundreds of downwinder victims, many to whom I am personally acquainted. They were unsuspecting pawns in this great American tragedy.

Sheldon Nisson, Bill Phoenix, and Stan Bostwick, friends that lived and died in those turbulent times.

Doug Gubler, Mitch Hafen, John Graff and Lee Ence, friends that lived and survived those turbulent times.

My wife Linda. Without her persistent prodding, her penchant for perfection and her willingness to shoulder the routine chores of living, this work might have never been completed.

ACKNOWLEDGMENTS

Thane Hafen for his gift of a treasured book that helped tremendously with my research.

Art Long for his skill in creating the maps.

John Graff for many donated hours. He read, proofread, criticized and praised the manuscript.

Alan Boyack for generous and competent legal advice.

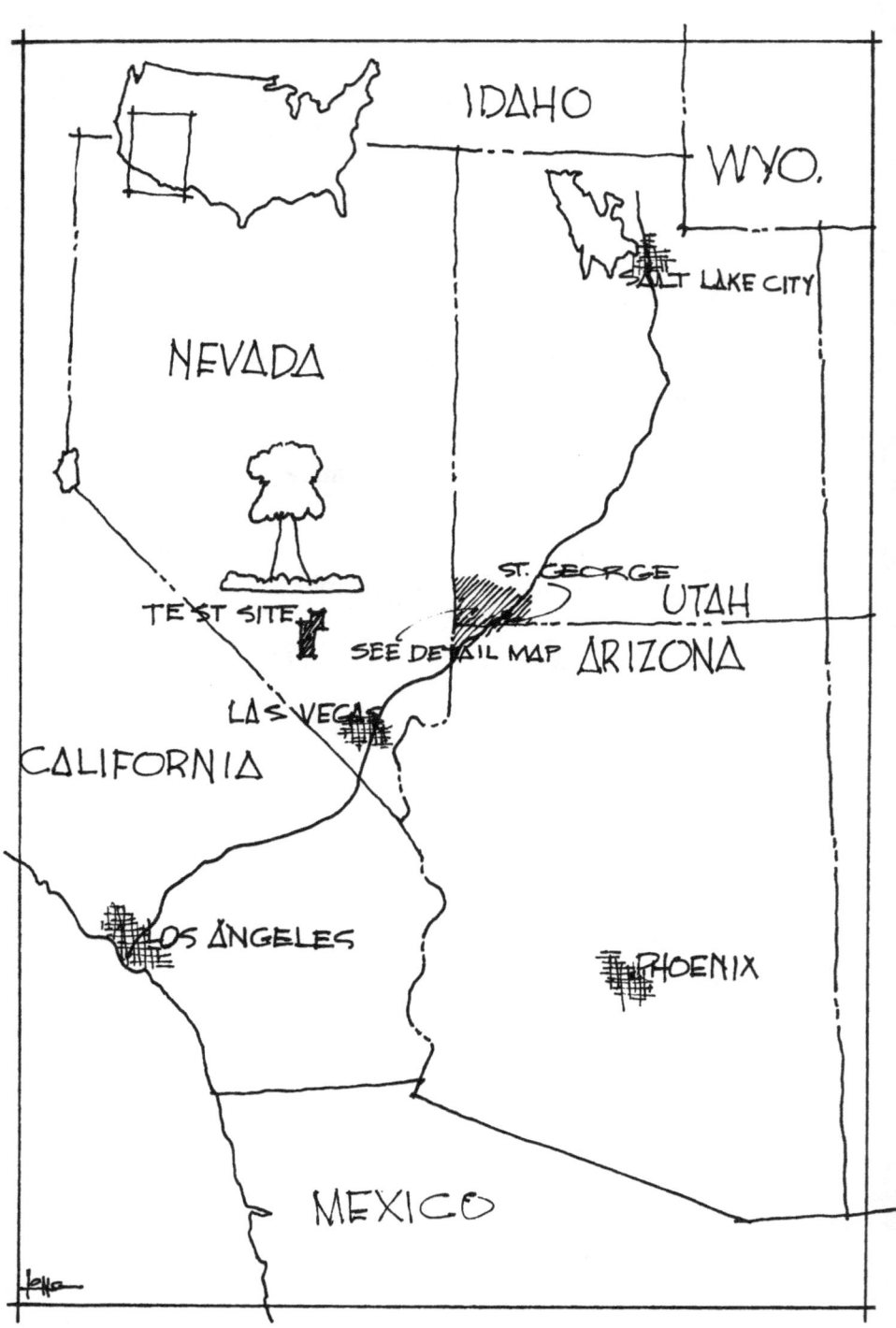

IDAHO

WYO.

SALT LAKE CITY

NEVADA

ST. GEORGE

TEST SITE

UTAH

SEE DETAIL MAP

ARIZONA

LAS VEGAS

CALIFORNIA

LOS ANGELES

PHOENIX

MEXICO

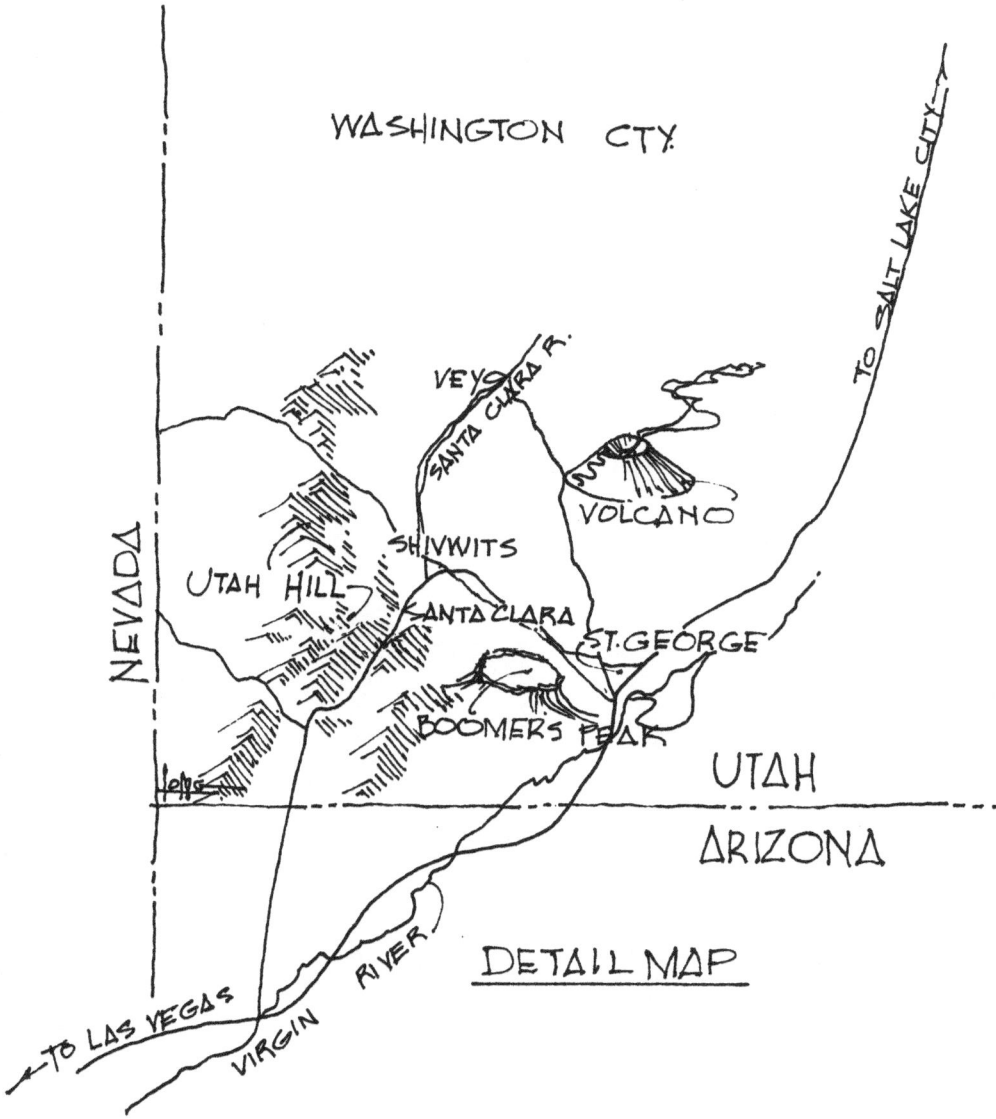

WASHINGTON CTY.

NEVADA

TO SALT LAKE CITY→

VEYO

SANTA CLARA R.

VOLCANO

SHIVWITS

UTAH HILL

SANTA CLARA

ST. GEORGE

BOOMERS PEAK

UTAH

ARIZONA

←TO LAS VEGAS

VIRGIN RIVER

DETAIL MAP

1

Adrenalin indiscriminately mixed with Colt 45 created a raspberry flush on the young men's cheeks and brought a reckless gleam to their eyes. The fire added a fierce golden glow to both. The six of them danced around it, howling into the empty night like spirits of perdition, their shadows ballooning large in the firelight which contorted wildly with each movement of the inebriated dancers.

The bonfire, like a nimble fencer, flirted with the darkness, alternating flamboyant charges with rapier swift retreats. When it flared, it outlined a circular ridge faintly visible against the slightly brighter backdrop of the sky. From every point on the horizon the curved ridge sloped evenly back to the fire, creating an inverted cone that doubled both as a fire pit and a primal, dusty stage for the dancers' sneaker-clad feet. The dance music did not come from tightly stretched leather drums but rather from a transistor radio that discharged the smudged strains of Bill Haley's *Rock Around the Clock*.

The fire was a foul thing. It spewed thick plumes of oily smoke accompanied by the harsh, pungent odor of burning rubber. The fetid fuel consisted of an assortment of Goodyear, Goodrich, Michelin, Kelly Springfield and Royal tires as well as a sprinkling of some lesser known brands. Other than being rubber, the only other common denominator was that they were all threadbare.

As he paced out of time with the music, one dancer seemed jittery. He cast a rueful eye at the group, then looked at his wristwatch. At times, the firelight buffed his sandy blonde hair, polishing it to a luminous bronze. When he turned, his facial lines deepened in shadow as the firelight bounced off the high ground, his forehead, cheeks and chin. The play of light and shadows accentuated the solid refined features of a Swiss-German heritage and at times gave a spark of color to his pale blue eyes. Slightly incongruous with this classical Teutonic image were prominent high cheek bones that reflected some minor American Indian lineage. The only flaws in an otherwise handsome face were twisted upper teeth that conjured the image of a run-down white picket fence. As a result, Jack Tobler Kunz seldom smiled, and he was not smiling now.

"Mick!" He hailed one of the dancers. "Hey, Mick, don't you think we oughta be going?" He again glanced at his watch then continued, "The fire's been going for twenty minutes. Surely, someone's spotted it by now."

Rather than giving him an immediate answer, Mick grabbed another Colt 45 from the icy slush in the wash tub and tossed it to Jack.

"Cm'om on J.T., lew—sum up. Don't see your dad, or by God the bishop or the fuzz heer yet," Mick blurted. His face flushed in the firelight, abundant freckles gleaming like stippled brass.

"But it's been twenty minutes," Jack said, tapping his wristwatch.

"An' affer the cops do get the word, still be twenny minutes more afore they can get here. An' are they gonna just climb right up here? Fuck, I think not. Shit, they're gonna pace around and jerk-off for a while, 'fraid the goddamn thing'll blow. We got at least twenny more minutes. Affer all, we are talkin' about Saint George's finest. Ya–hooo!" Mick bellowed at no one in particular, then danced away, jerking to the beat of the music.

With a sigh Jack sat heavily on a ragged, lava outcropping just outside the ring of light. The sharp angle of the rock bit at his buttock and the rancid smoke chafed his nostrils and burned his eyes. With growing apprehension he surveyed the neo-pagan dancers still frolicking around the fire. Perhaps his father was right after all. These constant pranks, this drinking and carousing were going to get them into serious trouble someday. Maybe tonight.

It had been Jack's idea to transform the extinct volcano into this, an active geyser belching black smoke and spitting darts of fire into the warm southern Utah night. According to Mr. McCormick, his geology teacher at Dixie Junior College, the last time this volcano erupted was forty thousand years ago. But even before that the area had already been inhabited by the Anasazi Indians, predecessors of the present day Paiutes and Navajos. Jack could imagine the catastrophic scene of the havoc, confusion and destruction this very volcano must have created for the early Indians. Instinctively, Jack touched his cheek bones. His mother had descended from those Indians. Or at least, half of her had.

After the geology field trip, Jack had mentioned this to Mick and said how cool it would be if they could turn this extinct volcano into an active one. Bad mistake. If Jack was the thinker of the group, Mick was surely the organizer. When Mick seized an idea he almost always saw it to fruition.

Jack swatted a waft of black smoke from his nostrils and remembered how he had brought Mick up here to plan the caper a month ago. They had selected a switchback, serpentine path up the vertical slope of the volcano but even at that their sneakers lost traction from the ball-bearing action of the cinders.

"Goddamn it, Easy," Alan whined. "Give me a fucking beer!"

Jack was shaken out of his reverie as Easy Earl held a six-pack above his head and Alan danced under him like a baited six-year-old.

It was Mick who had masterminded the midnight raids on the tire stores, virtually cleaning them out of everything that was used or discarded. And it was Mick who had selected this night and organized the other guys to bring their pickup trucks and haul the tires eight miles out of town to the volcano. Looking like an Egyptian foreman at the pyramids, Mick pleaded, cajoled and even cursed them into completing the task. Reluctantly, the six of them had dragged scores of tires and two five-gallon cans of gasoline up the five-hundred-foot almost vertical slope to the cone of the volcano. This in and of itself was a feat, like climbing a mountain dusted with marbles. Of course, three cases of Colt 45 didn't hurt. The malt liquor rapidly changed an impossible task into a party.

The end result, Jack had to admit, was spectacular. It was hard for him to visualize that an actual volcanic eruption could appear more real than this. Flames leaped thirty feet into the night sky accompanied by billowing plumes of thick black smoke. Surely molten lava would follow, slopping over the cone, coursing down the slopes, seeking out the dry washes as like water, it searched for lower ground. Without question, this spectacle would be seen from the highway and perhaps the flames would also be visible in Saint George itself, or even from their homes four miles to the west of town in Santa Clara. If it were visible from that far away, they certainly didn't have more than twenty minutes.

"Mick!" Jack half-pleaded, half-shouted above the din of the revelry. "Mick, we've got to go. They should be here any minute. I can't afford to get arrested and neither can you. We gotta go!"

Mick lurched toward Jack, still trying to keep time with the music. "Not even sure we're breakin' any friggin' law. There any law against startin' a bonfire and social—iz—ing with friends?" His tongue thickened like flour gravy as he tripped on the word.

"Shoot, Mick. There's more to this than just socializing. What about the tires? Someone's going to want to know where we got them. And I'll bet there's a law against promoting public panic. Like you can't stand up in a crowded theater and shout fire. This is going to make a lot of people nervous."

"Ye—eer right and they're not going to start climbin' the damn thing til they're sure it's not going to blow up in their friggin' faces and bury them asp—I mean ass-deep in burning ash. They'll probably set up a barri—barrica—those goddamn little white fences a half mile around. Shit, we're puttin' on as good a show here as they do at Yucca Flats. Maybe they'll give us a commend—a commenda—a goddamn metal for puttin' on a good show. Yeah, that's it. Were not criminals, we're en—ter—tainers." Mick doubled over and howled at his joke.

"Mick, what they're going to do is throw our butts in jail. We can't have a criminal record. Not if we're going on missions. You can stay if you want but I'm leaving," Jack said, his face hardened with determination. Then he softened a bit and added, "I would really feel a lot better if you would come with me."

Suddenly the melancholic wailing of police sirens faintly pierced the thick, smoky air and somehow they seemed oddly appropriate for this peculiar night. Abruptly, the young men, looking like a battalion of marines on a beachhead, wriggled to the crater lip, keeping their heads low. South of them on the valley floor Jack could see a long, broken strand of flashing red lights snaking up Highway 18 toward them. At this altitude the police lights looked anything but ominous. Instead, they appeared cheerful, almost festive, like a string of blinking Christmas lights. For a minute, the young men were mesmerized by the spectacle.

"Let's get the hell out here!" yelled Easy Earl, who looked every bit like the defensive tackle he was.

"Whoa, not so fast," Mick said, assuming his accustomed role as leader. "I wanna see what they do. See if they think this is a real volcano. See if they start climbin' up right away or if they block off the friggin' highway and start a damn dis—ass—ter drill or somethin'. Just keep low and out of sight. We've got plenny of time. If they start up we'll just slide our butts down the backside and hike over to Diamond Valley where the trucks are. By the time they git to the top we'll be in our trucks and outta here."

"I agree with Easy. We should leave right now," Jack insisted. He knew he was the only one of the group who had the guts to disagree with Mick once he had made a decision.

"No J.T., let's stay. We got plenny of time and this might be kinda fun. We might learn something, like how our offici—how cops cope with a stimulated—a simu—with a friggin' fake disaster," Mick slurred but his tone had the unmistakable inflection that there would be no more discussion.

It was just as Mick predicted. One squad car stopped about a half mile south. The other sped about the same distance north of the volcano. Ant-sized figures marched out of the cars and quickly set up road barricades. Four other squad cars roared past the south barricade and parked in a flat area just below.

The boys could see diminutive figures gesturing wildly and they could occasionally pick up a word.

"Do you think we should call—."

"Hell no—goddamn kids—."

"I don't know—could blow—."

"Blow—my ass—kids."

"I don't—up there." More gesturing from the stick figures below.

By now several cars had stopped behind the barricades and a small throng of frightened motorists had gathered at each check point.

Nervously, they pointed up at the spewing, belching pinnacle and some ran for their cars. Two ground their vehicles into reverse, then sped back down the road.

Flat on their bellies, the boys peered over the edge and giggled as they surveyed the panic below.

"Those crazy bastards don't know what to do!" Mick gloated, then almost shouted, "Run for your lives! Run for your bomb shelters, you damn fools!"

Flushed with excitement and alcohol, Easy Earl inched further over the lip and bellowed, "The Russians are coming. No—the Ruskies are here and they're blowing up the goddamn place!"

Below, the deputies ceased their gesturing. They had heard the over-exuberant Earl.

"I told—goddamn kids." One deputy pointed up, then continued, "Me and Clayton—up. You two—around." The deputies separated and two quickly started to scale the face of the volcano. Grunting and cursing, they skated on the cinders. Their hand-held flashlights bobbed erratically in the night sky with each slip of a foot.

"Well boys, it's time to go," Mick commanded. "Grab your shit. Jack, you get the radio. Greg, grab the wash tub and Easy throw the rest of that gas on the fire, can and all."

"That's too dangerous, Mick," Jack protested. "That thing'll blow in seconds. Earl just leav—"

"Then I guess we better get our butts in gear." Mick didn't let Jack finish. "When we go over the lip, throw the friggin' can on the fire Earl, then run like hell. Let's do it."

As the boys ran to the opposite side of the cone, one forgot to retrieve his jacket from the pile that littered the ground, shed in the fire's heat like the skins of molting rattlesnakes. Jack grabbed the transistor radio and in two leaps crested the lip and started sliding down the slope. The others, including Mick, were already ahead of him. All except Easy Earl. This was insane. Where was Earl? A wave of guilt stabbed Jack in the chest. He should have helped Earl or at least waited for him. Earl was much too drunk to pull off a stunt like this, or perhaps that was the very reason he was willing to do it.

Ka-boom! The night sky flashed a brilliant orange and the

ground beneath Jack convulsed, propelling him several feet further down the unstable slope. Instantly, the heavens were alive with flaming shards of burning rubber. Jack rolled to his right to dodge a blazing missile, then immediately had to brush another off his pant leg. Oh God, where was Earl? This was crazy. Then, just to his left, Jack sensed something huge slide past him in a hurry. It was a jubilant, jabbering Easy Earl.

"Jack! Did you see that? It was better than goddamn Fourth of July in Vernon Park." Still babbling excitedly, Earl passed Jack and hurtled down the steep slope.

At the bottom the young men assembled quickly, breathless but exhilarated from the chase and the spectacular explosion.

"You all right, Earl?" Jack asked, his face drawn with concern.

Earl thrust his forearm forward. "Singed the hair on my arm but wasn't that fucking beautiful? Blast knocked me right over the edge. Hit me harder than that so-called all-American from Ricks College ever did."

"There they are!" The words rang out from the darkness seemingly unattached to humans, like an edict from God followed by the blinding glare of flashlights in the boys' eyes.

"Let's get the hell out of here!" Mick roared and pivoted to his left. He crashed through a sagebrush, stumbled head-first to the sandy floor of the arroyo bottom, then sprinted down the wash. The other five followed.

With the advantage of young lungs and solid football-toned muscles, the youths easily outdistanced their pursuers. As they sprinted down the wash, Jack passed Mick. This was unusual, Jack thought. He'd never been able to outrun Mick before. As halfback on the football team, Mick could easily outrun the rest of the players, including his blocking fullback Jack. But lately Mick just didn't have the strength, stamina or wind. Probably too many Cokes, and of course malt liquor didn't help either.

The three trucks, two pickups and a flatbed were parked at the end of a double track that led from Diamond Valley. Mick and Jack vaulted into the flatbed and Mick hit the ignition. Earl and Greg jumped into one pickup, Alan and Curley into the other.

Mick slammed the International in reverse, grinding sagebrush and greasewood under his wheels, then headed down the road spraying double rooster tails of sand at the other trucks. Alan and Curley followed, and Easy and Greg brought up the rear. Once in Diamond Valley the fugitives turned left, then careened toward state Highway 18. Not bothering to even pause at the stop sign, they screeched right onto the highway and headed toward Veyo.

Almost immediately sirens and flashing lights from two patrol cars jolted their senses and the chase was on. Within seconds they were at the north barricade. Mick whipped the steering wheel to the right, careening erratically off the shoulder, spewing gravel like bullets from a Gatlin gun as the tires fought for traction. Even with that maneuver he still clipped the wooden barricade, sending it spinning and smashing into the first car waiting in line. When the convoy of trucks and police cars roared by, the stunned deputy stationed at the north barricade quickly regained his composure and jumped into his squad car to join the chase.

"Mick, this is nuts, slow down. You're going to kill us all!" Jack pleaded.

"I cud outrun those bastards, even in my dad's pig truck and wif one hand tied behind my back and the other'n cut off." Mick sneered, gripping the steering wheel tighter and punching the accelerator.

"We're almost to the Veyo Gorge. You know, where the road drops off to the bridge. There's some ugly curves. And the bridge is pretty damn narrow too," Jack said nervously. He should be driving. He was the most sober of the group.

"Come on J.T., you don't need to paint me a friggin' picture. I've bin down this road a thousand times."

As he spoke, Mick pointed the hurtling International down the steep incline toward the bridge. Screeching his tires, Mick rounded the last curve onto the bridge, the outer two wheels elevating briefly off the asphalt. He slightly over-corrected on the curve and the International thudded against the bridge guard-rail, staggered, then lurched forward.

Looking over his shoulder out the rear window, Jack saw that Alan and Curley had negotiated the curve with relative ease. Then came Earl and Greg.

Jack's gut clenched as he saw Easy career through the curve, badly over-correct, and skid sideways, violently colliding with the guard-rail. Though the rail was severely damaged, it had just enough structural resilience to throw the truck back onto the highway where it spun like a bottle finally coming to rest at a right angle with the road.

With no time to react, the charging patrol car broadsided the truck, propelling it laterally back into the already weakened barrier. With the second blow the crippled rail offered little resistance, crumpling as the truck slammed into it. Jack shivered as he saw the pickup catapult into the night sky and the crippled cruiser like it was being towed, followed the soaring pickup off the bridge. Then both vehicles plunged into the murky depths of the Santa Clara River Gorge. For one second Jack saw both vehicles float on air, suspended. Then like airplanes with engine flame-out, they nosed-dived, gaining momentum as they crashed to the canyon floor some hundred feet below. Twin fire-balls instantly rocketed up, piercing the darkness with an unnatural light. Through the rear window, Jack saw the other two patrol cars stop abruptly on the bridge and the deputies frantically scramble from their cars.

"Oh my God!" Jack gasped. "Mick did you see that? We've got to stop and help."

Mick pulled the International to a stop, rested his head on the steering wheel for a moment, then shook his head. "Shit, J.T. There's nothin' we can do. No way Earl, Greg or that cop is still alive. We could friggin' help haul up the bodies but they would be bodies. And if we do, there's no doubt we'll be apprehen—pprehend—you know, arrested and go to jail. Do ya want that?"

Jack contemplated the ramifications of going to jail. He would have to call his father who would be furious. They would probably have their driver's licenses revoked and maybe even do some jail time. Plus, they would have a criminal record, though Jack wasn't sure what the name of the crime was. A felony, probably. He was not positive but somewhere he had heard that you couldn't go on a mission with a criminal record. As far as college, medical school, or even future employment were concerned, a record would dog you the rest of your life and would probably close a lot of doors. But regardless of those more abstract concerns, he just couldn't stomach the thought of facing a disappointed Bishop Heinke or his accusing father tomorrow.

"Okay Mick, let's get out of here," Jack reluctantly agreed.

Sober now, Mick ground the truck in first gear, punched the accelerator and headed down the highway. Jack glanced through the rear window. Alan and Curley had decided to follow.

The cops paid them little attention as they searched for a path down the sheer canyon wall to the flaming cars below.

2

It had been a harrowing twenty-four hours. Jack's moods had swung wildly. At first he felt an odd mixture of claustrophobia and apprehension.

As a boy, he'd helped Uncle Milt with his trap line along Goldstrike Creek near Gunlock. Now, he felt like one of Milt's coyotes snared in steel jaws waiting for the trapper to arrive. But when the authorities didn't come, a sense of exhilaration set in. Maybe they had gotten away with it.

Jack had contemplated how the investigation might go, the moves and counter-moves he would make if and when they might match wits with the police. In spite of those giddy notions, his predominant emotion was guilt, billowing waves of suffocating guilt that left Jack woozy and filled with shame. It was similar to the nausea and dizziness he had experienced last year when hauling his father's hay on the hottest day of the year.

The air had been still and the thermometer topped off at 113 degrees with heat waves so thick they were almost visible as they bounced off the steaming hay field. Sweating profusely, Jack had pitched hay on the wagon, the cascading leaves mixing with his body sweat and salt sticking to his skin like postage stamps. Though he had felt lightheaded, he did not stop. He had to get the hay hauled or face the wrath of his father. Suddenly, he felt dizzy, vomited, then collapsed in the field. The newly cut hay stubble pricked and scratched his skin. Eventually, he gained enough presence of mind to roll into the thin ribbon of shade created by the wagon's shadow.

Feeling much the same right now, Jack flopped on his bed. Between surges of nausea, he considered yesterday's events.

After leaving the Veyo bridge, the four friends had stayed on the back roads taking a circuitous, sparsely traveled route to Santa Clara. At the only four-way intersection in Veyo, they turned west on the unpaved Sand Cove road, then thirty minutes later with headlights bouncing they had raced through the night into the tiny hamlet of Gunlock. From Gunlock the two trucks traveled south, winding down the Santa Clara River bed to the Shivwit Indian Reservation, eventually connecting with U.S. Highway 91. Here they had turned east and then ten miles later they were just outside Santa Clara.

Mick had pulled off the highway and parked the International but left the engine running and the headlights on. Alan and Curley followed. The four had clambered out of the trucks and gathered around the flatbed. The night was still and faintly illuminated by a one-quarter, witch's moon. Off to the side of the road, Jack could make out the occasional ghostly silhouette of a cedar tree.

"Do ya—do ya think they're dead?" Curley stammered, nervously running fingers through his crew-cut.

"What the hell do you think, Curley?" Mick lashed out. "The truck and cop car exploded in seconds. Even if they had survived the fall, which I doubt, they wouldn't have had time to get out before the explosion. They're dead all right."

"Maybe—maybe we should have stayed and helped. My God! After all it was Easy Earl and Greg. We've been friends since kindergarten," Alan whined.

"Help do what?" Mick demanded. "They're dead. We coulda helped the police haul the bodies up, then gone to jail for our efforts."

"We may still go to jail. A cop died trying to stop us." Jack said with a frown. His skewed teeth glinted in the headlights.

"Not if we stick together. This is important. We've got to get our stories straight. You know, we've gotta all say the same thing. Nobody can prove it was us up at the volcano, except for the four. So if we don't talk, the police can't prove a thing." With the headlight hitting the back of his head and his face in the shadow, Mick's freckles smeared together like smudged grease on a mechanic.

"I don't know, Mick," Jack replied. "Might go easier on us if we just go to the police right now and explain things. It's not like we planned on killing the cop."

"Goddamnit, J.T.," Mick fumed. "Can't you get it through your friggin' head? A cop is dead. They're not going to let you off with a promise that you won't do it no more. It's you who wants to go on a mission. Do you think that's goin' ta happen with a criminal record? And what about your dad? Jesus, J.T., think about it."

"Mick's right," Curley declared. "It's not going to help nobody if we turn ourselves in. Not the dead cop, or Easy or Greg. They're dead. Nothin' goin' help them. And it sure ain't gonna help us none."

"Then—then we've got to get our alibi, our stories down tight and stick to them," Alan said. His eyes glowed with fear in the headlights

"Damn right," Mick continued. "First of all, we were never with Easy and Greg tonight. We went to Cedar City to a movie and to chase girls. We invited Earl and Greg but they said they had something else to do, something big. I played in a couple all-stars' games in Cedar with Hank Bulloch. I'm pretty good friends with him. I'll call em' and see if he won't back us up. You know, verify our story in case the cops want to know if anyone saw us."

"Fine by me and Alan," Curley said. He had a habit of speaking for Alan.

"Then it's settled. Let's shake on it, then we can go on home." Mick intently scrutinized each friend as he groped for their hand. As his gaze came to rest on each of their faces, the young men ratified the agreement with a simple "I'm in" and a handshake. Reluctantly, Jack took Mick's hand but he couldn't speak or look him in the eye.

"Then it's done. Let's get the hell out of here," Mick decreed, then pivoted on his heel and started climbing into the International.

Jack stopped him before he got all the way into the cab. "Mick, I'm sure you've got a scrape, maybe even a dent on the driver's side of your truck when you banged into the guard rail. And I think you hit a barricade as we left Diamond Valley."

"This is my dad's truck, or at least it was when he was alive. Hell, it's a farm vehicle. There's dents and scratches everywhere. Anyhow, I never drive this on the highway and neither does anybody else. If I park it down on the farm, no one will know the difference, not even my mother. What's one more dent?" Mick gently touched Jack's shoulder. "Come on J.T., quit worrying. Let's go home."

"Mick, it's just—it's just that I feel so guilty. It's so unreal."

"I know, J.T., I know." Mick put his hand on Jack's shoulder for a moment, then climbed into the cab. "But we're not going to accomplish anything sitting here all night."

With the conspiracy firmly cemented in place, the four young men separated and headed home to finish the surreal night in sleepless beds. Quietly, so as not to wake his father or Mary, Jack had crept into his bedroom without turning on the light. It was a simple room with few amenities. There were two twin beds, a crude homemade desk and a scuffed dresser with the bottom two drawers askew on broken runners.

Jack had dropped onto the bed by the window, bypassing Chris's bed. Although Chris had died in Korea almost a year and a half ago, his father had refused to remove his bed from the room. One night Jack had made the huge mistake of sleeping in it. His father woke him the next morning and snapped angrily, "Sleep in your own damn bed." What difference it made to his father escaped him. But to Jack, the benefit of sleeping in Chris's bed was obvious. It was right under the swamp cooler's air outlet duct so it stayed cooler than Jack's on hot summer nights.

Jack had gotten up and stripped off his clothes. They reeked of tire smoke and tiredly he thought he should wash them but instead discarded them in a heap on the floor. Then in total disregard for his father's wishes, he flopped on Chris's bed under the cool air and starred at the ceiling all night.

The next morning Jack had learned that Easy Earl was not dead. Apparently, according to Jack's sister Mary, who had heard it from Alice whose husband was a policeman for the Saint George Police Department, Earl had been ejected twenty feet from the truck landing behind a huge boulder and had survived the explosion. He had however, suffered massive head injuries and was now in a coma at Dixie Pioneer Memorial Hospital. Greg and the deputy had not survived and were both taken to Desert Pine Mortuary to be prepared for their funerals. Mary had told Jack that Greg's service would be on Monday, in two days.

Last night's guilt returned immediately and this time it was acute and unrelenting. Earl was alive! They had not even bothered to stop and help him. And Greg was dead. Jack had known Earl and Greg since they were kids. In fact, the six of them had been friends as far back as Jack could remember. Even before kindergarten they had gone to Sunday school together and there they harassed the girls and tormented the teachers. Then in the first grade at Santa Clara Elementary School, they were it. The six of them were the entire male population of the first grade. They had grown close like brothers.

They had shared some good times together. Jack remembered how after finishing their farm chores on hot summer days, they would gather at the boy's pond to languish in the cool canal waters and swap stories. Here secrets were forbidden and any topic was acceptable, even welcomed. Wide-eyed they would trade tales about girlfriends, female anatomy, school, sports and even their limited, somewhat innocent view of God and the universe. Bathing suits were permitted but rarely used. They were not needed.

In Santa Clara there was a boy's pond and a girl's pond separated by enough distance so there would never be inadvertent mixing of the sexes. Furthermore, the unwritten code handed down by the town elders strictly forbade intentional mixing as well. This was not to say the six of them always obeyed this implied law.

On several occasions they had slithered through the tangle of tamarisks and squaw bushes to spy on the girls at the girl's pond. In the 1950s this was about the sum-total of their sex education for it seemed that wearing bathing suits was a nuisance for the girls as well. The boys were amazed at how pointy the girls' sprouting breasts were and how nothing protruded from their patches of pubic hair. After gorging their eyes with these amazing sights, the boys would retreat back to the boy's pond to discuss their fabulous findings. Though he was not sure, Jack suspected the girls had organized similar expeditions to their pond. They had never actually seen the girls but they had heard giggles from the bushes or at least thought they had.

That seemed so long ago. Jack supposed it was the immediacy and weight of present problems that made these past events seem more distant, more untouchable and more desirable. Certainly there had been some drastic changes lately.

In one careless insane night, Greg and the deputy were dead and Easy Earl was in a coma. For the first time in his life Jack felt mortal, even vulnerable. Perhaps life would not go on forever, at least it hadn't for Greg. The ephemeral quality of life troubled Jack. Could something so rare, so marvelous, really vanish in a second? No, it just didn't seem plausible. The teachings of the church had to be correct. There was life after death and Greg was probably in the Celestial Kingdom right now, smiling down on them and having a cold Coke. Something as magnificent as life just did not disappear in a foolhardy minute.

However, it wasn't just the metaphysical that disturbed Jack. Mick's attitude also troubled him. Of the six friends, Jack had always been closest to Mick. Through the years they had become inseparable. Even now that they were older and courting women, Jack almost always double-dated with Mick. But lately, Jack had become increasingly concerned about Mick's behavior. For the last year or so it seemed Mick had become more reckless, with more drinking binges and in general he was more out of control. When asked, he still agreed that they were going on church missions together but Jack wondered. Mick had become increasingly cynical and critical of the church's ordinances and doctrines.

At their last Aaronic Priesthood personal interview, a somewhat surprisingly empathetic Bishop Heinke had counseled them: "If you're going to be foolish, do so while you're young. Such behavior is glaringly out of place and much less tolerated by society when you are an adult." Now they were of missionary age, twenty-one, and Mick still showed no signs of reforming.

Even more bothersome to Jack now was Mick's apparent lack of grief or remorse about Greg's death and Earl's ghastly condition. It seemed to Jack that Mick had been just a little too quick to declare them dead and beyond help and too eager to leave the scene of the accident. My God, after all, it was Earl and Greg, their blood brothers! But in spite of these worrisome signs, Jack knew he loved Mick and always would.

The dead cop, however, was an entirely different matter. Jack had occupied the waning hours of the sleepless night by studying the dictionary. According to *Webster's*, murder first-degree was "the unlawful killing of a person, especially when done with deliberation or premeditation or occurring during the commission of a serious crime." Murder second-degree was pretty much the same as far as intent but was lacking deliberation or premeditation.

Jack had analyzed these facts in the light of his present predicament. There was no question the six of them had not planned to kill the deputy. There was no premeditation at all. But what worried Jack was that an officer was killed in the commission of a crime. Even considering this Jack doubted his crime would qualify as murder one. Also, because of the lack of intent, murder two would not be seriously considered either.

But what about manslaughter? *Webster's Dictionary* defined manslaughter "as the unlawful killing of a human being without malice or forethought." They were responsible for the killing of another human being but it was a careless mistake, almost a fumble of fortune. Certainly, they had not planned to kill the cop so there was definitely no forethought. It was an accident. But there was no arguing the fact that the fatal accident occurred during the commission of a crime, even though the crime was a misdemeanor if that made a difference. So with this logic Jack concluded that since it was an accident, there could be no malice. However that thought offered Jack little solace because there was a body and as best he could tell, what they were guilty of on the road to Veyo was manslaughter!

Unfortunately, what *Webster's* did not make clear was the penalty. Though Jack had very little legal experience, he was pretty sure manslaughter was a felony and typically felonies were accompanied by substantial prison time and often a considerable fine.

Just the thought of prison generated panic. It was not only the mental image of confinement that made him cringe. He had heard of other unspeakable things that went on in prison as well. Jack began to ooze perspiration. He gulped air like an asthmatic and his heart raced like a horse being whipped down a straight-a-way. Without even trying to sleep, Jack had watched the sunrise through his bedroom window never having closed his eyes.

Though his father didn't ask about his whereabouts the previous night—he almost never did—someone else did. Sheriff Meecham appeared that afternoon just as Jack was unhooking the locking pins of the hay mower from the Massey-Ferguson after having almost finished cutting the five acres of alfalfa in the old Loren Webber piece. With scattered alfalfa leaves flecking his sweat-soaked tee-shirt, Jack knew he smelled like an odd blend of freshly mown hay and day-old P.E. clothes.

"How you doing, Jack?" Sheriff Meecham greeted him as he hauled his big frame out of the patrol car. "Looks like you're about done for the day."

Jack took the pin from the center bar of the three-point hook-up, letting the mower settle to the ground.

"Hi, Sheriff. I'm finished cutting; mower's broke," Jack answered nervously. "I need to replace three busted teeth before I can finish." Jack pointed to the six-foot lever arm of the mower with three, serrated teeth snapped off.

"Kinda looks like my four-year old kid with her front teeth missing. That mower probably couldn't even cut the legs off'en a lame pheasant, much less them alfalfa stocks." Sheriff Meecham smiled. His fleshy jowls jiggled but his eyes were hard. "Jack, I guess by now you've heard about Greg and Earl?"

Jack knew he had to be careful and measured his words. "Yes, Mary told me this morning. At first I didn't believe it and I'm not sure I do even now."

"You been over to the hospital to see Earl yet?"

"No, I'm going over to Saint George tonight. Dad said I had to get the Loren Webber piece cut today. Once I get the mower fixed and get a chance to clean up, I'm going on over."

Sheriff Meecham looked surprised, reached down and scratched his groin. "I thought you and Earl was real tight." The sheriff paused again and cocked a dubious eye at Jack. "Anyways, do you know anything about the circumstances of the accident?"

"Not really, just what Mary told me. She said there was a high speed chase with the cops, and Earl crashed his truck off Veyo bridge," Jack said evenly as he took out a dirty handkerchief and mopped his forehead.

"Well, let me give you the details, Jack. There were at least three trucks involved and perhaps six or seven people. It all started when these six or seven guys started a fire in the crater of the old volcano last night, the one by Snow Canyon. I suspect they had been drinking. Anyways, when we tried to apprehend them, all three trucks raced down Highway 18 towards Veyo. Of course we followed them and that's when Earl lost control and rolled his truck over the Veyo bridge into the gorge. Deputy Saunders was right behind Earl and he had no chance. Saunders smacked Earl's truck and spun out of control and flipped off the bridge as well. Deputy Saunders and Greg Hafen were killed instantly and as you know, Earl sustained massive head injuries. You know anything about any of that, Jack?"

"Honestly, I don't," Jack declared. He hated lying and wasn't very good at it. "But Sheriff, why are you after these guys? It sounds like all they did was start a bonfire and have a party. Kids do that all the time. There's nothing to do in Saint George. We have to make our own fun."

"Fun's one thing. This is another. I got two people dead and another one damn near dead."

"Sounds like it's all a big mistake, that things just kinda got out of hand. That no one's really to blame. Maybe some minor laws were broken, but nothing major," Jack said as he tripped the latch and laid the mower arm flat on the ground.

"Well excuse me if I disagree. If these kids had been behaving themselves, none of this would have happened. And I don't think the crimes are so minor. We have drunk and disorderly, destruction of public property, driving under the influence, reckless endangerment and evading arrest. And for a topper," Sheriff Meecham said grinning, his fat lips drawn smugly across his teeth, "we got manslaughter. Anyways, in one night, we had more crime perpetrated here in Washington County than we've had in the last three years combined. So where were you last night, Jack?"

"Mick, Alan, Curley and me went to Cedar City last night. We did see Earl and Greg earlier and invited them to come along, but they said they had something else going. So the four of us went to Cedar and saw a movie and chased girls, but as usual we weren't very successful."

"What movie?" Sheriff Meecham asked. "Can anyone corroborate your story?"

Jack stomach's clenched and rolled. They hadn't talked about what movie they'd seen. His mind raced. What was playing at the Cedar Crest? Probably the same movie that was playing in Saint George the week before. He had to say something. "*Rebel Without a Cause* with James Dean at the Cedar Crest drive-in. Let me see." Jack contorted his face as though he were thinking. "Yes, I did talk to Hank Bulloch at the drive-in snack bar while I was getting a Coke and hotdog."

"*Rebel Without a Cause*, how appropriate." Sheriff Meecham twisted his flabby face in disgust. "Why don't you guys see something worthwhile, like Charlton Heston's *Ten Commandments* that's playing at the Gaiety right now? These damn movies give you kids ideas and that James Dean's a punk. He belongs in jail. Don't think I won't check out your story, Jack"

"I'm sure you will."

"I don't understand what's wrong with you kids nowadays. Your older brother Christian never behaved like this, God rest his soul, before he went to Korea. He never gave me a minute's trouble. I thought you six guys were going on missions."

"We are," Jack said and wiped his brow again

"Well two of you ain't. Anyways, this certainly isn't missionary behavior. I just don't understand your generation. You've had everything handed to you on a silver platter but you dump it on the ground and try to sell the silver." Sheriff Meecham shifted his .357 magnum laterally to a more comfortable position so that his overflowing stomach didn't rest so harshly on the hammer. He started to go but suddenly turned back.

"Oh, Jack?"

"Yes."

"Did you enjoy the fire?"

Jack climbed back on the Massey-Ferguson. "Like I said Sheriff, I was in Cedar City."

The sheriff backed up, then accelerated down the lane, his patrol car dragging a parachute plume of dust as he went. With the sheriff gone, Jack felt his neck and face muscles slowly relax. He selected a 5/8 inch wrench from his tool box and turned back to the frozen bolt holding the fractured tooth on the mower arm. There was no question in Jack's mind that the sheriff suspected he was at the volcano fiasco. If he had any evidence, the sheriff would have arrested him and would be hauling him off to jail right now.

But this conspiracy and cover-up was beginning to get to him. He wasn't any good at this. Jack wondered how the rest of the gang was handling it. Then a pang of conscience tweaked him. He really should go see Easy Earl. Maybe Mick would go with him. With any luck if he and Mick went to the hospital fairly late, they might not run into any of Earl's family. Jack was just not ready to handle the reproachful look of Easy Earl's mother. He would give Mick a call once he got this damn mower fixed.

"Jack," his older sister Mary yelled from the porch. "Telephone. It's Emily."

In all the turbulence Jack had forgotten about Emily. Just twenty-four hours earlier Emily had been the biggest excitement in his life. Only recently relocated from California, they had met at church a month ago. Jack had been immediately drawn to her. She was a very attractive young woman in a thoughtful, strong sort of way. Her face was pretty, refined and almost cosmopolitan as opposed to the girls in southern Utah who all looked like farmers' daughters. She had delicate features and her intelligent brown eyes always seemed tinted with a trace of sadness. Her figure was slight and athletic but nicely rounded in the appropriate places. Her hair was the color of desert sand with a hint of natural curl.

When she was just a kid, Emily's father and mother had divorced and through the years she had pretty much lost contact with her father. Jack was not sure why her parents had divorced. If Emily knew, she had so far kept it to herself. This seemed understandable to Jack. After all, divorce was a California thing and not well accepted here in Utah. Now her mother was seriously ill with rheumatic heart disease, basically an invalid. Hence the move to Santa Clara to live with her parents, Emily's grandparents.

"Jack, are you coming or shall I tell her to call back?"

Shaken out of his reverie Jack shouted, "Tell her to hang on. I'll be right there."

He mounted the porch in one leap. Another took him through the kitchen door and he grabbed the phone from his sister.

"Hi, Em. Sorry I haven't called but this has been an awful week."

"I heard about Greg and Earl. I'm sorry. I know they were friends of yours."

Frankly, Jack did not want to talk about it after the grilling by Sheriff Meecham but he was polite. "It's a terrible thing. They were both like brothers to me. We'd been friends for forever."

"Will Earl be all right?"

"I don't know. I haven't seen him yet but I hear he's real bad, in a coma."

"I didn't know Greg very well but he seemed like a great guy."

"Yeah, he was great," Jack said lamely.

"Anyway, I just wanted to tell you how sorry I am and to see if there's anything I can do."

"No Em, it's just going to take me a little time to get over it. I'm pretty tied up this week with Greg's funeral and all but maybe next week could we go out for a movie or get a Coke or something?"

"Sure, that's fine Jack. Whenever you're ready," Emily replied. "Are you okay?"

"Yeah, I'm fine. I'll give you a call next week."

Jack hung up, then picked the receiver up again to call Mick. "Hello, Operator, give me *ORCHARD—2255.*"

3

Dixie Pioneer Memorial Hospital was on the edge of town just southeast of the pristine, "ivory-castle" Mormon Temple. It was an unobtrusive single-story, sienna brown brick building with two wings that formed a right angle. One wing angled north, the other slanted east. The north wing contained ten patient beds, the east wing housed the operating room, the recovery room, the lab and x-ray. Though it was not a new building, it was neatly landscaped and had the overall appearance of a middle-class bungalow rather than a medical center.

The medical staff was small, only two family physicians, Dr. Seegmiller and Dr. Hilton. Dr. Seegmiller was in his seventies and wanted to retire so the bulk of medical care in Washington County was shouldered by Dr. Hilton who always looked haggard and had raw, red eyes from lack of sleep or Jack Daniels, or both.

At this hour, 8:30 p.m., there was no one at the reception window when Mick and Jack entered the foyer. Without stopping, they hurried down the hall to the north wing. It shouldn't be too hard to find Earl. He had to be in one of the ten beds. There were no private rooms; each cubicle was partitioned by ceiling-to-floor cotton curtains suspended from metal runners. The curtains and patient beds butted up against a plastered wall painted khaki-green. Time had blistered the paint, flaking it like a bad sunburn. As the paint peeled it revealed previously concealed layers of color.

Mick and Jack walked quietly down the center isle, Jack parting the curtains of each cubicle just long enough to verify its occupant. Jack could sense Mick was ill at ease around sickness and hospitals while he found it fascinating. Each time Jack had gone to the hospital or a doctor's office, he considered it a learning opportunity. Someday he would be doing this sort of thing. Ever since his mother had died, he had wanted to be a doctor.

Then they found him. Earl was stashed near the back of the wing on the right side of the aisle.

Easy Earl did look easy in an awful sort of way. Stretched out on the bed, he had no visible parts moving. His head was wrapped in a cocoon of white cotton bandages with two apertures for his eyes and two more for the nose and mouth. The only exposed skin was his upper torso and arms, and they were covered with dozens of cleaned and sutured lacerations, multiple purple contusions, raw abrasions and blistering burns. The burns were covered with a thick white cream. Attached to his right hand was an IV from which exited a tube that climbed up to a glass bottle that dangled from a metal standard. There were two other lines. One was an naso-gastric tube retreating like a tapeworm from his nose to a Gomco suction machine sitting on a bedside stand. The other, transporting yellow fluid, appeared from under the sheet at the groin level, then descended downward to a bag hanging on a bedside rail. Other than the faint aroma of musty, sweat-soaked linen, the predominate odor was rubbing alcohol. It suppressed all other odors, like a skunk in a flower patch.

Though Earl was breathing on his own, his respirations were labored and punctuated with alarmingly long pauses of apnea. When he would finally take a breath, his whole body would shudder, accompanied by a strident whistle as the air was sucked through his rigid vocal chords like wind whistling through a closed door.

However, the most disconcerting thing to Jack was not Earl's breathing, but his eyes. With his pupils fixed and dilated, Earl's eyes appeared vacant, dull and out of focus. When Jack peered closely into Earl's eyes, he noticed fine rapid, oscillating eye movements with the eyes slowly wandering far to the right, then suddenly correcting back to center, only to repeat the same drifting motion again and again.

Jack picked up Earl's left hand. This was unbelievable, he thought. Just yesterday, Easy was excited and laughing wildly as he slid past him down the volcanic slope after tossing those five gallons of gasoline on the fire. Now, he was this, whatever this was.

Mick stood several feet back from the bed as though he thought

Easy's condition might somehow be communicable. He paced and stared at the ceiling, at other patients, the IV bottle, the Gomco suction machine, anything but Earl. Finally Jack sighed, patted Earl's hand and rose to leave.

"Earl looks awful. Looks like he could die any minute," Jack moaned.

Mick brushed aside a pillow from the bedside chair and sat down heavily. "But what if he don't die?"

"What?"

"What if he don't die, and he wakes up and tells the cops everything?"

"If he does, he does. Sometimes, I wish he would," Jack said.

"We don't always have to leave everything to chance," Mick said. He had retrieved the pillow from the floor and was idly rotating it in his hands.

"What the hell are you suggesting?"

"Well, if he's going to die anyway, why let him suffer? Ah, forget it J.T. This whole thing's got me thinking a little crazy." Mick placed the pillow on the chair seat as he stood up and resumed aimlessly treading around the room. "Come on, let's go."

"Mick, what's bothering you?"

"I don't know J.T. This whole thing's kinda eerie. It gives me the creeps. Let's get out of here."

"But it's just Easy. We had to come. We owe Earl that much."

"That's not Earl; that's just a carcass. As far as I'm concerned Earl is dead and his spirit, if you believe in spirits, has gone to wherever spirits go. Probably nowhere," Mick said.

"What'a ya mean, wherever spirits go? The church specifically teaches us—"

"Can we just drop it!" Mick barked. "I know perfectly well what the church teaches and I don't need another friggin' sermon from you. Not tonight. Hell, let's just go. Anyway, I'm supposed to see Brenda tonight."

As they turned to leave, the curtains suddenly parted and in stepped Earl's mother with a gaunt face and swollen eyes.

"Oh. Hello, Mrs. Jaussi," Jack said. "We were just leaving. I can't tell you how sorry we are about Earl."

"Hi Jack, Mick," Mrs. Jaussi said in a husky voice, then brushed past them to Earl's side. "Oh God, I just can't believe this! Not Earl. He was always so big and strong and so—so happy."

As Mrs. Jaussi sobbed the silence became painful. "What did the doctors say?" Jack blurted out.

"Oh, they're not very—not very hopeful. I can only understand about half of what they tell me. But they say he has a broken skull bone about here." Mrs. Jaussi pointed to the back of her head. "Apparently, Earl has had some bleeding in his head from the break as well. They've talked about moving him to Salt Lake. Dr. Hilton called a brain surgeon today and if Earl makes it through the night, they're going to ship him up to Salt Lake tomorrow." Mrs. Jaussi started weeping again. "They might operate. Try to lift the bone and take some of the pressure off the brain and drain off some blood."

"They can do some amazing things nowadays with neurosurgery," Jacks said more hopefully than he felt.

"I don't know Jack. What if they save him and he is left a—a vegetable?" Mrs. Jaussi sighed, as she dabbed her eyes with a white-lace handkerchief. "I know he wouldn't want that."

Mick edged a little farther away. "Is there anything we can do to help?" he asked lamely.

"As a matter of fact you can. The sheriff told me Earl was involved in a high-speed chase and that's when he rolled his truck over the Veyo bridge. He also said Deputy Saunders was killed trying to stop him. After I prodded him some, Sheriff Meecham told me Earl had been drinking and there were two other trucks involved in the chase that got clean away. What happened that night? Why weren't you two watching out for Earl?"

Jack and Mick studied each other, neither knowing what to say. It was one thing to lie to the sheriff, but quite another to lie to Earl's mother.

Finally Mick answered. "Mrs. Jaussi we weren't even with Earl last night. We went up in Cedar City."

"You two are Earl's best friends. I can't believe you don't know anything about this. Who were in the other trucks?"

Mick reached for the curtains. "We've got to run, Mrs. Jaussi, but we'll keep an eye on Earl, and if there is any thing we can do—" Mick didn't finish the sentence. Mrs. Jaussi's icy stare cut him short as if to say, "Don't bother, you've done quite enough already."

Jack and Mick made the ten-minute ride from Saint George to Santa Clara in uneasy silence. Considering what had just happened, there wasn't much to say. Mrs. Jaussi's eyes had said it all.

"See you tomorrow at Greg's funeral," Jack said as Mick was getting out of the car.

"Yeah, I'll meet you at the chapel," Mick answered without looking back.

Jack drove home and crawled into Chris's bed. He fell into a fitful, restless sleep punctuated with frequent nightmares and numerous self-imposed bathroom breaks in an effort to wrench his mind from the disturbing dreams .

The next morning dawn broke without a single cloud to mar the azure sky. To the north, Pine Valley Mountain shimmered in the glassy air. By 10:00 a.m. it was already 100 degrees with heat waves waffling up from the parched and earth made the whole town look like a mirage. The asphalt was sticky and the air smelled of dust and tar. It was the kind of brutal heat that made life languid and listless and when one did have to stir, it was from one patch of shade to another.

Jack decided to walk to the chapel. The thought of getting into his sweltering 52 Ford Fairlane, then having to grip that gummy steering wheel and touch that blistering hot metal gearshift was more than he could deal with. Though it was the standard rule of his generation to never walk when you can ride, today it really wasn't a difficult decision. He would walk.

He headed down Main Street which also doubled as Federal Highway 91. With their seed balls hanging like Christmas tree ornaments, venerable sycamore trees lined both sides of the highway, their arching branches forming an almost perfect shaded canopy over the asphalt. On both sides of the highway at the foot of the trees were two rock-lined canals that served as irrigation ditches. As Jack trudged along, the sound of bubbling water was a pleasant contrast to the suffocating heat.

Jack was in a reflective mood. He thought about Easy and Greg, and about the intangible and fragile substance called life. What gave life meaning and value? Certainly the church was important and so was family. His own family unit had been shattered by the deaths of his mother and his brother Chris, and his relationship with his father was tenuous at best.

But he still had fond memories of his grandfather, Hans. On his father's side, his grandfather had been the first baby born in the new settlement when Santa Clara colonized almost a hundred years earlier. Life in Santa Clara must have been hard a hundred years ago. Jack contemplated what life was like when his grandfather was a boy and how the settlers had carved a town out of the harsh desert sands, fighting not only the elements but at times, also with his grandmother's people from his mother's side, over land and water.

His grandmother, Alice Tsosie, was full-blooded Navajo from Kayenta on the Arizona reservation. Those Navajos were not at all related to the local Shivwits band. In fact, they didn't even like them. Grandma Alice had married Levi Judd, a Mormon trapper-missionary, and they eventually settled in Kanab, Utah. There, Jack's mother Mary Alice was born and raised in the traditional Mormon fashion. Grandma Alice would occasionally smuggle, against grandpa Levi's wishes, some of the traditional Navajo folklore and customs to her daughter. Publically grandma agreed with grandpa Levi that Mary Alice should be Mormon, but privately grandma felt she needed to understand her Indian heritage.

After Mary Alice had grown to an adult, she worked at the Kanab Fruit and Vegetable Emporium. There she met Jack's father on one of his produce trucking runs. It was an immediate attraction. Mr. Kunz loved her liquid brown eyes and willowy figure, and her sense of peace with the universe. She loved his sense of humor (Jack had to laugh at that one) and his ambition. They were soon married in the Saint George Temple. It was sad in a way, but Jack knew very little about her side of the family, couldn't even recognize most of his Indian cousins, though they seemed to know who he was. Frankly, he was embarrassed by that whole branch of his family.

Jack surveyed what he could see of the small valley through the sycamore trees. The valley was a small kidney-shaped basin carved out by the diminutive Santa Clara River as it flowed from Pine Valley Mountain. Along its course, a relatively short journey of approximately seventy miles, the river fought through one mountain range and several lava flows to reach its confluence with the Virgin River about a mile below Saint George. Just north of the valley perched the craggy, red navajo-sandstone cliffs of Snow Canyon. To the east lay the awesome creamy-red steeples of Zion Canyon. Immediately to the south was the disjointed, ruthless, grey landscape of the vast Mojave desert. And finally to the west rested the less imposing desert mountain, Utah Hill. It was in this barren and inhospitable land that Jack's great-grandfather had settled years ago. Unquestionably, the harshness of the land and the constant struggle to survive had shaped and forged the personalities and disposition of the valley's inhabitants, including his, Jack reasoned.

Santa Clara was colonized in 1856 when Brigham Young called a small band of Swiss immigrant-converts to settle on the banks of the Santa Clara River. Apparently his motivation was two-fold. First, to establish an outpost on the southern border of the Territory of Deseret, ostensibly to use as a rest and re-supply station on the main trail across the Mojave desert to California. This would also further define and solidify the Mormon's southwestern boundary. Second, after being driven from their homes in Illinois, coupled with recent skirmishes with the federal government, Brigham Young had dreams of making the new territory self-sufficient, even independent. He had hoped the warmer climate would be conducive to growing cotton which the colonists normally had to import from the southern states. Cotton was essential in making clothing for the burgeoning number of Latter-Day-Saints arriving in their new land and it was not always easily available, nor easily transported from Dixie, particularly with the Civil War brewing at the time.

Immediately on arrival in the valley, the Swiss settlers constructed a dam across the Santa Clara River and dug canals to irrigate the thirsty soil. Each family was given a building lot and plot of land to farm. The building lots were centrally located adjacent to the main street, whereas the farms were scattered throughout the remainder of the valley. The canals, dredged down either side of Main Street, had several functions. Not only were they used to irrigate the vegetable gardens always located on the building lots, but the pioneers would also take drinking water from the canals at daybreak. Then an hour later, the livestock would be turned free to quench their thirst.

The raising of cotton met with limited success but regardless of that, the region became known as Utah's Dixie. The cotton fiber was short and of poor quality, and when transportation and the political climate improved, it could not compete with the cotton from the south. By happenstance, the Saints found the climate was favorable for growing alfalfa and fruit: peaches, apples, apricots and cherries, as well as grapes for the sacramental wine. Over the years, the Swiss band cleared more and more land for farming, and to accommodate this increased cultivation, the irrigation canals branched from the Main Street canal to form a web over the entire valley. In places, particularly where a canal would make a sharp turn, the current would eat away at the sandy banks creating whirlpools and eddies. Slowly the current would enlarge and expand these sections of the canals into small lagoons. This also resulted in forming two natural swimming pools, the boy's and girl's ponds.

Even in the 1950s, the citizens of Santa Clara continued to be fiercely loyal to the Mormon church and remained largely a closed society with family names still reflecting their Swiss heritage: Graff, Tobler, Hafen, Stucki, Reber, Gubler, Frei, Ence, Staheli, Leavitt, Kunz and Jaussi.

Due to isolation and the now forsaken practice of polygamy, the gene pool remained relatively pure and in general, the descendants of those Swiss settlers continued to retain similar physical, as well as mental characteristics. As a group, they were short to medium in stature with thick stocky torsos, and there was a tendency toward blue eyes and fair hair. They maintained their Germanic sense of industry with labor not only being a virtue, but almost a sacred attitude. As a society they valued loyalty and tended to be fervently devoted to their church and passionately patriotic with their country. Questioning and probing life's mysteries, while not strictly prohibited, was never encouraged. The prevailing attitude seemed to be that it was better to fix what was broken than to embrace the untested and the new. While radical or deviant behavior was tolerated in the young, it was rigidly discouraged in adults to the point of ostracization.

During the last twenty years, home construction building materials had gradually shifted from rock and adobe to brick and mortar. But there was still a smattering of adobe houses and granaries in town. Fastidious by nature, the inhabitants of Santa Clara regularly manicured their lawns and shrubs and patrolled their vegetable gardens for unsightly weeds. It was just their disposition to be neat.

Through this quaint hamlet that not only reflected but defined his existence, Jack finally arrived at the chapel. As usual, when the occasion was to mourn one of its own, the chapel was full, and as Jack entered, the service was about to begin. He spied Mick in the last pew on the right of the center aisle and slid in next to him. The chapel was heavy with melancholy and tears had already begun to flow, but Mick appeared dry-eyed and merely nodded to Jack as he sat down.

Jack made a cursory inspection of the congregation. Almost everyone from Santa Clara was there, everyone except his father. After his mother's funeral years ago, his father had vowed he would never attend another funeral, not even his own. The anguish in his father's face as he suffered through her service was still vivid in Jack's memory.

As Bishop Heinke approached the podium, the congregation fell silent. He placed two leathery hands on the podium and spoke with an educated, slightly German accent.

"Brothers and sisters, I wish I were not here. I would much rather be irrigating my fields or hauling my hay, but we are here. Here to commemorate the life of our brother, Gregory Hafen. I know the fundamental question you've been asking is why. Why would a bright young man approaching the prime of his life be snatched from us? Perhaps some of you will answer this question in your own minds with the obvious and most superficial of explanations: Greg was being foolish and paid the price for that foolishness. But I think there is more to it, more that is not readily visible from the surface or with casual inspection.

"Our Heavenly Father has a grand scheme, a master plan for mankind. Through the gospel we understand the general outline of the plan, but not every detail. This is where faith is essential. God wants us to trust him. And while it is true that God works in mysterious ways, someday we will understand the entire plan, it will all be revealed to us. I personally don't believe Greg died for nothing. God had a plan, a mission for Greg."

As the bishop droned on, Jack glanced over at Mick. He seemed unmoved by the Bishop's sermon. To Jack, the Bishop's words rang true. The Bishop's right, he thought. God needed Greg on the other side for some purpose. The accident was just a mechanism for God to recruit Greg. Like the Bishop said, we just need to have faith. We don't have to understand everything right now, but there is a purpose, a comprehensive plan.

Mick touched Jack's shoulder and muttered in his ear, "This is a bunch of crapola. What killed Greg was that he was drunk and going too fast. Mission in heaven—my ass."

With a hand laminated with work callouses, the bishop paused and wiped the sweat from his brow, then continued. "Let's concentrate on what we do know and leave the mysteries alone. I realize this is a service to commemorate the life of brother Greg, but what better time to review the foundation of our faith? To reflect on those principals that allow me to say with certainty that Greg is with our father in heaven right now."

Mick mumbled to Jack, "Why does he always have to turn everything into a sermon? This is a friggin funeral."

Jack put finger to his lips. "Shssst. He's the bishop, that's what he's supposed to do."

"We do know that God appeared to Joseph Smith in the sacred grove and revealed to him that none of the existing churches were true. Then subsequently through the Prophet Joseph, God did establish his true church and gave us another scripture, a companion to the Bible, the *Book of Mormon*. The *Book of Mormon* chronicles the ancient history of the people of this hemisphere and Christ's dealings with them. We also know that Jesus Christ is the son of God and that he gave his life for us to atone for our sins, thereby giving us a vehicle, a mechanism, by which we may return to our Heavenly Father's presence. It has also been revealed that if we live our lives as God has prescribed, not only will we return to his presence, but we may also become like him.

"This eternal plan, we call the gospel. And even though this plan is priceless, we are instructed not to hoard it, but to share it with the world. This is why the church has its vast missionary program. All young men of twenty-one years of age need to prepare to go on a mission. We need to give all people throughout the world the opportunity to embrace the gospel before the second coming of Christ. Young men, remain faithful to the gospel, attend your church meetings, abstain from alcohol and tobacco, and think pure thoughts. Lust and pre-martial sex are evil, and will inevitably devour you and detour you from the path of righteousness."

Again Jack reflected on the bishop's message. The bishop's correct again. He has an uncanny knack of zeroing in on my faults and weaknesses. I need to be careful with my relationship with Emily. It would be extremely easy for me to go too far, she's so feminine. No more booze or partying for me; I've really got to concentrate on preparing myself for a mission, Jack thought.

Mick was again muttering, "Why don't they just make us friggin' Catholic priests?"

The bishop concluded his remarks with the traditional testimony. "I know this is the true church. That Joseph Smith was a prophet of God and that David O. McKay, our present president, is also a prophet of God. I know Jesus Christ died for our sins and it behooves us to live our lives in accordance with the gospel, so he did not die in vain. Without question, I know Greg Hafen is with our Heavenly Father today and is just embarking on a glorious celestial mission. I say these things in the name of Jesus Christ, amen."

Greg was then eulogized by one of his Sunday school teachers, and then Coach Betenson, Dixie Junior College football coach, offered the benediction. Following the closing prayer the pallbearers, including Jack, Mick, Alan and Curley, hoisted the casket and the recessional began.

After placing the casket in the hearse, Mick and Jack stepped back to make room for Greg's family. Jack turned to Mick as the crowd dispersed. "Wasn't that a great service? Bishop Heinke certainly has a knack of explaining the difficult things."

"Yeah, it was okay, but—" Mick suddenly had a coughing spasm and doubled over.

"I don't feel so badly for Greg now," Jack said, offering Mick a hand. "He's in a far better place and already fulfilling his mission."

Through clenched teeth Mick blurted, "J.T., this is like trying to sweeten shit. Greg's dead and as best I can tell, the only thing he's going to preach to is some friggin' grubs and worms six feet under. There is no mission in heaven, no grand scheme to all this. Greg got drunk and fucked up; we all did. The only difference is Greg got caught. It's all chance. It could be any one of us in that casket, and if it were, they'd be saying the same thing: God had a mission for us. It's just the same old friggin' crap used to explain every death."

Jack was stunned. "What's wrong with you lately, Mick? You know that's not true. You can't believe something so fine and noble as the human spirit would cease to exist, just like that." Jack snapped his fingers.

"Fine and noble, huh?" Mick replied, getting his breath. "What about the Jews? For Christ's sake J.T., wake up. Men are killing each other for money, politics or just for a piece of ass. What about that old fucker Freeburg from Saint George who raped his own daughter? If I were God, I would look around, then flush the whole human race down the toilet as a bad mistake," Mike shouted, coughing so hard it doubled him over again. This time the coughing producing pasty-green mucous tinged with blood.

"Are you okay, Mick? That cough sounds awful."

"Just a damn summer cold," Mick replied as he wiped the green-red sputum into a handkerchief.

"Do you still feel like going camping tomorrow night?" Jack said, trying to change the subject. "We don't have to go, you know. There will be other test shots. I hear they've got em scheduled about every month."

"No. I don't want to miss this one. It's supposed to be the biggest yet. It should be quite a show," Mick said more cheerfully.

"You sure?"

"Yeah, this is nothing. I get one of these damn colds every summer." Mick wadded up the handkerchief and stuffed it in his pant pocket.

"Where do you want to camp? I know a place where my dad took me to cut cedar poles when we were fencing the Loren Webber piece. There's a spring there and it's right next to our BLM land. Dad wants me to check on our cattle, anyway. We're running about fifty-five head up there this summer."

"That sounds fine. We should get a great view from almost anywhere on Utah Hill. From there, you can almost see Yucca Flats. You gonna take your horses?"

"Yes, Dad wants me to do a head count on the cows, check on the new calf crop. Too big an area to cover on foot. Thought I would take A.C. and Ginger. You can ride Ginger.

"That's big of you. I wouldn't ride A.C. anyway. That damn mare is crazy. Loco. Belongs in a mental hospital. I don't know why you guys keep her. You want to take the girls?"

"I already told you I was." Jack looked puzzled.

"Not the goddamn horses, I mean Emily and Brenda."

"I don't know, Mick," Jack said. "Do you think that's a good idea? Anyhow, it's pretty short notice."

"J.T., it's just something to do. It's not like we're asking them to go to bed with us, though that's not such a bad idea. I've even got a spare tent for them. Anyway, what's the friggin' harm in asking?"

"I don't know."

"Just give Emily a call. She's crazy about you."

"Okay, I'll call her." Jack relented. "But either they both go, or neither goes. Deal?"

"Whatever. I have to spray the peach orchard tomorrow. I can be ready to go by four. It's a shitty job. I hate that damn DDT. Smells like an outhouse." Mick frowned.

"Four is fine by me. I've got to finish cutting the hay, then I want to run over to Saint George and check on Easy. See if they're going to ship him to Salt Lake City. That'll still give a couple of hours of daylight to make camp and ride the horses."

"Thought you'd heard," Mick said quietly.

"Heard what?"

"Easy died last night."

"Oh, God! Greg, and now, Easy."

"Hey, you two!" shouted a young man suddenly shattering the silence. "I want to talk to you." It was "Witless" Walt Hafen, Greg's older brother. What Walt lacked in intellect, he made up for with brawn. His well-sculpted muscles were chiseled on a six-foot, two-inch frame, with broad shoulders and a tight, lean waist. The only detracting feature was his eyes, a lethargic, dull green with a hint of meanness.

Jack, still shaken by the news of Easy's death, was the first to respond. "Hi Walt. I'm sorry about Greg. He was a good friend, almost a brother."

"Apparently a better friend to you than you were to him. What happened that night?" He spat, his face turning crimson.

"Wit, we weren't there. Jack and I was in Cedar City chasing women," Mick said sarcastically.

"Damn it, Mick. Don't ever call me Wit."

"I'm sorry Walt, I thought Wit was your name," Mick said with a straight face.

Walt's open palms suddenly landed on Mick's chest. Stumbling backward, Mick's feet tangled and he crashed to the ground, a striated grass stain now tattooed on the back of his gray Sunday pants. Slowly, Mick collected himself and stood up, ready for a fight. Walt responded with raised fists. After circling Walt for a moment, Mick shrugged his shoulders, dropped his hands, then turned.

"What's a matter Graff? Not man enough?" Walt sneered.

Mick whirled around, a right hook smashing Walt's left cheek and jaw, sending him cartwheeling to the right, onto the grass. Instantly, Walt was back on his feet, his eyes glazed with anger. Like a linebacker, he lowered his head and charged. His right shoulder thudded against Mick's chest, crushing the air from him. Mick staggered backward against the church wall but remained standing. Walt was on him in a second. The two young men grappled with each other, slapping arms away, trying to get leverage. Then Jack plunged into the fight and managed to wedge himself between.

"Come on guys. It's Greg's funeral! Let's show him a little respect."

"I know you two were with Greg that night," Walt shouted, backing away. "I know you did nothing to save him! You just drove off! You two turds are just as responsible for his death as if you had pulled a trigger. If the sheriff's not going to do nothing, I will. You two are going to pay for this!"

"Come on, Wit. Greg is responsible for his own death, not us," Mick replied, still gasping for air.

"All I can say is, you two better watch your fuckin' backs. There will be hell to pay for this. Count on it," Walt said evenly as he turned and left.

Jack quickly looked around and was relieved that they had attracted no attention. Everyone had already gone to the cemetery.

"Do you think he's serious?" Jack whispered, his face pinched with worry.

"Ah, hell J.T. You know Witless Walt is all hot air. What's he going to do? Kill us?" Mick's laugh was hoarse and raspy.

"He might, or he and his friends might just beat the crap out of us."

Mick shrugged. "If they do, then they do. But if they beat the friggin' shit out of one of us they had better get both, or they'll be the ones with trouble."

Jack's eyes became moist, and he put his arm around Mick's shoulders. "You know, we'll be doing all this again real soon—for Easy."

"I know," Mick said.

"You want to go on up to the cemetery?" Jack asked.

"No."

"I think we'd better go."

4

It hadn't been as difficult as Jack had imagined. Both girls were eager to go camping. The only conditions were those imposed by Emily and Brenda's parents: the girls must have a separate tent and the four of them were to conduct themselves in accordance with church standards.

In relatively good spirits considering the last three days, Jack had loaded both horses into the trailer, then stowed the tack and camping gear in the back of the pickup. The four of them then squeezed onto the bench seat in the cab. Jack didn't mind. He liked the feeling of Emily so close to him, especially with the floor-mounted gearshift positioned so seductively between her legs.

The road to Utah Hill was uneven. It meandered through multiple dry wash beds, then would abruptly scale an arroyo bank, only to descend again. This kind of broken terrain, to Jack's delight, required almost constant shifting. Second gear was usually accompanied by the "inadvertent" brushing of Emily's soft inner thigh.

Jack headed west out of Santa Clara on Highway 91. At the Shivwit Indian Reservation they turned north toward Gunlock. Just outside of Gunlock Jack turned left and bounced onto Goldstrike Road, steadily gaining elevation. About three-quarters up Utah Hill, they veered left again, connecting with Pahcoon Road that eventually led to the summit.

Adorned with gnarly cedars and the more aesthetic, conifer-shaped piñons, Utah Hill was a hill only by western standards. Straddling the Utah-Nevada border, it towered some 8,500 feet above the Mojave Desert floor. Yucca Flats, the above-ground nuclear test facility, was some eighty miles due west with no obstructing high terrain between it and Utah Hill. It was an excellent place to view the tests.

The foursome arrived at the summit a couple of hours before dark and hastily made camp. Nearby, a spring bubbled out of a limestone aquifer and tumbled into a shallow pond. On its banks the tents were erected and stakes were placed. Mick located several limestone rocks and placed them in a circle to form a fire pit. While the girls unrolled the sleeping bags and made the beds, Jack and Mick grabbed their .22 rifles. Time to go hunting.

Jack knew watering holes were the small eco-centers of the desert with the usual layers of interdependent life, plants, herbivores and carnivores. There was one striking difference however between desert springs and other more lush habitats. In the desert these strata of life co-existed in a relatively small geographic area. Consequently, desert springs made an excellent place to hunt for small game.

Within thirty minutes the hunters returned with two cotton-tail rabbits and a half dozen mourning doves. After skinning and cleaning the game and washing the feathers, fur and blood from their hands, the boys stored their take in an ice cooler. Jack then fetched the tack from the pickup.

The others tagged along as Jack began currying the loose debris from A.C.'s coat. "If you don't get this little straw and stuff off, it can rub em raw under the saddle blanket," Jack explained to Emily.

"I've never ridden a horse before," Emily said, her eyes wide with amazement. "They're huge!"

"Nothing to it. Easier than ridin' a bike. Don't worry I'll show you," Jack assured.

With a single graceful motion, Jack threw his prized Carl Darr saddle on A.C., then wedged a split-bit between her teeth. As he placed his left foot in the stirrup, A.C. dropped her head and flattened her ears. Jack knew he should have seen it coming but in the excitement of showing off for the girls, he had ignored these subtle clues.

Just as Jack bunched the reins and saddle horn in his left hand and swung his right leg over the saddle, all hell broke loose. Kicking her rear legs backward and skyward, A.C. vaulted forward, bucking furiously. Jack bounced hard a couple of times on the cantle, with nothing to protect his testicles from the jarring. In agony, he grabbed for the saddle horn, missed, and clutched only a handful of mane at the withers. With another jolt, he lost his grip on the mane and flew backwards off the rear of the horse. For what seemed like an eternity, Jack was suspended in air. Then he came crashing to the ground cracking his ribs on a cedar log just narrowly missing a protruding branch that might have impaled him.

Emily was the first to reach him. She cradled Jack's head in her lap, as he tried to get his breath. All he could manage was a gasping, "Uh—uh—uh."

"Are you okay?" Emily asked anxiously.

Still stunned and fighting for breath, Jack finally grunted. "Yeah—uh—I'm fine."

"You coulda been killed. How's your back? Can you feel your feet?" Emily pulled him tighter.

"I'm fine. If she hasn't been ridden for a spell, that damn horse always bucks. I shoulda seen it coming."

Mick and Brenda now closed in and Jack could see them hoovering over him."By God, that was a wonderful example of horsemanship, J.T." Mick's freckles bunched with amusement. "But I didn't quite get all the steps down. Could you give us that ridin' lesson one more time?"

"What a thing to say," Emily said, as her eyes fired darts at Mick.

"Uh—uh—uh," Jack moaned.

"Does it hurt a lot?" Brenda asked, as she bent over with her lacquered blonde hair slapping Jack in the face.

What the hell do you think? Jack thought, as he was finally able to get a lung full of air. Sometimes Brenda just plain irritated him, but he replied, "I'm all right. Just some bruised ribs." Jack struggled to his feet and gingerly touched his throbbing ribs.

"C'mon J.T., let's forget ridin' for today," Mick said. "It's getting late anyway."

"No, lets go. She'll be fine now she has it out of her system."

"I'm not getting on that horse," Emily laughed nervously, as she raised her hands and backed away.

Jack limped over to A.C. "Em, A.C. will be fine. Let me show you." Jack slipped into the saddle. Perfectly calm now, A.C. looked totally disinterested as she knifed off a tuft of grass and ground it between her teeth. To demonstrate his point, Jack rode A.C. around the camp, returning to Emily.

"Come on, Em," Jack said, extending an arm.

"I don't know, Jack Kunz." Emily laughed nervously. "Why do I think you're trying to kill me?"

But she gave in and slowly placed her foot in the stirrup, mounting behind Jack. Brenda and Mick got on Ginger and the four friends rode north following a well-traveled deer trail. To the right, an invisible coyote wailed at the fading light. To the left, the ebbing sun hemorrhaged then died as it slipped into the waiting jaws of the great Mojave Desert.

For the first time in days, Jack felt at peace. Up here, the volcano, the deputy, Greg and Earl all seemed distant and insignificant. How he loved this place. The coyote yipped again and somewhere to the back of them, he heard the hoot of a spotted desert owl.

The four friends rode in comfortable silence. Directly ahead, four or five mule-tail deer raised their heads, then silently bounded for cover. Slowly, the harmony of the evening dissipated to urgency and passion. Jack became acutely aware of Emily's body close to him and to his chagrin, he found himself aroused. With her arms flung firmly around him, the jarring motions of the horse made her firm breasts rub and sometimes flatten against his back. Subconsciously, Jack urged A.C. faster so Emily would cling tighter. He imagined Emily topless with her supple, firm breasts, each crowned with a pink, slightly raised areola and a succulent nipple and he pictured himself kneading them, bending over, his mouth all over them.

With a surge of guilt, Jack jerked on the reins of his mind. These were not the reflections of a prospective missionary. Sheepishly, afraid she could read his mind through the back of his head, Jack glanced back. Emily smiled, seemingly oblivious to his carnal thoughts. Jack then glanced at Brenda and Mick. They were enjoying each other and seemed completely unaware of his antics.

Eventually the gathering darkness made the trail difficult to see and the horses began to stumble on the rocks. Reluctantly Jack turned A.C. around and with Ginger in tow, headed back to camp.

The boys unsaddled the horses, brushed and grained them, then tethered them between two cedar trees. Jack and Mick quickly built a fire from needles, bark and branches gathered from the rotting carcasses of the dead cedar and piñon trees and within minutes the camp was bathed in amber light.

They peeled and sharpened green cedar boughs and skewered the rabbits and mourning doves. Mick placed the spit on two forked sticks staked on either side of the fire pit while Jack cut up onions and potatoes in a cast-iron Dutch oven. Smoke swirled and the distinct aroma of frying onions and roasting meat seeped through the camp. At regular intervals, Mick rotated the spit and the meat seared and sizzled, slowly turning golden brown. Occasionally, the fire hissed and popped, propelling small missiles of charcoal into the pot. Unconcerned, Jack blended them in.

When everything was ready, Mick cut the meat and Jack spooned each camper a portion of potatoes. Emily and Brenda retrieved bottles of Coke that had been cooling in the spring since their arrival.

"Hey, J.T., you got a church key?" Mick asked as he rummaged through the picnic supplies.

"Look in the box we had the Cokes in," Jack answered as he replaced the lid on the Dutch oven, then placed a few coals on top to keep the potatoes warm.

Mick finally found the opener, popped the cap, and with one gulp drank about a third of the bottle. Then he extracted a fifth of cheap rum from his pack and filled his bottle to the top.

"Anybody want some?" Mick grinned and held the bottle high. His eyes danced and the sweet smell of rum floated in the firelight.

Jack shook his head. "Not tonight. I'd think after all that's happened the last few days, you would of had enough of booze."

"For hell's sake J.T., lighten up. We're twenty-one, in the middle of nowhere, not driving nowhere that I know of. Why not have a good time?"

Brenda giggled. "I want some," she said and grabbed the bottle. "I've never tried rum and Coke before."

Yeah, I'll bet, Jack thought.

After splashing about a fourth of her Coke on the ground, she filled the bottle with rum. Slowly Brenda rotated the bottle mixing in the rum, then took a sip. Immediately she choked, spraying the beverage on the fire. "This stuff is awful." She sputtered, took another gulp, then passed the rum to Emily.

Looking unsure, Emily took the bottle, then glanced at Jack. Before Jack could speak, Mick cut him off. "What's it going to hurt, Em? One drink's not going to make you an alcoholic, and this party needs to be livened up. Bet you had booze at some of your California parties."

"Well, yes, but—"

"Come on Em," Brenda said. "I don't want to be the only girl drinking. It's not that bad, tastes like cherry Coke."

"Only if it's okay with Jack."

Not wanting to look like a prude in front of Emily, Jack shrugged his shoulders. "All right, just a little." He slowly took a swig, then filled the remainder of his Coke with rum. But silently to himself, he promised, this will be the last time.

The girls conceded the meal was good, or at least filling, but Jack noticed their plates were only half eaten and the only thing they asked for seconds was the rum and Coke. After they had eaten, as a reward for the men having done the cooking, the girls washed and dried the dishes. Then the campers settled back in their chairs of flat rocks and cedar logs to enjoy the fire and sip their drinks.

"This is wonderful," Emily sighed. "My father split when I was young and with my mother's heart problems, I've never been camping."

"Me neither," gushed Brenda. "The only time I've been camping was when my family took me to Yellowstone and we had to stay in those awful little cabins. That was really roughing it. Couldn't do anything with my hair the next morning."

"That must have been terrible," Jack said, smiling at Emily.

"We've been camping a lot," Mick said. "J.T. and me, Greg, Earl, Alan and Curley used to saddle our horses, pack our gear in saddle-bags and ride up to Snow Canyon. There's a side canyon, Clarie Canyon, that has water and a natural arch. We'd camp there."

"You six did a lot together," Emily's said, then frowned. "I was sure sorry to hear about Greg and Earl."

"I guess you know Earl died night before last. Both of them. Both of them gone." Jack said, as he stared vacantly into the night. "Greg had a very nice funeral. Now we gotta do it all over again."

For a moment Mick seemed lost in his own thoughts, then his voice hardened. "For one night could we not discuss what happened? We had some good times together. That's the way I prefer to remember them."

To change the subject, Brenda said brightly, "Em and I haven't known each other nearly as long as you guys, but we've had some good times. Tell them what we did the other night, Em."

"Which other night?"

Brenda pointed to her ears, then giggled.

"Oh, yeah. It was nothing that great, we just pierced each other's ears." Emily replied, flipping her hair back to reveal a white cotton string threaded through a tiny hole in her ear lobe, tied into a loop.

"You did that yourself? Didn't it hurt?" Jack asked.

"Nah, not really," Emily said as she smoothed her hair back into place.

"I thought it did." Brenda giggled again. "Anyway, our parents would never let us get them pierced, so the other night when Em stayed over, we just did it. First we numbed up the earlobe by sandwiching it between two ice cubes. Then we sterilized a needle with a match and threaded the string through the eye of the needle and just jabbed it through the earlobe and pulled the string. After that, we tied the string in a loop to keep the holes open. We have to put alcohol on it and slide the string back and forth each day so it doesn't stick." Brenda paused to take a breath. "And our parents still don't know."

"I don't think I could do that. I can't stand needles," Jack said.

"You'd better get over your fear of needles, J.T., if you're going to be a doctor." Mick stirred the coals, then abruptly broke into laughter. "J.T., you remember that time in church? When we were about twelve or thirteen?"

"You tell it Mick. I'm not sure which time you're talking about."

"You remember when those cracker balls were popular?" Mick asked, looking around at the group. "You know those little balls filled with black powder, and when you threw them on the sidewalk, they would explode like a little firecracker? Well, when we were twelve or thirteen, Jack, myself, Alan, Earl and Greg, I don't remember why Curley wasn't there, snuck into the church about a half hour before the service. At that time in the chapel they had those wooden pews with the individual folding seats. You know, the kind that when you sit down, the seat comes down to rest on a metal platform, and when you get up, the seat springs up again." The girls nodded. "Anyway, like I said, we snuck in before the service began and planted cracker balls on the metal platforms so they would be crushed when the seats came down."

Mick chuckled at his own story. "You should have seen it! It was better than the fourth of July in Las Vegas. I never knew those blue-haired old ladies could move so friggin' fast. They would sit down, their seats would explode, and they would jump up so fast it's a wonder they didn't have a heart attack. It was like holding church in a battlefield. Those old ladies were hopping around, holding their behinds and looking bewildered, like they weren't sure where the sound was coming from."

Holding their aching sides, the four howled with laughter. "There's no way to top that one," Emily said, as she caught her breath.

Mick, still laughing at his story, got up and stirred the coals again, sending a geyser of swirling sparks billowing into the black night.

"Not to change the subject J.T., but what's this one gonna be called? Peter or Paul? Something biblical?"

"No Mick, you're thinking of the last one, that was Simon. The one before Simon was Nancy. This one is called Harry, Shot Harry," Jack said. He was fascinated by the nuclear tests and had read everything he could find on the Yucca Flats experiments.

"I hear the Russians are way ahead of us," Emily said. "They've got bigger bombs, something called an H-bomb. And they have a lot more of them."

"That's why these tests are so necessary," Jack declared. "This batch, the Upshot-Knothole series, is critical for us to keep pace with the Russians. The hydrogen bomb is about a hundred times more powerful than the atomic bomb, but Em, as far as I know, the Russians don't have one yet. We've got to get it before they do, or we're all goners. The Russians will annihilate us," Jack said, his voice strong with conviction. "Shot Harry is supposed to be 32 kilotons, the biggest yet. That's three times the size of the bomb dropped on Hiroshima. Tomorrow ought'a be quite a sight."

"Now, is Shot Harry an atomic bomb or a hydrogen bomb?" Brenda asked.

"I just got done saying we don't have a hydrogen bomb," Jack said tersely.

"Don't you think the government and the Atomic Energy Commission are overplaying this Russian angle a bit?" Mick asked. "Why would the Russians want to wipe us out? Just so they could occupy a country that was fried with radiation and wouldn't be habitable for a hundred years or more? It makes no sense to me, J.T." Mick shook his head and tossed a cedar log on the fire. "I think the government, and all of us for that matter, are acting just a little paranoid."

"The Russians are not like us," Jack replied. "They're a patient people and are not into individualism. They plan for the future. Their whole society will sacrifice now, so in the future their great-grandchildren will have control over the entire planet. To them, a hundred years is nothing." Jack sounded convincing, even though he had never met a Russian.

"I'll bet they would wipe us out in a minute if they thought they could get away with it," Brenda said, not to be left out.

"Whatever," said Mick. "I'm just not convinced that Russians are all that evil and that our military, government and Atomic Energy Commission are so lily white. They're just people. I'll bet they're just running scared like we are. And what's more, I'm not at all sure these damn tests are safe."

"Of course they're safe," Jack said. "Do you think the AEC would purposefully harm us? I think in general we are right and, in general, the Russians are wrong and evil. Mick, they don't even believe in God They're atheists!"

"So? J.T., don't you think it's just a bit naive to think that every person who believes in God is righteous? History certainly doesn't support your position. How do you explain the Crusades, the Spanish Inquisition or even the persecution of the Mormons? These things were all done by friggin' religious people, most of em Christians." Mick glared. "And just for the sake of argument, name me one atheist that's committed atrocities."

"I'll name you two: Stalin and Lenin," Jack snapped.

Emily stepped in. "You two are probably both right. Anyway, you're not going to settle this argument tonight. Not an argument that has been raging for centuries. There are evil people regardless of their religion. Let's just mellow out a bit and enjoy the evening."

Suddenly, Mick was seized with a violent coughing fit, which he finally squelched with a swig of rum and Coke. A trickle of blood flowed from Mick's left nostril and he looked pale and tired. "Goddamn it, another nosebleed." Mick brushed the blood away with the back of his hand, then pinched the bridge of his nose. "Gang, I'm bushed. I think I'll hit the sack. What time's the blast tomorrow, J.T.?"

"Supposed to be just before dawn, 5:00 a.m. Don't worry, I'll wake you up."

"I never worry, at least not when you're around," Mick said dryly, then looked over at Brenda. "You coming?"

Brenda blushed, "You don't look like you're up to it tonight."

"Whatever," Mick said, tossing aside his empty bottle and crawling into the tent.

"What'ta you guys wanna do now?" Brenda said with a nervous giggle.

"Five o'clock comes awfully early. You know how you hate to get up," Emily replied as she arched an eyebrow.

"Yeah, I don't think I've ever been up at five o'clock before."

"If we go to bed now, we'll get plenty of rest," Emily urged.

"Let's talk. I saw John Sedgely at the Polar Bear last week and you'll never believe who he was with."

"Brenda! Go to bed," Emily commanded

"Oh yeah." Brenda got the hint, excused herself and squirmed into the girls' tent.

"I sure like Mick," Emily said. "He's funny. Is he okay?"

"I don't know if you call it funny or just cynical, but I think he's all right. Says he's got a summer cold, but it seems to hang on forever." Jack put his arm around Emily and felt the cotton string in her ear. "I still can't believe you did this yourself."

"It was nothing," Em said softly. "Jack you were magnificent today, the way you handled A.C." She placed her head on his chest. "I would never have had the nerve to get back on her. You sure know horses."

The faint perfume from her hair and the pressure of her breasts once again aroused him. "When you get bucked off, you've just got to get right back on. Otherwise, the horse senses you're afraid and from then on he's the one in control."

"You afraid of me, Jack?" Emily asked, tilting her face upward.

Looking down at her, Jack noted that her cheeks were flushed from the warmth of the fire and the top button of her shirt was undone, revealing the crests of her rounded breasts.

He bent over and kissed her and without hesitating, Emily responded. She wedged her tongue in his mouth and sensually braided it around his tongue, a sensation Jack had never experienced. He reached down through her half-open shirt and cupped his hands around her breasts. Moaning softly, Emily burrowed closer. Jack then pressed her already hard nipples and Emily responded by unzipping Jack's Levis and massaging his penis through his underwear. Fumbling with desire, Jack quickly unzipped her pants and thrust an exploring hand inside. He felt Emily's soft pubic hair, then the firmness of her pubic bone. Emily began thrusting her pelvis against Jack's. Thrusting and rubbing, again and again. He tugged her pants and panties down, then pulled her close as she spread her legs.

Suddenly, Jack stiffened. "Emily, I'm sorry, I just can't do this. I promised my mother before she died that I would stay true to the church and go on a mission. I'm so sorry, Em, I've got to stop." Jack buried his head in his hands.

"I understand, I think," Emily said, still breathing hard. She then put her arm around Jack's shoulders. "Jack, as you know my mother is very ill, and I respect any promises you made to yours."

"Em, sometimes I'm not sure what's right anymore, but I just don't want you to think that I—uh—that I don't want you."

"I don't, Jack. I can tell."

5

Jack joined Mick in the tent at around midnight but sleep did not follow. He was aware of Mick's harsh, labored breathing but his mind sprinted like a riderless horse along several paths.

He was embarrassed by his moronic behavior with Emily. What must she think of him? The serious, prudish, religious guy who is no fun at all. After all, what would have been wrong with making love? It was the most natural thing in the world. On the other hand, the church taught that Satan often packaged sin to look natural and attractive, the old wolf in sheep's clothing trick. But sex was biologic, as fundamental as breathing and eating, and the human race would die out without it. It was a force of nature that could not be denied.

The church insists that we learn to control our appetites, become masters of our bodies as well as our minds, Jack thought. That is a big part of the reason we are placed on earth, and self-control is an integral component in achieving our ultimate goal, the growth of our immortal spirits until we become gods, like the church teaches. Bitterly, Jack wondered, what exactly did gods do? Certainly, he could not imagine God engaging in lustful sex. On the surface, it seemed that they must live a pretty mundane existence of self deprivation, like the Catholic priests. But regardless of all that, it would have been nice to make love to Emily.

Jack's restless mind then veered to Mick. Undeniably Mick is a classic cynic, Jack thought, he questions everything. Nothing is as it seems on the surface and everybody and everything has an ulterior motive. Even things that should be beyond reproach, like the church and even God. Mick even challenged the integrity of the AEC and government itself. There was no doubt in Jack's mind that these organizations were looking out for our welfare and the good of the country. If the Atomic Energy Commission said the tests were safe, they were safe. What possible motive could they possibly have for lying?

After all, the citizens of Washington County and the AEC had a common goal, Jack thought, the preservation of our land and freedom. And as a country we were in some serious trouble, we had to beat the Russians in the development of the H-bomb. This was not just hysteria or paranoia, this was real. Regardless of what Mick said, God is on our side.

But even more troubling to Jack was Mick's cynicism toward the church. When they were kids, they had made a pact, that they would go on missions together. Lately, this was looking doubtful. The church had designated twenty-one as the age to go on missions, and now they were of age. It was time to stand up and be counted Jack thought, but Mick seemed disinterested, almost antagonistic. Mentally, Jack doubled his resolve to encourage Mick to go with him on a mission.

Then there was Mick's health. Lately he had been tired and irritable, and that damn cough would not go away, and now tonight, the nosebleed. When they got back home, Jack would insist that Mick see Dr. Hilton. Probably some penicillin would do him and his summer cold a world of good.

Jack's thoughts wandered to the volcano, Easy and Greg, Deputy Saunders and the manslaughter charge. That benign prank had left three people dead. How could innocent horseplay blow up in your face like that? To Jack, these events only served to confirm the fleeting and transitory nature of life and life's circumstances. One day it looked like you pretty much had a handle on life, attending college, majoring in pre-med, preparing for a mission, and starting to date a terrific girl. The next day you could be going to jail, doing one-to-five, or, as in Easy's, Greg's and Deputy Saunders' case, be dead.

With a flashlight, Jack checked his watch. It was 4:15 a.m. Thank God, it was time to get up and wake the others. He pulled on his faded Levis and rotated his navy blue T-shirt in the dark, trying to sort out front and back. For the first time he noticed a jagged tear, probably from a barb-wire fence, on the back of his shirt. That must of really impressed Emily. With a sigh, he parted the tent flaps and went outside to re-start the fire.

In the chill morning air, Jack nursed the coals back to life. A hint of light sneaked past the craggy shoulders of Pine Valley Mountain to the east and seeped like blood into the raven-black night. To the far west, thin streaks of russet light outlined wispy, rooster-tail clouds that dozed unsuspectingly high above the Mojave desert. With a growing sense of excitement, Jack put a pot of water on the fire. Hot chocolate would be perfect for watching the test.

When Jack shook Mick's shoulder to wake him, he noticed his shirt was damp with perspiration and the front of his white T-shirt was flecked with blood.

"How you feeling?" Jack asked, his hand still resting on Mick's shoulder. "Your shirt is spotted with blood."

"Just that nosebleed. I'm fine. What time is it?"

"It's 4:30. About last night, I'm sorry," Jack said.

"No big deal. We just differ on certain things. Friends can do that, you know."

"Lately, seems like we disagree on everything. We're still going on missions, aren't we?"

"J.T., we're different people. We're supposed to disagree. For now, forget the missions. If it happens, it happens. If it don't, it don't. That's not what our friendship's about. Let's get the girls. I certainly don't want to miss that shot. You get any last night?"

"Any what?"

"Nookie. You know with Emily."

Jack flushed. "Nah, after you went to bed we just talked for a while, then we all hit the sack. Brenda seemed disappointed that you left so early."

"I'll make it up to her. We better wake them up or we'll miss the show."

As the rumpled girls came out, Jack greeted them with steaming mugs of hot chocolate. A wave of embarrassment pierced him as he handed Emily hers, but she squeezed his hand and smiled. Feeling better, he tilted his watch to the firelight. It was 4:45.

"We ought to get over to the edge of that high point, where it drops off. We'll have a good view from there." Jack pointed to a spot about twenty yards to the west where the terrain rose slightly, then pitched precipitously to the valley floor.

"This is exciting. I've never seen an atomic bomb test before." Emily said.

"J.T. and I have been watching them on and off for about two years now. From here you can't actually see the mushroom cloud but you can sure see the flash and feel the earth shake." Mick took a sip of his chocolate. "Then a couple hours later, what's left of the mushroom cloud will float over. Sometimes they're pink. It should be quite a show. I just don't know why they set them off at this ungodly hour."

"I'll second that," Brenda said with a yawn. "I'd heard of five o'clock in the morning but until now, I never really believed it existed."

"Well, bring your mugs and let's go over and get the balcony seats before they're all taken." Jack laughed as he started walking toward the ridge.

Ninety miles to the west, Shot Harry was detonated at exactly 5:05 a.m. at Yucca Flats, Nevada. Hanging like an outlaw from a gallows, Harry dangled above the desert from a 300-foot aluminum tower and when the prevailing winds were exactly right, blowing due east, Harry was exploded.

Within milliseconds after the switch was pulled, Harry shattered with an atomic rage three times that of Hiroshima, instantly produced a blinding white-orange fireball. As it shot upward, a giant root-bearing stem instantly appeared as if to support the ascending fiery mass. Standing on the valley floor like an enormous water tower, it was, for one paralyzing minute, a thing of terrifying beauty. Then the base of the stem began to disappear as a billowing ashen-gray dust cloud was sucked from the valley floor.

The loose soil and rock of the desert floor, the tower and the cab that contained Harry were all instantly vaporized. As the fireball rose and began to cool, the gaseous vapors within condensed to form a vigorous updraft called afterwind. This afterwind vacuumed the remaining loose debris from the valley floor and thoroughly mixed it with the vaporized material and radioactive products. It created a suspension of particulate matter that varied in size from that of an atom to about a half inch in diameter. As Harry's cloud floated downwind, these airborne radioactive particles would systematically fall out with the grip of gravity. The heavier particles would plummet to the earth first, and the lighter particles would take hours or even days to descend.

At the time of the blast, a small thunderhead had been perched directly over the top of the tower at about 10,000 feet. As the bomb exploded, the mushroom rose and swallowed it up, transforming it into a thing of eerie beauty. It instantly turned an iridescent pink, rapidly intensifying to a flaming orange, then deepening to a crimson red, rifling through the colors of a sunset in milli-seconds.

Meanwhile, the stem started to blur. Hanging from the fireball like gray beards, apron-clouds began to appear, ringing and obscuring the upper stem.

Ten minutes after the detonation, the soaring mushroom cloud collided with the troposphere. It flattened and layered out at 42,000 feet, while the bottom remained steady at about 27,000 feet. The cloud and its stem held their mushroom shape for a short time, then began to break apart. As the cloud islands drifted east, they continued to glow. Their pink color was created from the residue of nitrous acid and oxides of nitrogen that formed in the caldron of intense heat and catalytic radiation generated by the fireball. All in all, it was a breathtaking scene.

Straightaway, the entire ghoulish family of fissionary by-products was released to seep into the atmosphere. This deadly clan consisted of the virulent triplets: Alpha rays (positively charged particles consisting of two protons and two neutrons), Beta rays (negatively charged particles with approximately 100x more pene-trating energy than alphas), and Gamma rays (similar to x-rays, but with 10,000x more penetrating power). Unfortunately, none of these emissions could be seen, heard, tasted or smelled. Some radioactive particles were short-lived and decayed in hours. Other fissionary elements, like plutonium, had a half-life of some 24,000 years.

This spectacle amazed and appalled, inspired and dismayed the four campers. In awe they watched as the brilliant, blinding white flash chased the residual blackness from the morning sky. The intense brightness had forced them to blink and close their eyes and within seconds they heard a low-pitched roar that seemed to come from the earth. As the ground shook, the horses reared and lunged at their restraining ropes. The campers flinched as the rolling sound waves hit the surrounding hill with a series of explosions, like echoing cannon fire. The thin cirrus cloud that floated over the valley instantly effervesced, radiating a metallic-pink that caused the group to gasp in amazement.

Then as quickly as it began, it was over except for an ominous dark cloud that was gathering on the western horizon.

"God, that was beautiful!" Emily exclaimed. "So powerful. Words just can't describe it."

"I've never seen anything like that in my entire life," Brenda said. "It's just like in the newsreels."

"Amazing! Something so magnificent, so glorious, kinda makes you believe in God," Jack added almost reverently.

"Believe in God, hell!" Mick fumed, as he stared at the mottled western sky. "What you've just witnessed is one huge fucking mistake. Shit, we could wipe out the whole human race with this. If there is a God, which sometimes I doubt, he don't want his name associated with the likes of this."

"Come on Mick, you don't need to use the f-word, not in front of the girls."

"I'm sorry, but that's how I feel. It's beyond me, how can you attribute this to God."

"Well, God made man in his own image, to be inquisitive and inventive. The atomic bomb is a testimony of God through man's genius. A lot of good will come of nuclear power, and maybe someday we'll be able to harness some of this power for peaceful purposes."

"If God has a hand in this, he'd better be prepared to accept liability for his actions. More people are going to die from this damn thing than Stalin and Hitler combined," Mick said.

"When God made man, he gave him great potential and ability. What man does with that potential is his own responsibility, not God's."

"You mean to tell me that God, on purpose, made man imperfect with the ability to do evil as well as good, and when he does do bad things, then God accepts no responsibility? How convenient for God. He purposefully makes a defective product, then assumes no liability.

That's like when Steve Hardin knocked-up Peggy, then told her it was her problem and not his," Mick said, his face distorted.

"Mick, it's not the same. You don't understand the principle of free agency."

"I damn well do understand free agency and also know when your arguments make no sense. J.T., we'll never agree on this one. Let's just drop it."

"I think it was wonderful," Brenda gushed, oblivious to the tension between Mick and Jack. "I'm glad I came, but if I was in charge, the tests would be scheduled for a more reasonable hour. Say ten o'clock or so. At least give us time to put on some make-up and do our hair first. Can you do something about that, Jack?"

All four laughed, then Emily said, "Forget the make-up. How about some breakfast?"

As they headed back to camp, the first shafts of sunlight pierced the eastern ridge top and fought through the piñon and cedar boughs, splashing the camp in dappled light. After adding fuel, Jack stirred the white-crusted coals with a piñon branch and they erupted into flames. Before long, they had prepared a ranch hand's breakfast of sizzling uncured bacon, scrambled eggs mixed with what was left of last night's onions and potatoes, and fresh baked Dutch oven biscuits topped with butter.

"Mick, Jack, this is delicious." Emily said. "You can cook for me anytime. And where did you get the butter? It's great."

"Actually, we make it ourselves," Jack answered.

Emily arched her eyebrows. "Growing up in La Puente, I always thought butter came from the grocery store. How in the world do you make butter?"

"We have a Guernsey cow I milk every morning and night. Guernsey milk is high in fat, so we run the milk through a cream separator. Once it's separated, the cream is poured into a butter churn. After what seems like an eternity of working the plunger up and down, you have butter. Then just add salt to taste. It's a lot easier if you just get it at the grocery store," Jack laughed.

"I'll bet most of this food Jack raised on the farm,"Brenda said. "My dad buys some of their stuff to sell in the store."

Mick joined in, "Most families in Santa Clara are pretty self-sufficient. The bacon is fresh, uncured, and is probably from a pork Jack's dad butchered in the last couple weeks. The eggs are from their own hen house, and the milk for the hot chocolate is from that same Guernsey cow. And, I'm sure the biscuit flour is from wheat that Jack's father traded to the miller for flour. Only thing not from Santa Clara is the chocolate."

"Wherever it comes from, it's scrumptious," Emily said, impressed. "Anyway, in case we have a nuclear war with the Russians, I think it will be the self-sufficient that survive. I hope you guys remember who your friends are."

Jack nodded. "That could happen. Anyway, I'd hate to be a Russian invading Santa Clara. There's more guns and ammunition there than in the Utah State National Guard Armory."

"And I can't wait til I kill my first Russian. Those godless bastards," Mick quipped.

"Actually, they do have a plan to invade—" Jack said, but Emily cut in.

"Let's get everything cleaned up."

A few minutes later as they were washing dishes in the spring, the campers noticed that the sky had suddenly darkened. The dark cloud, once innocently gathering on the western horizon, was now directly overhead, appearing thick, angry and ominous. They quickly finished washing, drying and packing away the tableware.

Suddenly, the wind shifted and the cloud dropped to the ground. The campers were instantly engulfed in a dense, murky fog. The air smelled metallic, like a welding shop, and Jack could feel the hairs of his arms and the back of his neck tingle and stand up. Silently, a gray ash, like the soot produced by forest fires fell all around, the gray flakes flashing and flickering like Fourth of July sparklers. Within minutes, the ground was lightly covered, and their boots and sneakers left footprints in the dirty snow.

Abruptly, the feathery ash became grainy, like hail.

"My God! This shit is hot. I think we're in trouble!" Mick screamed as he brushed a small burning particle from his arm. "Let's get to cover."

All four sprinted for the truck and once inside the cab, Jack asked with a nervous laugh, "What the heck is that stuff?"

"It's fallout. This is fucking radioactive fallout," Mick barked.

"Mick, cut the profanity," Jack replied, staring out the window.

"Look at my hair. It's a mess. I just had it done yesterday," Brenda sobbed, as she strained ash from her hair with forked fingers.

"This is kinda scary. How long will it last?" Emily asked, her eyes wide.

"Who knows? I've never been in friggin' fallout before," Mick answered.

As he spoke, the cloud began to lift and a few scattered rays of sunlight penetrated the gloom.

"Think it's safe to get out?" Emily asked, as she scanned the sky.

Jack, though he knew he had nothing to confirm his reply, answered, "We should probably wait. Maybe thirty minutes to an hour. By then, it should be safe."

"Yeah, right. A couple of physics classes, and now you're an expert," Mick said.

"It looks okay to me right now. The sun's shining," Brenda said. "I need to get my mirror and things out of the tent."

"Let's wait a bit," Jack said firmly.

"Whatever," Mick grunted. "You still planning on riding over to your dad's land and check on the cows?"

"Yeah, I've got to. We put those cows up here three months ago, before they calved. We still don't have an accurate count on how many calves were born this spring."

"Fake it," Mick said. "Just figure one calf for every pregnant cow you had."

"I wouldn't dare do that. Sometimes we lose an odd calf to cougars or coyotes. My dad would throw a fit if my count wasn't accurate. It won't take long. We'll saddle up and ride double. Might even be fun." Jack thought of Emily's breasts poking him in the back.

"Are you sure A.C. will behave?" Emily asked. "I'm still nervous about riding that horse."

"Yeah, she'll be okay. It's just when she hasn't been ridden for a while that she acts like that," Jack answered.

"That horse is mental," Mick said, "and I've never heard of the crazies being cured overnight, or at all, for that matter. Unless radiation fallout is a cure for mental disease, that horse is still psychotic."

In an hour, Mick and Jack eased out of the truck. Mick scooped up a bit of ash. He tried to make a snowball but it wouldn't stick. Jack then motioned for the girls.

As Mick and Jack saddled A.C. and Ginger, they noticed white splotches on their backs. Even after Jack vigorously brushed and curried the horses, the chalky stains remained. They smelled like singed hair, but did not seem painful. With a shrug, Jack covered the patches with saddle blankets, then threw on the saddles. The four then rode a mile north to the Kunz's summer range.

Jack opened the barb-wire gate and looked around at the land he had worked on for so many years. It was not their land at all, but belonged to the United States government and was administered by the Bureau of Land Management. Years ago, the BLM had leased this tract to his grandfather, like many ranchers in the west, for the grazing of cows. As long as the leasee did not abuse the land, made periodic improvements, and was conscientious about maintenance, the leases were long term, open-ended contracts, and were even inheritable. Though still legally a lease, the owner of these contracts was also able to sell them at his discretion and they were very difficult, if not almost impossible, for the BLM to revoke.

The Kunz's range had four sections, roughly 2,600 acres, on the high western slope of Utah Hill about ten miles north of U.S. Highway 91. As it turned out, about half was in Utah, the rest in Nevada. In a wet year, the range was covered with native grasses that lapped at the trunks of cedar and piñon trees. The trees were grouped in island clusters as if this offered them protection from the aggressive grass. Like reverse veins on the back of a hand, arroyos dissected land indiscriminately, carving out a drainage system through the grass land. The gullies and tree islands gave cattle a thousand places to hide, making fall round-up an arduous and sometimes exasperating task.

On all 2,600 acres, there was only one source of standing water, a small, year-around spring, tucked away at the base of a bluff, in the northwest corner of the property. The cows had to make a daily pilgrimage to the small pool to drink. It was a good place to start a head count.

While they were still some distance from the spring, Jack noticed three large mounds on the ground only yards from the spring. That was odd; Jack didn't remember these rocks. As they approached, Jack realized they were not rocks at all, but dead Hereford cows. With mounting apprehension, they reigned and dismounted. The late-morning air was hot and reeked of rotting flesh. A swarm of blue flies flitted and darted above the lifeless carcasses. As they approached, two scavenger crows, clamoring and cawing, awkwardly launched into flight, then patiently wafted above them on thermal currents of rapidly warming morning air.

"What the hell is this?" Mick exclaimed.

Jack walked cautiously over and kicked one with his boot. "Dead cows."

"No Shit, Jack! I can see that. No doubt your two years of pre-med hasn't been wasted. What killed them, doctor?" Mick asked, anger in his voice.

"Probably kids from town, or Shivwits."

"Any bullet holes?"

Without answering, Jack took a closer look. All three cows were bloated like helium balloons. There were no bullet holes, but there were other odd findings. "Come over here Mick. What do you make of these open sores on their necks and backs?" As he spoke, Jack circled the carcass and examined the head. "The same sores are around the eyes and mouth."

The girls stayed back, watching in horror.

"Never saw nothing like it," Mick said as he grimaced and pinched his nose. "It don't qualify for scabies or hoof-and-mouth disease, and milkweed poisoning don't cause no raw open sores," Mick shook his head. "This is strange. Never saw nothing like this. We're probably going to have to get the vet up here to tell us what the hell this is."

"We better check the rest of the cows," Jack said, his voice hollow. "I hope they're not all dead."

They spent the rest of the morning searching the thickets, arroyos, and occasional dense stands of cedar and piñon trees. Three more cows were found dead. But what was even more disturbing was the calves.

Seven were dead, and two appeared to have been stillborn. As Jack dismounted to inspect the carnage, he winced. It was a grizzly sight. The fetuses had been born with no hair, giving them an albino appearance. They had grotesque, dried-prune, wrinkled skin, with huge potbellies and no legs.

"J.T., what do you make of this? I've seen stillborn calves before, but I've never seen none that looked like that," asked Mick.

"They're mutant. Something damaged the embryo. Either a virus or bacteria, poor nutrition, or they got into something toxic," Jack said with the confidence of someone who had studied the biological sciences.

"I think it's all those goddamn tests at Yucca Flats. Shit, they've set off thirty or so of them already, and if they all had as much fallout this morning, I think we have to consider they might be the cause," Mick said, not bothering to get off the horse.

"Seems to me you blame everything on the tests. I don't think they'd tell us those tests were safe, if they weren't. There's gotta be another explanation," Jack said, then scanned the now faultless blue sky, as though it had the answers.

"That fallout today was hot. It burned. Those sores on the cow's backs were from the same thing, radiation burns. And that same toxic shit caused these mutant stillborns," Mick argued.

"There's at least a half dozen other expla—"

"Could you two shut up!" Emily interrupted. "Brenda's not feeling very good. I think we should start back."

Mick's face softened. "Gee, I'm sorry Brenda. Maybe you're getting my cold."

"My head throbs, and I feel a little sick to my stomach. Maybe its from sleeping on the ground last night, or the sight of all these dead cows but, I just don't feel good. I'm dead tired and my bones ache."

"Let's head on back," Jack said. "We're pretty much done here and I got my head count." Jack plucked a scratch pad from the back pocket of his Levis and reviewed his notes. "Of the original fifty-five head, we got forty-nine left. And we lost seven of this year's calf crop."

"Knowing your dad, he's not going to be happy about them losses, and somehow, he'll figure out a way to blame you," Mick said.

"And you need to get a vet up to look as this mess. Anyway, there's not a friggin' thing we can do about it now."

"For once, you're right," Jack replied. "There's no question my dad's going to be angry. He'll have to come back with the vet to figure out exactly what's happened here, and what can be done to save the rest."

"Do you ever listen? That's what I just said," Mick declared.

"What?"

"Forget it. Let's get out of here before we all get friggin' sick," Mick said as he turned Ginger and nudged her in the flank

As they rode back to the camp, Jack became increasingly aware that he also had a queasy stomach and a hellish headache that pounded with each jolt of the horse.

6

They drove the thirty-mile ride back to town in weary but pensive silence. Each was immersed in their own thoughts as they reviewed the disturbing events of the last two days.

As the truck jolted over the dusty washboard and crater-sized potholes of Pahcoon Road, Jack's thoughts bounced along also. He realized it was normal for a twenty-one-year-old man to be confused about life, but until now, he had pretty much mapped out the route he would take for his life's journey.

Jack knew his father would be furious and in some way, blame him for the dead cows. Since Christian had died in Korea, his father had not been the same. And the death of Jack's mother a few years earlier had left his father angry, bitter, resentful and humorless. Jack had the feeling his father would have preferred it had been him who was lost on the battlefield in Korea rather than Chris.

Chris had been a model son. Prior to Korea, he had taken over the farm and run it efficiently and profitably with little help from his father. Also, Chris had been devoted to the church, never did any drinking or partying, and certainly his father never got any reprimanding calls about Chris from church or civil authorities. In a way, his father and Chris had seemed more like buddies, like business associates, than father and son.

Jack remembered how proud his father had been the first time Chris put on his Army dress uniform. His pants were starched and creased, his boots buffed to a high gloss like a new car. He looked handsome and invincible. But of course, he wasn't. Now his father was resentful and seemed to blame everyone for Chris's death, the North Koreans, the Army, the U.S. government, and Jack. At times, Jack could understand his father's negative slant on everything. Life had not been kind to him. Even though Jack could empathize with him, one fact remained unchanged. Their relationship was miserable at best.

Twelve years back, right before his mother died of cervical cancer, she had called Jack to her bedside. That was when she made him promise her that he would always be faithful to the church, and start preparing to fulfill a mission. Jack could remember it vividly. The room smelled of impending death and with the curtains drawn, it looked like a tomb. Her skin was loose like old carpet that had lost its tacking glue. The cancer had robbed her of all nutrition, including the fat pad behind her dark eyes, making them sink into her skull like two potholes in a road. Her voice was weak and strained as she had called for Jack.

With the conviction of the dying, she explained to Jack that she had been visited by angels and they were preparing to take her. In a way, he found it curious that his mother, near death, had pretty much abandoned any remnants of her Indian religion in favor of the Mormon's. Jack always took this as a sign that the Mormon Church was true and was God's church. With tears flowing and more than a little frightened, Jack had promised her he would stay loyal to the church and fulfill a mission. How could he not?

Now he was twenty-one and it was time to keep those promises. There wasn't much left to do, just complete his application and have a personal interview with the bishop. Not that Jack did not want to go on a mission. He was pretty sure he did. But it was a big sacrifice, two years out of the irreplaceable and carefree part of his life. That would mean two years without women, two years further behind in his pre-med studies, and two years without football. Jack had been offered an athletic scholarship to play football at the University of Utah at Salt Lake City, and that would be lost.

And, the unknown was always frightening. The church's general authorities could send him anywhere on the planet. A mission to some region of the United States would not be too bad, but Jack could also end up in Bolivia, Japan, Norway or Austria. With his Swiss heritage and two years of German in high school, there was a fair chance they would send him to Switzerland, but he couldn't count on that. It was like Bishop Heinke had said, the church would send him wherever God directed, wherever God needed him.

Forget about being two years behind with his pre-med studies. What about medical school? If he went on a mission, he would be twenty-nine by the time he graduated, and that did not include internship or residency. Ever since his mother had died, Jack had resolved to make medicine his career. His mother's slow, painful death had left a mark on him. In his mind, there had to be a cure, or at least a prevention for cancer, and he was determined to help find it.

Jack rounded a corner, then headed the pickup down a sloping bench dotted with piñon trees. Those next to the road were caked with dust. It had been a while since it rained. Off in the distance he could see a large animal in the road. Wasn't that old Smoky Grayman's paint horse tied to the piñon bough, and his butt sticking out into the road? Actually, Smoky was a relative, being his mother's first cousin from her mother's side. As they got closer, Jack spotted Smoky in the shade, propped up against the trunk. Next to him, against the tree, was Smoky's 30-30 carbine.

"J.T., isn't that old Smoky's horse blocking the road?" Mick asked, rubbing the sleep from his eyes.

Jack grunted and ground the gears as he downshifted to a stop in front of the brown and white paint. "I'll take care of this. It will only take a minute. You guys can stay here and sleep," Jack said as he quickly opened the door and stepped out.

Smoky was an embarrassment to Jack, along with Indians in general, and he didn't want Emily to know he was related to that bunch. It was irritating to Jack that Smoky always showed up, uninvited, at most of the major events of his life. He was there when Jack was eight years old being baptized; he attended most of his football games; was there for his high school graduation; and just recently showed up for his graduation from Dixie Junior College. Hell, his father didn't even attend half these functions, including his graduation.

Sometime before her death, Jack's mother had told him there were two reasons Smoky felt such a kinship: one, because Smoky was always fond of her; and two, he and Jack were born on the same day of the year. Smoky had said that being born on the same day was an omen, whatever that meant. Jack did not believe in omens. Regardless of the reasons, Jack wished he wouldn't show up quite so often, and not in public places where everyone could see. It wouldn't be quite so embarrassing if he would bathe and clean up.

Ginger and A.C. caught a whiff of the other horse and started neighing and fidgeting, and rocking the trailer.

"Hi, Smoky. Thought I recognized your horse," Jack said. The sweet smell of alcohol floated through the air, grating at his nostrils.

"*Yaa' eh t'eeh*, Jack," Smokysaid, greeting Jack in his native language.

"You're quite a ways from the reservation. What you doing up here?"

"Hunting deer," Smoky said, as he pushed his sweat-stained, black, reservation-style Stetson further back on his head, then peered up at Jack with his black eyes .

"It's not deer season," Jack said, then shook his head. He immediately realized his mistake.

"It's government land, ain't it?" Smokey asked, and Jack nodded. "Then I don't need no *biligaana* license and you don't neither, 'cept you don't look much like an Ind'an. Not much like your mutter."

"I'm not an Indian, Smoky," Jack said. "I'm Swiss."

"Whatever you say." Smoky shook a cigarette from its pack and stuck it between his brown cracked lips. "What'cha doing up here, Jack?"

"Came up to check on dad's cows, and watch the bomb go off. That test was something!"

Smoky was silent for a moment, then took a drag on the cigarette. "*Chindi*. Work of skinwalkers. That nuclear is bad stuff, smells bad, feels bad, and burns the skin like hell. No good."

"Come on, Smoky. What's this talk of skinwalkers and smoking cigarettes? I thought you were Mormon."

"I am. In a lifetime, you can be many things."

Jack knew exactly what Smoky meant. It irritated Jack that Indians never seemed to abandon the old when they embraced the new. Somehow, they just mixed it all together. It was like when they painted the walls of their government reservation houses. They never stripped or sanded, just slapped on another coat of paint. In time the paint blistered and the old layers would show through again. To a certain extent, he'd seen some of this spiritual dichotomy in his mother. One minute she would talk about the spirit of Jesus Christ, a half-hour later she would talk about the crafty spirit of the coyote or Great Spirit of Pine Valley Mountain.

Smoky ashed his cigarette. "What'ta bout you, Jack? What are you?"

"Sometimes I wish I knew," Jack said, his voice trailing off. "Well, anyway, can you move your paint? His butt's blocking the road."

"You move em, Jack. His butt's not bother'n me."

Jack untied the reins and moved the horse to the opposite side of the piñon tree, waved to Smoky and returned to the pickup.

"Smoky drunk again?" Mick sneered as Jack slammed the door.

"Nah," Jack said and let it go at that. Right now Jack did not want to get in a lengthy conversation with Mick about Smoky, not here with Emily in the truck. Smoky was a disgrace, with his long hair, reservation hat, dirty clothes, and drunk half the time. Of course, Mick knew he was related to Smoky, but Jack didn't want Emily or Brenda to know. The less said, the better.

Anyway, what was the use in trying to talk to Mick, or anyone for that matter, about Indians? Jack thought. No one understood Indians but Indians. Not that he understood Indians, being he was three-quarters Swiss. But what had Smoky said about the bomb? Work of skinwalkers. That was a laugh, Jack thought, but felt a shiver crawl up his spine anyway. Almost as big a laugh as Smoky saying he was Mormon with a cigarette dangling from his mouth and talking of *chindis*.

Or, as big a laugh as him going on a mission or to medical school. With a possible manslaughter conviction hanging over him like thick winter's fog in the Virgin River Valley, all his plans might become a joke. As an ex-con, Jack was sure he would be an attractive candidate for a mission or medical school. Probably be the first one snapped up.

Another thing however, that was not a laugh, was Mick's attitude. Over the years they had formed a bond that had been unbreakable and never questioned. They had experienced their share of disagreements, even some of them with bloody fists, but there had been a link between them that was hard to explain. When there was no one else in the world Jack could count on, he could always rely on Mick. It didn't matter if that assistance required money, time or brawn, or even if Jack was in the right. If he really needed him, Mick would be there. There was no question, Jack relied on Mick more that he did his own family. Mick depended on him as well.

Then there was Earl, Greg and Deputy Saunders. As Jack thought of them, a thick sense of guilt squeezed at him like newly-washed Levis. Of course he and Mick were partially responsible for their deaths. And it was only balm for the conscience to assume that God had called Greg and Easy back, and that he had missions for them in heaven. That way it was all God's will and had nothing to do with the fact they were all drunk and acting like jerks. What possible mission could God have for Easy Earl and Greg? Who knew what went on in heaven? To Jack, the only plausible function the tragedy could possibly serve was to make them feel a sense of guilt for their actions and maybe be a catalyst for them to reform. In that respect, at least, the tragedy may have served some purpose.

Tired of feeling less than honorable, Jack struggled to change thoughts as they thudded over another pothole. What about Emily? It was undeniable he was becoming extremely fond of her. Not just the physical attraction, though without question, he was sexually drawn to her. Quickly, the mental image of Em with her blouse open and her Levis pulled down flashed before Jack's eyes. But, it wasn't just the sexual thing. He enjoyed her sensitivity, her slightly irreverent sense of humor, her air of the city and cosmopolitan nature. After all, she was from California, which was miles ahead of Santa Clara, Utah in sophistication.

And, Jack had to admire the way Emily cared for her invalid mother and their relationship. Jack wished he had that kind of relationship with his father. With a sudden sense of dread, Jack realized he would truly miss Emily, if he did go on a mission. Would she wait for him? Probably not. Though girlfriends always promised, they almost never did.

As they bounced back onto the paved asphalt of Highway 91, Jack ground the transmission of the floor-shift into high gear, again grazing

Emily's thigh. Immediately, he felt a stirring in his groin. Disgusted with himself, he stomped the accelerator and the pickup lurched toward Santa Clara.

Through the Shivwit Reservation, the road snaked along the river bed, then about a mile from Santa Clara it abruptly climbed out of the river bottom, bore left and leveled out on Ivins bench. The upward grade, coupled with the abrupt turn, limited Jack's visibility to just a few feet. Suddenly, Jack slammed on the brakes but the horse trailer kept coming. Its weight and momentum jack-knifed it at an acute angle, bringing it alongside the rear bed of the pickup. The weight of the buckled trailer pushed the pickup on a slant to within a couple of inches of a new 55 Buick Roadmaster parked right in the middle of the road.

The horses, frightened by the commotion, fought for footing, violently rocking the trailer and the truck.

"What the hell is this?" Mick exclaimed as he viewed the stationary line of vehicles ahead of the Buick. "There's cars stopped all the way to Santa Clara."

"Whew, that was a close one," Jack said, letting out a breath and wiping his brow. "That Buick almost got crunched."

"I see some flashing lights. Maybe a cop car or ambulance or something," Brenda said.

"It's probably an accident. This sort of thing happens all the time in California," Emily said.

"Or they're looking for an escaped convict," Mick laughed. "Any of you got a criminal record?"

Jack did not laugh or answer. In a week or so I might have one, he thought.

Brenda's face knotted with concern. "Well, I hope they don't keep us long. I'm tired and I have Young Women's tonight. We're doing a quilting project for the bishop's storehouse, you know, for welfare. And my hair's a mess. I need some time to get ready."

Just as Jack was about to get out and investigate, the cars started to inch forward. Suddenly the automobile behind them hit the horn. Jack waved at the impatient driver, then inched forward with the pack. After thirty minutes of starting and stopping, they were at the front of the line. Ahead was a wooden barricade painted a striped black and white. Next to it was the sheriff's car with flashing red lights.

A burley officer approached. It was Sheriff Meecham. After eyeing them through the window, he nodded at the ladies, then asked, "Where you boys been this morning?" He spied the camping gear in the bed of the pickup, then looked back again at the girls. "You spend the ·night? Looks like you've been camping."

"We've been up at Mule Springs, north of Pahcoon. You know, up at my father's summer range," Jack answered evenly.

"You mean, up on Utah Hill?" Sheriff Meecham asked again. "You spend the night?"

"Yes we did, though I can't see where it's any concern of yours," Mick answered.

"You better watch your mouth, Mick. I haven't forgotten that volcano fiasco. Don't think for a minute, I've finished with my investigation. And, fornication is still illegal in Utah. Anyways, what were you four doing up there?"

"Dad wanted me to go check on our cows, do a head count," Jack replied. "We're kinda in a hurry, Sheriff. Brenda's not feeling good. How about letting us through?"

"You see the test?" Sheriff Meecham asked, as he pushed his belly against the truck door and peered in at them. Before Jack could answer, a small, bespectacled man whose official-looking white lab coat flared like a rain slicker when he walked, came up and waved a small instrument over the truck. Periodically, he would stop and check the needle-gauge, then continue with his sweeping motion. Everyone watched, mesmerized by his actions. As the man leaned over and brandished the noisy, ticking instrument across the windshield, Jack noted the name tag on his left breast pocket, Rudy Popovich, Atomic Energy Commission.

Rudy scratched his head intently, then spoke. "Sheriff, this car is hot. Have it pull over into the line going to the carwash." Then Rudy jerked the cab door open and scanned up and down each of the campers, about four inches from their bodies. "Clothes are hot too, as well as the hair. They can't go into town with those clothes and they'll have to shower. And rinse off those horses," Rudy commanded, as he turned and headed for the next car.

Mick leaned out the window and yelled, "Hey, Rudy, what was our count? How many rads?"

Rudy turned, adjusted his glasses, then in a voice laced with irritation, he replied, "Not high, well within the safe range."

"How about giving me a number? So I can go to the library and look it up to make sure," Mick said.

"That information is confidential, national security reasons. But I can tell you, you're in no danger."

"National security, my ass," Mick muttered.

Rudy whirled around. "What was that?"

Jack quickly waved at Rudy and smiled. "The ash. He just asked about the ash." Jack pointed to the gray soot clinging to the running board.

"Hose it off," Rudy said, then pivoted on his heel.

Jack eyes narrowed. "Sheriff, what's going on here? What did he mean, hot?"

Mick did not wait for the sheriff's answers. "What he meant by hot, is radioactive. We're all covered with that friggin' nuclear crap. I'll bet we'd glow in the dark."

"Na, it's not that bad," Sheriff Meecham said. "This is purely precautionary. The Atomic Energy Commission has assured me that the only place where you can get enough radiation to cause trouble is in the restricted area of the proving grounds itself and that's fenced off." Meecham cocked a wary eye at them. "You guys didn't sneak over there, did you?"

"We told you where we were, Sheriff. Mule Springs. But we did find some of Jack's cattle dead with weird open sores on their backs, eyes and mouths, and we also found some freaky stillborns. You still sayin' this stuff's safe?" Mick asked.

"I don't know nothing about them cows. Anyways, like I said, you are not in any real danger here. We'll just have you wash your truck, shower yourselves, and change your clothes before going on into town. You'll have to leave your dirty clothes here as well."

"This is my best pair of Levis. Will we get them back?" Jack asked.

"I don't know—probably," Sheriff Meecham answered.

"Where does this shit go once you wash it off? Jack says some of this stuff stays radioactive for thousands of years. It doesn't just dissolve like sugar in water or evaporate into thin air. It has to go somewhere," Mick persisted.

"How the hell should I kno—" Sheriff Meecham was cut off by the shrill blast of a horn from one of the cars. The others in the line were getting impatient.

"Well, I sincerely doubt it disappears," Mick answered his own question. "And it's not like washing off battery acid with baking soda. Water doesn't neutralize it. Maybe it goes into the soil and our drinking water. What do you think, Sheriff?"

"I don't know where the hell it goes, college boy. All I know is the AEC says it's safe, so it's safe. Come on guys, move it along before I give you a citation."

"Don't you think this is a lot of fuss, the carwash and all, for something so harmless?" Mick continued the argument as he wiped sweat from his brow.

"Goddamn it!" Sheriff Meecham said. "I don't make the rules. You four, do as you're told." Then he waved them into the left-hand lane leading to the Texaco station.

It was another thirty-minutes of stop and go just getting to the car wash. As another white-coated official watched, Mick hosed down the pickup and trailer. Jack unloaded, then rinsed off the already jittery horses and tied them to the trailer.

The AEC officials directed them to a telephone booth and told them to call someone to bring them clean clothes, then they were shown to the showers.

Two portable, green-canvas showers that looked like standard Korean War issue had been erected on a flat field adjacent to the Texaco station. Each shower was labeled with a cardboard sign: MEN and WOMEN. Taking the lead, Mick deliberately sauntered straight for the women's shower. As he pulled the flap aside and ducked his head to enter, Brenda grabbed him.

"Not this tent Mister, unless you're wearing a bra."

"But, there's a line at the other one," Mick laughed, as he pointed to the men waiting at the other tent. "Thought you were in a hurry."

"I am, but not that big a hurry. Anyway, I'm so dirty, I'd scare you." Brenda still had her arms around Mick.

"I doubt it," Mick said, his eyes dancing. "C'mon J.T., you can share a shower with Emily. It'll save time."

Jack turned red and stared at his feet. "Uh–uh Mick, we'd better get in line."

Emily smiled as she entered the tent. "Nice thought, Mick."

While they waited for their turns, Jack noticed Mick eyeing two officials standing behind the Texaco station, close to where the horses were tied. Even at a distance, he could tell they were engaged in serious conversation, accompanied by a lot of gesturing and nervous pacing. Being as unobtrusive as possible, both walked casually over to check the horses. Jack could catch pieces of the discussion.

"We should alert the town—evacuate or stay indoors."

"God damn panic—meter is wrong."

"—checked—okay."

"Got to—wrong."

"But—if the reading—correct—danger."

Jack and Mick inched closer.

"We've far exceeded the maximum allowable of 3.9 Rads for a thirteen-week period."

"Nobody knows for sure where the fuck they came up with that figure, probably from white rats. Safe levels could be a lot higher."

"Or a lot lower, but we're not just marginally exceeding the safe limits, we're blowing them all to hell. I'm recording 5.2 Rads of gamma radiation per hour!" The man jabbed a finger at his notebook.

"I don't accept that figure and that's not going into the official log until you've double-checked it with another meter. And even if it is true, what the hell we going to do about it? We can't stop it from falling any more than we can stop the rain from falling or the wind from blowing."

"But we could evacuate or at least warn them to say indoors."

"Goddamn it, we've been over that. It's too late to evacuate. And, how the hell am I supposed to warn them? They don't even have a radio station in this hick town, much less television. Maybe, I could ride up and down the street like fucking Paul Revere in a pickup truck with a megaphone. Shit, Dale, I'm just as concerned as you, but there's not a goddamn thing we can do about it."

"Well, I still think we need to do something."

"We are. Just record the data and collect the badges from the school kids tomorrow. And don't forget, the boss wanted you to buy a couple quarts of local milk for testing."

"Is this shit getting into their food and water supply?"

"We don't know nothing about the milk yet."

Mick suddenly exploded into a fit of coughing, startling the two AEC men who quickly moved away.

As they retreated, Jack heard one say to the other. "Damnit Dale, you should be more careful what you say."

Mick took a breath and this time did not try to stifle the cough. Finally, he hacked a big lunger and spat it at the base of the mulberry tree.

"Mick, tomorrow you need to see Doc Hilton. You're getting worse."

"To hell with Doc Hilton and to hell with the cough," Mick snarled. "We need to hurry and get the hell out of here. Didn't you hear? This place is alive with friggin gamma rays."

"Mick, those two guys couldn't agree whether there was a danger or not. Rudy Popovich said it was safe, and he had a Geiger counter." Jack smiled tightly, so as to not expose his crooked lower teeth.

"J.T., I heard them. One said we were blowing the safe limits all to hell."

"That was probably just his opinion," Jack said.

"No, he had the data in his notebook. If I could get my hands on it I could prove that the goddamn AEC is not playing straight with us," Mick said. "You know where those AEC pricks are staying?"

"At the Big Hand Motel in Saint George. Why?" Jack answered without thinking. Then Mick's question hit him. "Mick, I hope you're not thinking what I think you're thinking. That's stealing government property. That's just plain crazy."

"Yeah, you're probably right, J.T. It's just that I know they're lying. Anyway, humor me and let's get the hell out of here. We probably ought'ta stay indoors tonight."

"Okay by me. But we gotta shower first and wait til Brenda's mom gets here with our clothes. That could take a while. You know Brenda's mom. She's a lot like Brenda."

"What do you mean by that crack?"

"Nothing, they—they just march to their own drum."

Hours later, Jack dropped Brenda and Mick off. Emily wanted him to meet her mother, so the two of them first unloaded the horses at the Kunz corrals, then drove over to Emily's grandmother's house. On the way Jack turned on the radio to KSUB in Cedar City. Broadcasting from fifty miles away, daytime reception was always scratchy. Through the hiss Jack heard the broadcaster announce, "I've been informed by AEC officials that fallout is occurring in Saint George right now. The authorities have requested that residents of that town take cover and remain indoors until further notice. Too hot to be outdoors down there anyway. Now back to our regularly scheduled program," he concluded as if he had been reading baseball scores.

"Looks like Dale got his way," Jack mumbled.

"Who's Dale?" Emily asked

"Oh, he's just an AEC guy Mick and I overheard. He wanted to put out a warning."

"Jack, don't you think it's odd?" Emily said. "The very people that hear this warning are the ones who are already inside. The people outdoors, the ones who really need to hear it, never will."

"I don't think it's a big deal. Anyway, we're in Santa Clara. The KSUB announcer only mentioned Saint George."

"Jack, they're only five miles apart."

"I know that, Em, but the announcer said, Saint George."

Emily shook her head. "Do you always take things so literally? Don't you ever make deductions?"

"They have Geiger counters. I think, they mean what they say."

7

"Your mother grew up here in Santa Clara but you were born in California," Jack said, changing the subject. "How did she get to California?"

Emily sighed, relieved with the change in Jack's tone. Her mother, she told him, was born fifty-one years ago to Rachel and Emil Stucki of Santa Clara, Utah. Yes, she was raised in the typical Mormon fashion, and at age eight considered by Mormons as the age of accountability, she was baptized into the church. Through her adolescent years, she faithfully attended the required church meetings including Sunday school, sacrament meeting and all the functions of the Mormon youth organization. Like all young Latter Day Saints girls, Irene dreamed of a Temple marriage. Not a temporary one like Catholic or Protestant marriages, Temple marriages were not to be only for this life, but for time and all eternity.

Unfortunately, that didn't happen for Irene, Emily told Jack. She met Edwin at a dance at the Santa Clara Pavilion. After a whirlwind courtship, she married the career Navy man and moved to San Diego. Though Irene didn't really care for the ship anchor tatoo on his right forearm and even though he wasn't a Mormon, she felt in time she could change that. What she didn't foresee was that her groom was well on his way to becoming a devout alcoholic and a dedicated womanizer. While he was at sea, Emily was born, and when he docked two months later in San Diego, Irene served him divorce papers.

After the divorce, Irene remained a single parent and never again seriously considered marriage. Through the years, she drifted away from the church, though she still considered herself a non-active Mormon, a jack-Mormon. But in spite of her Mormon background, Irene had raised Emily completely non-denominational. That's why she knew very little about the Mormon Church. Now they had resettled back in Utah, and Emily had started going to church and was quickly picking up on doctrine, but she admitted that it didn't all make sense to her.

Though Irene was never really totally healthy, she managed to work at her job as a telephone operator until age forty-five, then her deteriorating heart condition forced her to retire early and return to Santa Clara. It was ironic, Irene had confided to Emily, that she should languish her remaining days in the same bed in which she was born. Maybe it was some kind of punishment for the sins of her early years, she had told Emily.

"But," Emily concluded. "I've never really understood rheumatic heart disease."

"If I remember right," Jack said, as he parked the truck in front of the Stucki house. "It's a problem of identical protein."

"I don't get it," Emily said.

"When the Strep bacteria invade, the body fights back by producing antibodies. Unfortunately, the protein in the wall of the bacteria is identical to the protein in the heart valves. The antibodies can't tell the difference, so they attack both. Kinda like what happened to my brother Chris in Korea."

"You've never told me what happened to Chris."

"He was killed by friendly fire, whatever that means, at Pork Chop Hill."

"Tell me more. You never talk about him."

"Maybe, someday," Jack said, then quickly got out of the pickup to open the door for Emily.

Inside, her mother's room was sunless and dreary, and the air was thick and stale. It reeked of Vicks rub, medicinal alcohol and stale sputum. Almost inconsequential in the presence of these overpowering odors was a tiny emaciated Irene propped up and almost swallowed by the large pillows.

Emily quickly moved to her side and gave her a light kiss on a gaunt cheek. "Hi, Mom, I brought someone for you to meet. This is Jack Kunz. Jack's the one I went camping with last night."

Irene flopped a shriveled arm from beneath the covers for Jack to shake, then whispered in a weak, raspy voice. "Nice to meet you Jack. I'm pleased Emily is finally dating such a fine young man. From what I hear, you're not at all like some of the boys she ran around with in California." Irene paused for air. "And certainly nothing like the man I married."

Jack's face flushed and stung like a sunburn. If she only knew about his drinking, carousing and the events of the past week, he was pretty sure she wouldn't be so enthusiastic. "I'm pleased to meet you, Mrs. Vasser," he said with a weak smile. "You've raised a wonderful daughter. How are you feeling?"

"Like hell," Irene wheezed, the words trailing of to a whisper.

"Nothing the doctors can do?" Jack asked awkwardly.

"Yes, they could give me a new aortic valve," Irene laughed, choking on her joke.

"Perhaps, someday they will be able to do just that," Jack replied as he looked around the room. A half-full glass of water with an assortment of medication vials was strewn on the night stand. Behind the glass was a photograph of Emily and a fit-appearing Irene, both smiling broadly with their arms entwined. Jack picked up the photograph. "You two look like sisters in this picture."

Irene's face softened as she glanced over. "Em's always been a good kid and as she grew up, we were in some ways like sisters. No, more like buddies." She reached over to Emily. "As a single parent, with working and trying to spend some time with your kid, you don't have a lot of time for making outside friends or socializing. I was fortunate. In Em I not only had a kid, but also a friend and social partner as well. We had some good times, didn't we Em?"

"Remember the time at the movies, when those two young business types in black suits tried to hit on us? The handsome one was after you," Emily said smiling at her mother.

After a moment of silence, Irene turned to Jack. "Be good to her Jack. Take care of her."

"Of course I will," Jack said, grasping her hand.

Emily quickly looked way, but Jack noticed the mist in her eyes. In an odd way, he was envious. He'd never developed that kind of relationship with either of his parents. "From what little I've been around her Irene, I agree. Emily is an incredible person."

The conversation had exhausted Irene, so Jack excused himself, promising Emily he would call. As he drove home, Jack wondered if he would shed a tear if his father died tomorrow. Probably, but he didn't think his father would if the reverse were true.

As Jack wheeled his truck into the driveway, the sun was just setting. To the east the sky was deepening from navy blue to sable black. To the south, Venus was the only star visible in the twilight. But to the west, the sky was ablaze. Utah Hill was still crowned in light even though the sun had slipped behind the horizon. A maverick, feathery cloud was hanging directly above the mountain and catching the dying sunlight. It literally glowed, sending shafts of golden light from its portholes. Then the golden shafts unfurled, turning the western sky into a variegated dome of crimson. It was a splendid effort, as if nature, feeling upstaged by Shot Harry's effort, was playing with colors to regain her honor.

However, nature's stunning pageant was immediately shattered by a more earthy scene. Sheriff Meecham's patrol car was parked in the driveway. As Jack climbed out of his pickup, he prayed his father wasn't home from his produce run yet.

When Jack entered the house, his father's voice echoed from the living room. "Jack, come on in here. Sheriff Meecham wants to talk to you."

Jack plunged his hands into his pockets as he entered the room. "Hi, Dad. Hello Sheriff. Did you finally get that line of cars cleared out?"

"Yep, the AEC lifted the road block at 7:00 p.m. Probably didn't need it anyways. They were just enforce'n standard precautions. There was never any real danger."

Not wanting to start an argument, Jack replied, "You're probably right. It never hurts to be cautious."

"Jack, the Sheriff has been tellin' me some damn disturbin' things about the other night. The night Earl, Greg and Deputy Saunders were killed. What do you know about that?"

For a moment, Jack thought of coming clean. He was growing weary of the lies and the cover-up was becoming complicated, but he thought better of it. "Like I've already told Sheriff Meecham, we, Mick, Curley, Alan and myself, went to Cedar City to see a movie. I was fifty miles away when it happened."

"I don't know why the hell you guys always want to drive to Cedar for a movie. Goddamn, gas is up to twenty-five cents a gallon. What's wrong with the Dixie Theater?"

"Just something to do. Anyway, the girls are prettier in Cedar."

"Girls is girls," Mr. Kunz snorted.

"You ever see these things before?" Sheriff Meecham asked, reaching into a burlap bag and pulling out a Levi jacket with several irregular holes burned in it.

Jack had seen it before. It was Mick's. "No, I don't recognize it. I've never owned a Levi jacket," he said.

Sheriff Meecham looked to Mr. Kunz. "I don't know," he said, shrugging his shoulders. "With his mother gone, Jack buys his own clothes and Mary does the laundry. Most of the time I never know what he wears."

"How about this?" Sheriff Meecham asked, producing an aluminum flashlight with a ribbed handle.

Jack's heart raced. He knew that was their flashlight, but his father answered for him. "We used to have a flashlight like that, but I haven't seen it in a while."

"That's a pretty common flashlight. I'll bet half the people in town have one," Jack hastily added.

Sheriff Meecham stared at Jack for a moment, then extracted a book of matches. The match cover displayed a scantily clad show girl wearing only fishnet nylons and pink feathers in the appropriate places. Below her high heels, the inscription read, Flamingo Hotel. "Been to Vegas lately, Jack?"

"Come on Sheriff. Anybody can pick those things up almost anywhere. And no, I haven't been to Vegas since we played basketball down there in the church league."

"Anyways, it doesn't matter. I think we got some partial prints off both the flashlight and match book. We're just waiting for confirmation from the state criminology lab in Salt Lake City. Don't be surprised if I give you a call to come to the office for fingerprinting Jack."

Jack's mood soured, but he smiled lamely. "Whenever you want, Sheriff. I'm not going anywhere."

"Anyways, I'll let you know," Sheriff Meecham said as he rose to go, tucking his shirt back into his pants.

As the sheriff lumbered out, Mr. Kunz declared, "Damn it Jack, you'd better not be involved. I don't have time for it. If it was your brother Chris, I wouldn't have a minute's worry about it, but with you I never know. And don't forget, you still have cows to milk. I milked for you last night and I'll be damned if I'm going to do your chores tonight." Then cooling a bit, he asked, "How were the cows?"

"Dad, we've got real problems. Something's killing the cows. We've got thirteen dead, seven of em this year's calves."

"Thirteen? My god! Cougars?" Mr. Kunz's face contorted in anger.

"No, they hadn't been attacked or slashed. They were sick, probably bad water or poisonous weeds. Most of them have funny raw sores on their backs, mouths, and eyes and their hide-hair came off in clumps. A lot of the calves were stillborn with body parts missing. I think you need to get the vet up there to check on them."

"Shit! That's all I need. It's not like I don't have enough problems. You know I got the truck run tomorrow. Anyhow, them range cows are your job. You should have been keeping a closer eye on them. How many times you been up to check on 'em since spring?"

"This was the first time. I've been busy too. With school, graduation and farm work, when was I supposed to go?" Jack said, as he rose from the sofa.

"When you have a responsibility like that, you make time, not excuses. How about all of that time you spent carousing to Cedar, or all the time you spend farting around with Mick? You could have gone up and checked on them cows ten times."

"But those times were at night."

"Go milk your cows, Jack. I'll call the damn vet. Jesus, from now on, I guess I'll have to do everything around here." Mr. Kunz stormed off.

Jack headed for the kitchen, grabbed the milking bucket from the sink and stomped off to the coral. It was just as Mick had predicted. His dad had found a way to blame him. Even if he had gone up a month earlier, what could he have done to save them? Jack hobbled the Guernsey, found the milking stool and positioned the bucket under the udder. As he squezed the teat and heard the first spray of milk jangle in the bucket, he bitterly compared relationships. He and his father to Emily and her mother.

Again, Jack did not sleep well. He thought of Emily, Shot Harry, fallout, deformed calves, prison, his promise to his mother, and his ever diminishing chances of going on a mission. Did Sheriff Meecham really have fingerprints, or was he bluffing? Would they be his? If they were his prints, there definitely would be no mission, only jail time. If they were not his, in spite of their pact, the others would probably rat on him. Either way, if the sheriff had prints, he was going to jail.

And this fallout stuff was becoming scary. Was it as Mick had said? Were the dead cows and calves a result of radiation fallout? If so, what other effects could they anticipate? Washing all the cars was a little strange, but maybe it was like the sheriff had said, just precautionary.

But in spite of the potential danger, Shot Harry had certainly been beautiful. There was no denying that. Jack could still see the blinding flash, feel the coarse, powerful rumble of the earth beneath his feet, and hear the shock wave bounce off the canyon walls. The technology of such a feat was incredible, mind-boggling, and certainly humbling.

Finally, he thought of Emily, of her naked, supple body pressing against his. Though guilt started to surface with that erotic image, it was slowly chased by the opium of sleep. Playing with different angles of that pleasant thought, Emily naked, Jack finally drifted into unconsciousness.

Sometime after dawn, Jack was suddenly awakened by the simultaneous discordant sounds of the telephone ringing and his father bellowing, "Goddamn it, Jack. Aren't you up yet? The phone's for you."

Dazed, Jack glanced at his watch. It had stopped. He'd forgotten to wind it. Turning, he looked at the electric clock on the dresser. It flaunted a tardy 8:30 a.m. Though he didn't feel rested, Jack guessed he'd gotten some sleep after all. He dragged himself out of bed and plodded into the kitchen to answer the phone sprawling on the counter.

"Hello." Jack yawned.

"Oh God, Jack," Emily sobbed. "I hope I didn't wake you."

Now he was alert. "What's wrong, Em?"

"Oh Jack," Emily said between sobs, "Mother passed away last night."

There was just no good way to respond to this kind of news. Jack could think of nothing appropriate to say. "Em, I'm so sorry. I know how hard this is."

"She died in her sleep, and I wasn't even at her side. I was asleep in the other room," Emily sobbed.

"Em, she knew how much you loved her."

"I know Jack, but what am I to do? This has me overwhelmed. Not only the funeral, but I still feel like a guest in this house. What will I do?"

"When's the funeral? Can I help with the arrangements?" Jack asked.

"I don't know yet. My grandparents are making those arrangements. But with tomorrow being Sunday, I suspect the funeral will be Monday or Tuesday of next week," Emily's said, her voice quivering.

"Em, I've got to do morning chores. It'll take me about an hour. Then I'll be right over," Jack said gently.

"Thanks Jack. I guess I just need some moral support."

Turning from the phone, Jack realized his father had been listening. "What was that all about?" he demanded.

"Do you know Emily Vasser? I think I've mentioned her. Her mother was a Stucki, Emil's daughter. Since they moved from California, they've been staying with Emil and Roseanne. Anyway, Emily's the girl I've been dating. Her mother died last night. It was kind of expected, but after the chores I need to go over and help her."

"Damn it Jack," Mr. Kunz exclaimed. "You know I've got to haul a load of peaches to Panaca and Pioche today. Then I'm supposed to meet the vet on Utah Hill on the way back. We're going to drive together over to the summer range and look at those dead cows. It's Saturday and we've got our field watering turn. Who's going to irrigate the Loren Webber piece if you go traipsing around? That's your responsibility."

"What time do we get the water?"

"Ten. And you've got to divert it from the vineyard canal, you know, up by the Gubler fields, then run it on down to our place."

"I know where we get the water," Jack fumed. "Don't worry dad, I can do both. In between water turns, I'll go over and see Emily."

"If you go over to Stucki's," Mr. Kunz insisted, "You'd better make damn sure every row of hay gets watered." As he started to leave, he turned around and added, "What the hell has come over you lately?"

Though it was not any less irritating, this time his father did not invoke the name of the deceased brother Chris, but instead used Mary as the shining example. "Why can't you be more like your sister? She's never given me a minute's grief. In fact, she's been a great help since your mother and Chris died. And I'm sure your mother, God rest her soul, is not pleased with what she sees you doing."

Mr. Kunz scratched his groin. "The big problem Son, is you need to be more active in the church and serious about your obligations. What about your mission? Have you even filled out your papers yet? They're certainly not going to send you if they don't know you want to go. You can't be drinking and carousing if you're going to be an Elder. That group of guys you're running around with is a bad influence on you, particularly that Michael Graff."

For a fleeting moment Jack thought about lashing out at his father. After all, it was Jack who daily worked the farm and did the chores. Maybe he didn't enjoy farm work like Chris had, but nevertheless he did it. Without his help, his father could not operate his produce trucking business. Jack couldn't count how many school activities, dances and football practices he had missed over the years to accommodate that damn farm.

Jack bit his tongue and remained silent. The painful memory of several leather belts lashed across his buttocks for assorted childhood offenses, including insubordination, kept him quiet. But when it came to his mother, Jack had to reluctantly agree with his father. She probably was not in the least pleased with his recent behavior.

It seemed to Jack that lately he could please no one, living or dead.

8

The next day as he dressed for sacrament meeting, Jack thought back on the events of the last twenty-four hours. In short, it had been almost impossible. Trying to divide his time between his farming responsibilities and a grief-stricken Emily resulted in the expected. He did little justice to either.

As for the farming there was never enough water in the field stream to irrigate the Loren Webber in one turning. Jack constructed a dam of canvas tarp, wooden support poles and mud in the main ditch to divert the water into feeder canals. Usually, he had enough to irrigate thirty to forty rows at a time. Once he had nursed the water down each row, he would go downstream and build another dam for irrigating the next section. He patrolled constantly for gopher holes. A gopher hole would rob the furrow of its water. As a consequence, the alfalfa plants down-furrow would go dry, wither and die. This was the sort of thing his father always noticed.

In between rotating the irrigation water onto each segment of the Loren Webber field, then nursing the stubborn water down every row, Jack had little time to spend with Emily. Her mood had been labile. She vacillated between profound grief and self-indulgent anger.

Finally, at midnight, feeling physically drained and emotionally depleted, Jack had said goodnight to Emily, turned the field irrigation water back to the vineyard canal, and tumbled into bed. Six hours later, he was up doing morning chores, and now he was getting ready for church. This morning, he'd rather have just stayed in bed, but it was Sunday and he had church obligations.

Fighting with his tie, Jack glanced at his still unwound watch. What time was it? He was running late, he thought, but this Sunday he had to be on time. He had promised to meet Emily for fast and testimony meeting. That thought made his stomach grumble. There would be no food today until after church, but it was for a good cause. The dollar amount in savings from skipping two meals was to be donated for the food and clothing for the poor and needy. Mary loved fast and testimony Sundays since she only had to prepare one meal.

The service had already started as Jack slid into the chapel's rear-most pew beside a brushed, scrubbed and almost immaculate Mick. After a quick salutatory nod, Jack quietly noticed seated next to Mick were Brenda, Alan and Curley, but no Emily. He cranked his head around and scanned the congregation. Just then she eased in and sat down beside him, looking drained and haggard but composed. Perhaps she was already coming to terms with her mother's death, he thought, as she slipped her small hand in his and gave him a gentle squeeze.

At the same moment, Mick nudged Jack's shoulder, then nodded down at the small space of bench between them. Mick had brought a small, wooden travelers' chess set and hidden it with an open hymn book tilted over the game like a pup-tent. This was nothing new for the two friends. He and Mick often whiled away the hours of sacrament meeting boredom by playing chess. It was not as though he had never heard these sermons before. He knew them by heart. Just once, Jack thought, he would like to go to church and hear something original.

"It's your turn to start," Mick whispered.

"I've got too many things on my mind. Em's mother died last night."

"I'm sorry Jack, but this is therapy. It'll take your mind off your problems."

"But it's disrespectful to Emily's mother."

"Disrespectful, hell. She never went to church anyway. It's friggin' fast and testimony meeting. I'll go nuts if I have to listen to another sobbing lady tell me about how much she knows the church is true."

Jack looked over at Emily. She seemed absorbed with her own thoughts. Meanwhile, Bishop Heinke had started the testimony portion of the service with his own. "I know this is the true church, that Joseph Smith is a Prophet of God, and that he was unjustly persecuted and murdered at Carthage, Illinois by an unruly mob of gentiles. I also know that God called upon Brigham Young—"

Jack shrugged his shoulders. After all, he had heard the Joseph Smith speech a thousand times before. Pawn to K-2. Mick and Jack had become passable chess players and remained fairly evenly matched, Jack holding a slight edge.

The Bishop droned on. "Brigham Young was chosen by God to be the next prophet and he led the saints on that arduous journey across the plains to the Salt Lake Valley in 1846, much like Moses led the Israelites out of Egypt. After declaring 'this is the place', Brigham Young began the monumental task of colonizing Utah and the intermountain west."

Mick's opening was consistent with his usual pattern of defense. Queen Knight to B-3.

"Polygamy was necessary in those early days," Bishop Heinke was saying. "Many men were killed by gentile persecution, Indians and disease, resulting in many destitute and defenseless widows that needed to be cared for. To solve this problem, God allowed polygamy. Not just allowed, but even commanded the saints to practice polygamy. Polygamy was not unique to us. It was widely practiced in the Old Testament as well."

Queen to R-5. Boldly, Jack slashed into enemy territory. Meanwhile, the sermon droned on. "Our Swiss ancestors, having no oxen or wagons, crossed the Great Plains by pulling handcarts, and though a rest in the Salt Lake Valley would have been welcomed, they all enthusiastically responded when Brigham Young asked them to travel another three hundred miles to settle on the banks of the Santa Clara River." Bishop Heinke dabbed the moisture from his eyes, as though he could feel his ancestors' suffering.

King Knight to B-3. Laboriously, Mick constructed his elaborate defense. Jack looked for weaknesses in Mick's defense. A pattern was developing. Each time the Bishop paused for a breath, it acted as a signal for one of the player's move.

Queen to B-7. Jack had suddenly attacked and removed Mick's

exposed Pawn. Now the game was all-absorbing and Jack barely heard the bishop's final remarks. He did not hear him open the meeting to the congregation, nor did he see the bishop sit down. Sister Reber was rising to speak as Jack pegged in his move that immediately placed Mick's unprotected Queen in jeopardy. Jack took the hymnal, as was their usual routine, to cover the game while Mick pondered. Jack cast a quick glance at Emily. She was totally absorbed in what Sister Reber was saying. While waiting for Mick, Jack caught some of Sister Reber's testimony.

Sister Reber's voice was strong with conviction. "I know in my heart, God hears and answers prayers."

Finally, Mick made his move. Immediately, Jack saw Mick's mistake and acted quickly before he could change his mind.

"Shit!" The word spewed from Mick's mouth like rancid milk, then hung suspended in the chapel air like winter's fog along the Virgin River. Jack had just captured Mick's Queen.

Horrified, the congregation gasped, then sat stiffly in a long uncomfortable silence. After a few moments, Bishop Heinke rose and approached the pulpit. Time slowed like cold molasses. He scanned the rear pew, then opened his mouth and tersely hissed. "I hope this is not too much to ask for a sacrament meeting, but if the young men in the back could possibly refrain from further profanity, we'll let Sister Reber continue." Staring at the two in rebuke, he said, "I apologize for them, Sister Reber. Please continue."

Mick and Jack sat motionless in humiliating silence. To atone, Jack even tried to concentrate on Sister Reber's testimony, but as she began, Mick started coughing. Emily seemed unaffected and, though he could not tell for sure, Jack figured there was a possibility that she was not even aware he and Mick had caused all the bedlam with the chess game.

Slightly wounded, but resilient, Sister Reber had recovered and continued. She was an older woman with a bland, trusting face, orange-peel thick make-up, glacier blue hair, and a facial tic that became especially pronounced when she was nervous. Her left eye was twitching rapidly, creating intersecting, crow-feet fissures in her gelatinous make-up.

"Like I said, Brothers and Sisters, I want to testify to you that God lives and that he hears and answers prayers." More eye twitching. "Last week I lost a priceless family heirloom, a gold-cast hatpin my grandmother gave to me on her deathbed. I was devastated." Tears were running down the cracks of Sister Reber's make-up like water in irrigation ditches. "Well, I got down on my knees and prayed, really prayed to my God, and you'll never believe it, but I found my hatpin the very next day. It had fallen in a crack of my hardwood floor." Now tears were dripping off her chin. "And I know in my heart, beyond a shadow of a doubt, that it was God who led me to that hatpin." Sister Reber dabbed at her eyes with a white-lace hanky, looked around at the congregation, then plopped down on the rock-hard pew.

After a stream of testimonies that lasted an excruciating two and one-half hours, fast and testimony meeting was finally over. Immediately after the closing prayer, Jack and Mick with Emily and Brenda in tow bolted, not wanting to face the reproachful stares or sharp reprimands of the congregation. Unfortunately, they bumped into Walt Hafen in the foyer.

"That was some performance in there," he scoffed. "I hope you two assholes don't think I've forgotten about you."

"I really haven't given it much thought, Wit," Mick answered.

Walt pushed his face right in Mick's and sneered, "You two sons-a-bitches are going to pay for what you did to Greg. Maybe with your own lives. An eye for an eye."

"Wit, we're shaking in fear, but we're ready any time you are," Mick taunted.

"Better watch your ass, Mick."

Jack grabbed Mick's arm. "Come on, not in church. We're in enough trouble already."

Jack turned Mick over to Brenda's care, and told her to keep him away from Walt. Then they split up and Jack and Emily headed back to his house, dodging the cruel sun by keeping to the sycamore's marbled lattice shade. Mary, Jack thought, would be at choir practice and his father was on his usual produce run to Pioche and wouldn't be back for an hour or so. He and Emily would have the house to themselves.

The Kunz's living room was simple. The floor was covered with short-pile, stained chestnut carpet. Next to the picture window was an over-stuffed chair with golden-yellow upholstery. The cloth was wrinkled, loose and ill-fitting. Against the opposite wall from the picture window was a sofa with the same cloth. Jack remembered how his mother had spent weeks re-upholstering the chair and sofa. Other than a ship-clock on the mantle over the fireplace, there were no other decorations.

As they sat on the sofa, Emily instantly erupted into tears. A kind of rhythm was developing, sobs followed by tears, then sobs, then tears.

"Was it sacrament meeting? The chess match?" Jack asked, exasperated. "I'm sorry I embarrassed you with that game. I know it was insensitive."

Emily shook her head, followed by more sobs.

"Was it something Bishop Heinke said?"

No answer.

Getting up, Jack eased over to the window and looked at the sycamore trees, their seed balls starting to break open and scatter fluffy, cotton-like seeds. A few congregation members were walking by on their way home. "Come on Em, I know this is a trying time, but I can't help if I don't know what is bothering you. Was it the thing with Walt in the foyer?"

"No Jack, it was the second lady."

That would be Sister Reber. What could she have possibly said? "I didn't hear all she said. But what I did hear, seemed harmless enough to me. Just how she lost a hatpin, prayed to God, and God helped her find it. Nothing too controversial about that."

Emily's sobbing vanished, instantly replaced by indignation. "I prayed just as hard, to the same God, for my mother's life! Why, Jack, why, would God answer a prayer so trivial as Sister Reber's and ignore me?"

Jack did not have an answer..

"Jack, God is supposed to be kind and just. Where's the justice in that?"

After a few moments Jack said quietly, "Em, I don't think that's a fair question."

"I think it's a very fair question. My mother died in spite of my prayers for help. Yet he responded to Sister Reber's hatpin crisis."

"My feeling is that God doesn't get involved in the day to day operation of the universe or mankind. We have to learn things for ourselves. It's part of our training to become like God. How would our own children grow if every time they had a problem, we solved it for them?"

"But Jack, you can't have it both ways. You can't have on one hand a loving, caring God who is deeply involved in mankind's welfare, including helping to find hatpins, while on the other hand, you have an aloof God who distances himself from mankind and says take care of it yourself. So basically what you're saying is that we have an indifferent God, not a caring God, but one that pretty much has the same attitude that my own father had. I gave you life, so now my part is done."

Jack was getting irritated. "I'm not saying that at all! All I'm saying is that we don't always comprehend or understand the workings of God. Perhaps someday we will."

"Well Jack, I can tell you this. I surely don't understand the workings of this God. The only explanation that makes any sense to me is, there is no God! Caring or otherwise," Emily said, as tears surfaced again.

Jack knew he was floundering. "Emily, all I can say is it all comes down to faith. You've got to have faith before you can have anything else."

"That's a cop out, and you know it. Faith is just another way of saying we know this doesn't make any sense, but you must believe it anyway."

"Emily, you're just playing with words. And words don't change the facts. Of course, there is a god, and I can't believe you said there isn't. Perhaps I'd better take you home."

"That's the only original idea you've had all afternoon," Emily replied.

Silence dominated as Jack drove Emily to her grandparent's house. Jack could appreciate that Emily was bitter, with the death of her mother and all, and it was understandable that she would want to blame someone, but to attack the church and God like that—that was blasphemy! Jack could not believe that the universe and mankind were random accidents of nature. Undoubtedly, he thought this whole argument with Emily was just another thinly disguised assault by Satan to foil his mission plans and break his promise to his mother.

After they parked in front of the house, Jack opened the door and walked Emily to the front porch. For an awkward, uncomfortable minute, neither said anything. Then Jack made a clumsy attempt to kiss her. Emily turned her head quickly and pushed him away.

"Jack, we just think differently. I think it's best if we don't see each other. I really can't see a future for us."

Jack felt woozy. His foundation, his chance of happiness, began to crumble like wet sandstone. All he needed was another rejection in his life. Desperately, he wanted to plead with her, beg her to change her mind. But his pride surfaced and he mumbled, "Whatever you say, Emily."

"I think it's for the best," Emily said as she disappeared into the house.

On the way home, Jack realized how much he was starting to depend on Emily. Subconsciously, he had even started to include her in his future plans.

But he didn't have much time to brood. As he walked through the kitchen door he found an irate father waiting for him. "Where ya been, Jack?"

"We've been at church. I just took Emily home. What did you and the vet come up with?" Jack asked, slumping down on the sofa.

"Goddamnest thing I've ever seen. The vet said the same. Said it didn't look like nothing he'd seen before. He was pretty sure it wasn't bacteria or virus. And didn't think it was contaminated water, poison weeds or malnutrition. Took one of them dead stillborns back with him, said he was going to do an autopsy. Maybe even get the government people involved."

"Any ideas at all?" Jack persisted.

"Well, it's kinda hard to say, since nobody's ever seen it before but it might be radiation sickness."

Instantly Jack suddenly felt a cold chill and his stomach churned. Just two days ago, they had been exposed to that same ash, that same radioactive fallout that the cows had. His right arm still tingled where that glowing ember had landed. "Did you find any more dead cows?"

"One more calf dead, about a hundred yards west of the spring, another yearling up in the cedars. This is a goddamn catastrophe, Jack. This could wipe us out. There's no way I can absorb these losses."

"Maybe the vet will come up with something." Jack knew his father always over-exaggerated their lack of money, but fifteen cows were a lot, he thought to himself.

"Won't help for the already dead. I hate to do it, but if it is radiation sickness, I may have to ask the government for some compensation."

Jack was shocked. In twenty-one years he'd never heard his father talk about asking the government for anything. "Yeah, if it is radiation, you probably should ask for help, but I doubt that it is," he replied, getting up.

"Not so fast Jack. There were two calls for you. Bishop Heinke wants you to come to his office tomorrow afternoon at two for a personal interview, and Sheriff Meecham wants you to drop by the jail sometime tomorrow for fingerprinting. Goddamn it, Jack. Nothing had better come of this fingerprinting business."

In his room, Jack's thoughts were racing. The Utah State Lab must have recovered some identifiable fingerprints. Otherwise, Sheriff Meecham wouldn't be bothering him. But even if he did have prints, they could be from any of the six of them, including Greg and Earl. He was ashamed of himself for thinking it, but it would solve a lot of problems if the prints were from the two already dead.

Jack's thoughts turned to the other message. He didn't have to think very hard about what Bishop Heinke wanted. A personal interview, that was a laugh; more like a personal reprimand.

Jack flopped on his un-made bed. His life was stampeding out of control like a nervous cowherd in a thunderstorm, racing frantically along without purpose. He felt powerless to stop the onslaught of time and events. Didn't even know where to start.

And what about Emily? How was he going to live without her? Just the thought brought him to tears. He thought of his promise to Irene to take care of Emily. Why the hell were women always making him promise things on their deathbeds? Did he look like some kind of obedient dope? First his mother, now Irene. Anyway, there was no way he could fulfill his promise to Irene when Emily was refusing to even see him.

But Emily had been right. They were very different people. Today's argument only confirmed that. Anyway, if he went on a mission he would be gone for two years. Probably the break was for the best, even though it didn't feel like it.

Emily's assault on the church and God still bothered Jack. However, it also troubled him that God had not helped Irene. Why was God so arbitrary? So callous? Irene was a good person, and the hatpin— well, it was just metal.

9

Mick had received the same two phone calls as Jack. Alan and Curley had dodged the Bishop, but they had been summoned for fingerprints. Jack and Mick would go the Bishop's interview together, then pick up Alan and Curley for the five-mile ride to Saint George.

The next morning Jack was up at 5:00 to rake the newly mown hay in the ten acres next to the creek just south of the Loren Webber field. Jack's father had inherited these from his father Sam and they were part of the original Kunz farm dating back to the first division of land in 1856. The alfalfa had to be raked into long rows before the scorching July sun vaporized the dew. Functioning like a natural glue, this moisture kept the alfalfa leaves from dropping off the stalks as the hay was windrowed. Once the alfalfa was raked, the rows would be dissected into smaller portions, then each segment heaped into piles to be pitchforked onto the flatbed wagon. Jack had heard of remarkable labor-saving machines that gobbled, chewed and bundled the hay into large rectangular cubes called bales, but his father said they were too expensive. Jack suspected that his father considered him to be his own private labor-saving device, and after he was gone, his father would probably purchase a baler.

Jack used an old horse-drawn trip rake with long semi-circular tines. The rake had been retrofitted with a hitch and rubber tires so it could be pulled behind the Massey-Ferguson. When pulled by a horse, the operator sat on a seat positioned on the rake and controlled both the horse and tripped the rake from that same position. However, when pulled by a tractor, the operator had to sit on the tractor, so this required a second person to sit on the rake seat to trip the lever, which then raised the tines to dump the hay. Jack had rigged up a rope tied to the trip lever so he could operate the rake from the tractor, eliminating the need for a second person. This, he thought cynically, was another less expensive labor-saving device.

By the time Jack had finished forking the hay into individual piles, it was 10:30 and the thermometer was topping 100 degrees. He was drenched in sweat. It was too hot to continue. And the hay was drying in the brutal heat, the delicate alfalfa leaves beginning to cascade from the stalks like sycamore leaves in an autumn breeze. He wiped the sweat from his brow and with a flourish of finality stuck the pitchfork in the last pile of hay, then headed over to the Boy's pond to splash off before his afternoon appointments, both of which he suspected would be unpleasant.

*　*　*

Patiently, Jack waited on the stone-hard metal folding chair outside the bishop's office in the chapel foyer. Mick had been inside for nearly thirty minutes. A half-hour for a personal interview was incomprehensible to Jack. What could they be talking about for a half-hour? In that amount of time, the bishop could cover almost everything, including the personal embarrassing stuff. Just thinking about the potential questions made Jack flush.

Finally, the door opened, and a still defiant Mick came out shaking his head. Rolling his eyes, Mick indicated the interview had been unpleasant, then with his thumb he motioned to Jack to go in. With sweat beading on his forehead, Jack took a long look at his friend, then entered.

Bishop Heinke was cordial, perhaps a bit too friendly. He smiled broadly, then thrust his hand at Jack to shake.

"Come on in, Jack. Glad you could make it. I know you're busy. Have a seat." Bishop Heinke pointed to the chair in front of his austere but intimidating oak desk.

Jack glanced around the room. Other than three pictures (one of the present Prophet, David O. McKay; another of founding Prophet, Joseph Smith; and the third, a picture of Jesus with a kind face and long flowing chestnut hair), the walls were bare. There was one window on the west wall set with opaque glass. The only other furnishings included two more chairs against the east wall and a matching oak file-cabinet in the corner of the room. The floor was covered with brown, short-pile carpet.

"How's the farm doing this summer, Jack?" Bishop Heinke asked.

"Okay. We're on our third cut of hay. Should get five if the water holds out. I just thinned the peaches, looks like a fair crop, and the tomatoes are starting to produce," Jack said nervously.

"You're a little ahead of me. I haven't cut my third yet. I wish I had a son like you to help out." Bishop Heinke sighed. "Jack," the Bishop said abruptly. "As you know, members of the Aaronic Priesthood are required to have annual personal interviews. Though it hasn't been quite a year since your last one, in light of yesterday's spectacle, I thought we should conduct yours a little early this year."

Swallowing hard, Jack remained silent. Bishop Heinke leaned forward in his chair, placed his elbows on the desk and gave him a penetrating look. "Jack, I'm not going to say much about yesterday. I'm sure it won't happen again. But regardless of that, I've been a little concerned about you lately. From what I hear, you've not exactly been leading a life of which Christ would be proud. Now, I can understand some youthful exuberance, but it's easy for that to get out of hand and jeopardize your opportunities for advancement in the gospel. Are you still planning on a mission?"

"Absolutely," Jack declared. "It's always been a goal of mine. I promised my mother."

"She was a fine person. A hard worker and sincere about her faith in Christ, while never forgetting her roots. Jack, as you know, before you can be called to a mission, you must be worthy to advance in the priesthood to office of an Elder in the Melchizedek Priesthood." Bishop Heinke paused and dabbed the sweat from his brow, then rose to crank open the opaque window. "So, let me ask you the questions necessary for advancement to that office. Do you believe in God?"

"Yes, Bishop, I absolutely do."

"Do you believe that Jesus is the son of God and that Joseph Smith was a prophet of God?" Bishop Heinke asked, returning to his desk.

"I do."

"Do you affirm that this is the restored and true church of God? That all other churches are false?"

"I do," Jack said confidently.

"Do you keep the commandments and live the covenants of the church?" Bishop Heinke asked, staring directly into Jack's eyes.

Jack paused, losing some of his poise. "I try to most of the time."

"Do you pay your full tithing? That's ten-percent of all your earnings before taxes."

"I do."

"Do you keep the Word of Wisdom? That means no smoking, drinking alcohol or caffeine."

"Well Bishop, I don't smoke," Jack gulped.

"What about alcohol and caffeine?"

"I do enjoy a Coke once in a while. And, I have had a drink on one or two occasions," Jack answered, looking down at the floor.

"Just one or two?"

"More like three or four." He hesitated, then mumbled, "Almost every weekend since graduation."

"Jack, you need to give those things up, and I mean today. Those things are bad for the body and the spirit, and can become habit forming. Can you do it?"

"Yes, Bishop, I can and I will," Jack declared, his jaw muscles clenched.

"Are you morally clean?"

"I'm not sure what you mean by morally clean." Jack stalled.

"Do you engage in masturbation?" Bishop Heinke gave Jack a look that withered lies.

Jack was awash with shame. He replied, "sometimes," as he continued to inspect the floor.

"Jack, self-gratification is not good for you. It shows a basic lack of discipline and loss of self-control. Plus, it's associated with some serious health problems," Bishop Heinke said with conviction. "How about heavy petting or sexual intercourse?"

"Well," he stammered. "There was one time the other night. We didn't have sex, but we did go pretty far."

"How far, Jack?"

"We—we undid our clothes and did a lot of touching. But that was all," Jack stuttered.

"Is the girl a member of this ward?" Bishop Heinke asked sternly.

Slowly Jack shook his head. "I can't tell you that Bishop. If she wants to come forward and confess, that's up to her."

Bishop Heinke took a moment. "I can understand your wanting to protect this girl, but one of the major principles of repentance is confession. A full and honest confession is cleansing to the conscience and pleasing to God. Jack, without a full confession, you can't truly repent. And if you don't honestly repent, then the sin is not forgiven. It is still with you to carry for eternity."

"I'm sorry, Bishop," Jack choked. "I just can't give you her name."

"Remember, the sexual act is consecrated and is reserved for the sanctity of marriage."

Jack nodded.

Bishop Heinke sat quietly for a minute. "Jack, you think about what I have said. Based on our conversation, I think I can recommend you for advancement in the priesthood. I can tell you have a good heart." Bishop Heinke ambled over to the cabinet and rummaged through his files. He returned with some papers and handed them to Jack. With disbelief and relief, he recognized the papers. It was the long awaited mission application form. Jack quietly thanked Bishop Heinke for his understanding, then joined a scowling Mick outside.

Looking up, Mick glanced at his watch. "Come on J.T., we've got to hurry. We need to pick up Curley and Alan and get over to the sheriff's office. He said the fingerprinter went home at five."

"I'm hurrying as fast as I can, Mick. I have no control over how long those interviews last. How did yours go?"

"The usual crap," Mick said.

"I thought the Bishop was very understanding."

"Right. You think whacking off is associated with serious health problems?" Mick demanded.

"Well—uh, I don't know," Jack stammered, his face flushing.

"Come on J.T., you're pre-med. You've studied biology."

"I don't know. Probably not."

As they left, Mick pointed to the papers. "What's that? Did Bishop

Heinke want a friggin' written confession?" Mick laughed.

"Nah, this is a mission application. Didn't he give you one?"

"He offered one, but I turned him down. Told him it was a waste of paper to give it to me," Mick boasted. "Don't look so damn disappointed."

"But Mick, we've planned to go on a mission together for years."

"No, Jack, not we—you. Face it, J.T., missions are not for everyone, and you have to admit I'm not exactly missionary material. Sending me on a mission would be like transplanting gophers in a hay field."

They drove in silence to pick up Curley and Alan. Jack was glad when their two friends climbed in, glad to have a distraction.

"Man, that was some performance in church yesterday, Mick. Profanity echoing in the house of God. That's gotta be a first for Santa Clara," Curley laughed.

"Ah, I just forgot where I was. Can't stand to lose my Queen, particularly on a sucker play."

"I thought Sister Reber was go'n to faint," Alan chuckled.

"Where you guys been?" Curley asked, as the laughter died down. "Other than church yesterday, we haven't seen much of you since the volcano."

"We went up on Utah Hill to see the blast and check on Jack's cows," Mick said as he steered the car onto Highway 91 heading east out of Santa Clara.

"How was it?" Alan asked. "Like all the others?"

"No, Shot Harry was awesome. It lit up the sky, like the resurrection," Jack said softly.

"Jack, could we drop the religious references for a while. Alan, it wasn't no resurrection, it was ghastly, like watching a hanging. Then to top it off, we got smothered with a radiation cloud and doused with fallout."

"How do you know?" Curley asked. "I didn't think you could see radiation."

"Well, we could certainly see this cloud. The ground got covered in ash and it rained bullets that burned our skin. Shit, a dozen of Jack's cows were killed by it."

"We're not sure what killed the cows," Jack said quietly.

"You may not be sure, but I am. Oh, I talked to Brenda about noon today, and she said her hair is starting to fall out in clumps. The same thing's happening to Emily," Mick said.

"What did you say, Mick, about Emily?" Jack asked.

"I said that damn radiation is making her hair fall out."

Jack was concerned. Should he call her? What would he say? I'm sorry for taking you up there and I'm sorry about a lot of other things. Maybe she wouldn't talk to him. Before he could brood about it any longer, Mick stomped the brakes and the car screeched to a stop in front of the county jail, which also served as headquarters for the sheriff's department.

"You think they have anything?" Alan asked nervously, as Mick turned off the engine.

"Sheriff Meecham said they had recovered some prints, but I doubt it," Mick answered. " I think they're just trying to make us sweat, hoping we'll crack. The important thing is that we stick to our story."

"But if they do have fingerprints," Alan insisted, "I've heard bad things about prison, like they screw you in the butt and things like that."

"If they have prints, then that narrows our choices. We can go to jail and turn into fags or we can run. Personally, I would rather run," Mick said flatly. "But don't worry, they don't have a thing. Come on, let's go in and get it over."

The jail and the sheriff's office were constructed of steel reenforced and grouted cement block. Troweled with a lime green stucco, it was an unimposing, single story building. Over the years, the rain and frequent sand storms had weathered the original green to a seedy turquoise.

It was basically a large studio room that had been sectioned into four smaller chambers. The first space was a general receiving, booking and office area. Visible in the rear were two cells with formidable, flat steel bars. To the left of the receiving area, a space had been partitioned to create a modest office for Sheriff Meecham. The basement, accessed only from outside, contained a larger holding and over-flow cell.

With no forensic lab on the premises, any evidence requiring criminology, though that was infrequent, had to be shipped to Salt Lake

City for examination. The fingerprinting station was located at the east wall next to photography. It was not elaborate, a simple folding table equipped with an ink blotter and some white cards used for obtaining fingerprints.

As they trudged in, Jack winced. He had never been in the jail before under these conditions. The next time, it might be as a felon, he thought to himself.

Sheriff Meecham was standing at the receiving desk talking to a seated deputy when they opened the door. He waved them in. "Glad you came by, boys. Saves me a trip. I've just obtained constraining warrants to have you fingerprinted." He waved some official papers in their faces. "But now, I guess they won't be necessary."

"We wouldn't miss this shindig, not even for church or cheerleaders," Mick said.

"Mick, you've got an attitude. If I get you in this jail doing time, we'll work on that," Meecham sneered.

"Well, let's get on with it. It's not like we have all day," Mick replied.

"Deputy Fowler," Sheriff Meecham pointed to the man seated at the receiving desk, "is our fingerpinter. He'll take care of you."

In a foul mood, Deputy Fowler growled, "Since Deputy Saunders was killed, I'm also the booker, dispatcher, photographer, receptionist and warden. So don't give me no shit and let's get this done as efficiently as possible."

Deputy Fowler was slightly built with a hatchet face, pocked in his youth by what might have been an astounding crop of pimples. His mahogany hair was oiled, parted in the middle, then swept harshly back at the sides. This gave him a vicious, surly appearance that belied his reputation for compassion and fair play. It was rumored that Deputy Fowler served as a moderating influence on the acrimonious and sometimes rash Sheriff Meecham.

"All right you Santa Clara Dutchmen, have a seat. You," Deputy Fowler pointed at Jack, "you come on back with me."

It still amazed Jack that the people from Saint George called them Dutchmen. The nickname either arose from Santa Clara's reputation for being frugal, or the obtuse Saint Georgians didn't know the difference between Swiss and Dutch.

As Jack trailed the deputy, he noted with a sense of foreboding that the two cells seemed to be waiting for him with barred doors open wide. Deputy Fowler recorded Jack's vital statistics, then seated him at the folding table. Systematically, the deputy dabbed each finger into the ink blotter, then rolled each digit onto a white card that had been sectioned into ten equal squares. Then Fowler handed Jack a towel to remove the ink while impatiently waving back the next suspect.

The fingerprinting took the better part of an hour, and it was 5:15 when the foursome climbed back into Mick's Chevy.

"You—you still think they're bluffing?" Alan asked, obviously unnerved. "They seemed pretty serious to me."

"They didn't ask any questions like they were trying to trick us," Curley added.

"How the hell should I know?" Mick growled as he fumbled for the keys. "We'll find out soon enough. In a couple days they'll have the results, and I suspect we'll be among the first to know."

"But suppose they just have fingerprints on one or two of us. Are we still all in this together?" Alan inquired.

"Are you saying, will those incriminated rat on the others? The answer is hell no. There's no need for all of us to go to prison if we don't have to. If they have fingerprints, I doubt they have all of us. The ones fingered will be on their own. The rest of us will try to help but there is absolutely no reason for us all to go to jail. Do we all agree on that?" Mick said emphatically as he cranked the engine. They all mumbled in agreement, though Jack could barely be heard.

"Anyway, I still think they're blowing smoke." Mick slammed the Chevy in reverse, then pulled out.

"Where do you want to go now?" Curley asked, hoping to change the subject.

Jack was glad of it. He was tired of worrying about life, prison, fallout and Emily. "Let's drag Main. See if any of our football buddies are out and about."

"To hell with football buddies. Let's look for some cheerleaders or Rebelettes," Curley said, slapping the back of the seat in front him.

As the Chevy Fastback slowly rolled past Ferg's Service Station, Mick exclaimed, "There's that dumb bastard Witless Walter Hafen.

Looks like he's washing his car with that worthless turd, Rapid Ray Reagan. Ray's the only guy I know who's never won a race and still thinks he's got the fastest car in town."

"What you got against Walt?" Curley asked. "He's too big and mean to mess with."

"Not much, only the son-of-a-bitch has threatened to kill Jack and me. Holds us responsible for Greg's death. Why us and not you two, I'll never know," Mick answered, sticking his head out the window to gawk at Walt. Distracted, he had steered the Chevy across the median stripe.

"Shit!" Jack grabbed the steering wheel, pulling the car back into the lane. "Watch where you're going."

"He used to date my sister," Alan said from the back seat. "Then he dumped her and smeared her name by telling everyone he'd had sex with her. He's an asshole."

"It sure would be nice to teach that dumb ape a lesson," Mick said. "Now's the perfect time. There's four of us and only two of them."

"They'd never fall for that," Curley said.

"They would if they didn't know there was four of us," Mick said, his freckles bunched in thought. "I could drop Alan and Curley off at the old airport hangar. Then Jack and I get them to chase us. That shouldn't be too hard since Witless hates us anyway. We'll lead them back to the old airport, then the four of us will beat the crap out of them."

"It might work," Alan said.

"I don't think this is a good idea. We're already in enough trouble," Jack said.

"Jack, quit being such a pussy. He has it coming," Curley replied.

After voting three to one in favor, Mick dropped off Alan and Curley, telling them to hide. Then he and a reluctant Jack returned to Ferg's Service Station. Wit was as slow at washing cars as he was at mental calisthenics. He was still scrubbing the side nostrils of his Buick Roadmaster.

Mick slowly cruised up to the station, then quickly stuck his head out the window and yelled, "Hey, Wit! You dumb bastard, take this." With that, Mick poked his left hand out and gestured emphatically, up and down, with his middle finger firmly erect.

Walt jerked around, uttered some obscenities, tossed his sponge and vaulted, along with Ray, into the Buick. Making sure they had time to follow, Mick turned the Chevy around, then spun his tires and raced toward the old airport road. A thundering Walt and Ray were in hot pursuit. Mick screamed through the curves and roared down the straightaways, negotiating the three paved miles to the airport with ease.

Tires howling, Mick screeched to a stop in front of the shabby, sheet-metal hangar. With adrenalin pumping, Jack and Mick burst out of the car. The air reeked with the smell of burning rubber and hot steam from an over-heated radiator. Seconds later, Walt jolted to a stop, ramming his Roadmaster against the Chevy's rear bumper, blocking any chance of retreat.

Having trapped their prey, Walt and Ray took their time. They sauntered confidently out of the Roadmaster and confronted Mick and Jack.

"What was that all about, asshole?" Walter shoved Mick, sending him reeling backwards.

Mick recovered, then smiled. "It was nothing. I just was expressing my general opinion of you."

Becoming even more agitated, Walt shouted. "Well, it's judgement day, shit head. I told you two fuckers I was going to get you. Now's as good a time as any."

"Well Wit, you've got us where you want us." Mick smiled, baiting Walt.

Just then, Ray reached out and slammed Jack into the wall.

"Ah, what the hell," Jack exclaimed. "I might just as well get this over with."

Using a vicious hook, Jack smashed his fist into the left side of Ray's face, accompanied by the unmistakable snap of bones breaking. As Ray staggered backward, Jack realized the broken bone was his. Immediately, his hand became encased in an excruciating glove of pain.

As Walt momentarily glanced over to see what happened, Mick slammed a lightning-quick uppercut at his arrogant jaw, slicing his tongue that was hanging out. Like a broken water pipe, blood gushed from Walt's mouth.

Now a wounded beast, Wit charged, striking Mick with his shoulder and grinding him into the ground. Once on top, Wit pounded Mick's face with both fists.

Ray then attacked again. With a flurry of brutal jabs to the stomach, Jack doubled over in pain. A savage knee-butt to the jaw sent Jack catapulting through the air, slamming him to the asphalt gasping for air.

Alan and Curley had almost waited too long before joining the fray. Finally, as if he had been awakened by an alarm clock, Alan jumped in and pulled Wit off Mick, pummeling him on the face and abdomen. At the same time Curley, with perfect football form, tackled Ray from behind, the two ending up in a crumpled heap in front of Jack. Protecting his injured hand as best he could, Jack stomped and kicked at Ray while Curley pulverized him with his fists.

When it was all over, Witless Walt and Rapid Ray lay bleeding, mangled and moaning on the airport runway. In just slightly better condition, the four friends weakly congratulated each other on their victory, then limped back to Mick's Chevy. The four of them were bruised, battered, and broken but Mick seemed particularly fatigued. Wearily, Mick did something he had never done before. He gave Jack the keys, then crawled into the passenger's seat.

"We sure taught that son-of-a-bitch a lesson," Mick said as they drove home in the slanted evening light.

10

The next day Jack's right hand was swollen, fiercely sore, and had turned a marbled purple. He had tried to fork the piles of hay onto the flatbed trailer, but succeeded in hauling only one partial load. The hand was just too painful to grip a pitchfork. Finally, he surrendered and called Dr. Hilton.

Thinking Mick might want to go with him to get checked out, Jack gave him a call. Mick refused, said his cold was much better, and anyway, he had Alberta peaches to pick today. "Unlike you," he said, "I don't have the time to gallivant off to Saint George."

After a quick look, Dr. Hilton sent Jack for an x-ray. While waiting for the technician, Jack couldn't help but wonder how x-rays were related to gamma rays and if they too were capable of doing harm. Surely not, x-rays were so widespread. Every time he bought a pair of shoes, he stood in an x-ray box to see if the shoes were a good fit. Obviously, they were not harmful. There was just too much fuss made about radiation these days, he thought.

Slapping the film in a view box, Dr. Hilton confirmed that Jack had fractured his fifth metacarpal, appropriately christened, the "boxer's fracture." Strange, Dr. Hilton had said, this was the second boxer's fracture that he'd seen today. Ray Reagan had been in earlier.

Dr. Hilton recommended plaster casting. It would heal better, and with immobilization, would be less painful. However, in Jack's mind, immobilization would get in the way of his hauling hay, and furthermore, Dr. Hilton did not have to deal with his father. So, after some negotiation, they compromised. Dr. Hilton splinted and taped his hand, and Jack promised to be careful.

By the time Jack got back home it was almost 3:00. Irene's

memorial service was at 4:00. As she had wished, there would be no church service, just a brief graveside remembrance. This seemed appropriate to Jack, considering Irene's lack of church attendance. Jack had debated on whether to go or not. On the one hand, he was not sure Emily wanted him there. Would she totally ignore him? On the other, maybe Emily would be offended if he didn't go and anyway, he liked Irene. The deciding factor, Jack admitted to himself, was his aching need to see Emily.

The Santa Clara Cemetery was located on a forlorn, red-quartz bluff just above town. The graveyard soil consisted of an eight foot layer of sand which made the digging of graves precarious; there was always the fear of a cave-in. The rust-colored sand resulted from the constant erosion of a massive bank of Navajo sandstone cliffs about one mile to the north of town. Wind, rain and frost had scarred and fractured the sandstone, leaving in its wake an array of red-pink pinnacles, vertical gorges, hollowed-out caves, dry gulches and sand dunes along with the thick mantle of sand that covered the cemetery.

Vegetation was sparse. The graves were not neatly blanketed with manicured lawns, but instead were punctuated by a few runty chaparral, an occasional prickly pear cactus and scattered bushy blue sage. It was as if the early Santa Clara settlers had purposefully chosen the most barren, forlorn plot of land in the entire valley, not wanting to squander precious fertile farmland on the dead. To Jack's way of thinking, if one had the time and means to search, it would be difficult to find a more forsaken, more inhospitable looking place.

At 4:00 it was still a sweltering 105 degrees. With no shade except an assortment of personal umbrellas, the service, out of necessity, was brief. Irene's father, Emil, offered a tearful opening prayer, then Sharon, an older sister from Provo, delivered a short eulogy. Bishop Heinke, sweating heavily in his navy blue suit, tight-collared white shirt and pencil-thin tie, ran a calloused finger between the waddle of his neck and his tight collar, gripped his bible, and hurriedly dedicated the grave and committed Irene's soul to the mercy of God.

Jack cautiously watched Emily throughout the service. The prayers, when everyone's eyes were closed, gave him time to study her more openly. She stood at the graveside with her grandparents, submersed in grief. With head bowed, she wept through the whole ceremony. During the dedicatory prayer, Jack eyed her more closely. He could see no signs she was losing her hair but it was impossible to say for sure. She had her hair done up in a bun, and her head was covered with a stylish black straw hat. Once, Jack caught her eye, but she quickly turned away. After it was over, she was immediately collected by her grandparents and whisked away.

Instantly, a mantle of melancholy descended on Jack like the closing curtain of a bad high school play. His life was turning to shit. Emily was gone from his life, he was probably going to prison, there would be no medical school, but there would be a couple of unkept promises. Also, according to Mick, he had been exposed to harmful levels of radiation, and now he'd fractured his hand. Oh, hell, Jack thought, regardless of the fracture of his hand and the other monumental rifts in his life, he'd better get his clothes changed and haul the rest of the hay before sunset. His father was due back tonight and the first thing he would ask would be about the hay.

But the fracture would not co-operate. By dusk, he had only managed to haul one more load. All things considered, Jack didn't think that was too bad. Not only did he have to fork the loose hay on the flatbed trailer, but when the pile got too high, he had to crawl on top and stomp it down. Then, when he'd crammed as much hay as possible on the trailer, he had to drive it two miles over the rutted furrows, then fork it into the barn.

By the time Jack got back to the house, Mary had the evening meal sitting on the dining table. The smell of freshly boiled and buttered corn filled the room, and there was his father impatiently drumming the table with his fingers, waiting for grace.

"Jack, I believe it's your turn."

Mechanically, Jack began. "Our Heavenly Father, we thank you for the food and bless it that it will nourish our bodies. We thank you for Mary's labor in preparing the food, and that we could share it as a family. We thank you for all other blessings, and we say this in the name of Jesus Christ, amen."

Mr. Kunz and Mary responded, "Amen."

Mary quickly started serving. T-bone steaks were still sizzling as she forked them from the frying pan. Jack heard the clink of the serving spoon as Mary heaped mashed potatoes on the China plates, then poured thick flour gravy with floating lumps of steak drippings. Then she added freshly picked corn-on-the-cob and steaming dinner-rolls with homemade butter.

As he ate, Jack glanced around the room. They were seated around the same metal table with the floral Formica top that was new when his mother was alive, except now there were no napkins or tablecloth. But they still had the china, a fine, cream-colored porcelain with a poppy floral pattern his father had given her on their wedding day. How his mother had cherished that china. She said it made her feel refined, like a lady. But Jack suspected it was more than that. To her, the china had been a symbol of her husband's love and commitment.

The once comfortable chairs, padded and covered with vinyl, now had tears and two permanent buttock grooves carved in each of them.

Jack looked at his father, then broke the silence with his announcement. "I met with the Bishop yesterday. He said he would recommend me for advancement to an elder and he gave me the application papers to fill out for a mission."

"I thought you'd already filled out the papers. You got enough money saved to pay for this?" his father asked, pouring himself a glass of milk.

"Depending on where I go, the mission will cost between sixty and seventy dollars a month. I got enough saved to last about a year, but I'll need some help for the second one." Jack grinned, exposing his crooked teeth.

"It's going to be tough on us. I'll have to hire someone to help me with the farm work and Mary is going to have to do more as well. If you hadn't squandered so much money carousing and drinking, you probably would have enough saved by now for the full two years," Mr. Kunz said, as he shook his head. "It'll be a hardship, but I guess, somehow we'll manage."

Jack's enthusiasm was crushed. Most of my friends haven't saved half as much, he thought. And their parents were more than willing to pay for the whole mission.

Mary bounced in her chair. "Where do you want to go, Jack?"

"If I had my choice, I guess I would go to Switzerland."

"Well, if you do, I'm sure you'll probably run into some of your distant cousins. The Kunz name comes from around County Bern, I think," Mr. Kunz said. "Mary, did the vet call while I was gone, or any of the government people?" he asked quickly changing the subject.

"Yes sir, the vet did." Mary replied and went into the kitchen to get the messages. "He says he's finished with the autopsy. He's pretty sure the cows died from radiation sickness. Says nothing else makes any sense." She flipped through her notes. "Oh. He says he's heard from the Cedar City vet that the Bulloch brothers lost a bunch of sheep with the same sores and symptoms. The government vet who looked at them said they died of malnutrition, so I guess, they're refusing to compensate the Bullochs." More shuffling of the notes. "Here it is. The Bulloch brothers want to start a law suit against the government and the vet thinks you might want to be part of it."

"And the government people, Mary. Did they call?" Mr. Kunz asked.

"No sir, they didn't. But an AEC man by the name of Popovich dropped by, said they were looking into the matter and would get back with you in a couple days. He said the preliminary investigation showed the cows probably died of malnutrition." Mary smiled, pleased that she delivered the message so accurately.

"What the hell are they talking about?" Kunz exploded. "I've been in the ranching business for fifty years, and they're telling me my cattle are dying of malnutrition? I'll bet that son-of-a-bitch has never even seen malnutrition before. Goddamn insult for him to say I let my animals die of starvation. Shit!"

"It sounds like the Bulloch brothers' sheep died of starvation. The AEC wouldn't lie about that," Jack said.

"For hell's sake, Jack!" Mr. Kunz shouted. "What are you talking about? You got some special source of information I don't know about?"

"Well, I just thought, maybe they had assumed our cows were like their sheep and when they check it out—"

"My cows," Mr. Kunz cut in, and them sheep both died from the same damn thing, radiation fallout. For some reason those bastards are trying to cover it up."

Mary quickly pushed her chair away from the table. "Maybe it's all a mistake, Dad," she said, frightened at her father's outburst.

"In my opinion, once the investigation is completed, I'm sure the government will do the honorable thing, they always do," Jack said, hoping to calm his father. "I see no need to join the lawsuit. That will just cost us more money."

"No one asked you for your opinion, Jack," Mr. Kunz said.

Jack started to strike back, then thought better of it. What good would it do, he thought. The room lapsed into an uneasy silence, the only sound being the occasional jangle of silverware. Finally, Mary asked, "Jack, what happened to your hand?"

Jack looked up, surprised. He took a quick bite of potatoes, trying to formulate an alibi. "The trip lever on the rake got stuck. I knocked it loose, but when it released, my hand was in the way. I had Doc Hilton take a look at it. Said I broke the hand bone of my fifth finger, the bone fighters usually break, called a boxer's fracture. No big deal."

"You broke your hand on the hay rake?" Mr. Kunz arched an eyebrow.

"Yeah, one of those stupid accidents," Jack said, still looking at his plate.

"Is this your way of saying you didn't get all the hay hauled?" his father demanded.

"Yes, that means I still have three loads left. I'll get them done tomorrow," Jack replied through clenched teeth.

"Well, as long as it gets done. But Jack, things are starting to back up. The peaches are almost ripe now. You've got to start on them tomorrow or they'll be falling to the ground. The birds are already picking at 'em."

Stinging with anger, Jack did not trust himself to answer. He gulped down the rest of his meal, excused himself and stomped off to his room. He flopped on Chris's bed, fuming. In the quiet, he could hear the ceramic clink-clink of Mary doing the dishes, and the garbled sounds from the television.

Jack tuned out the domestic sounds as his thoughts focused on his father. This was just another in a long series of events that confirmed how unappreciated he was in this house. It would be great to leave for a couple years, a mission or even prison. If neither of those options worked out, he'd join the army and go to Korea, like Chris had done. It didn't really matter as long as he got out. Once he was gone, his father would realize how much he did around the house and farm. Especially when he had to hire someone. He might even have to hire two people to do my work, Jack thought, smiling to himself. Once gone, he would never come back.

The next day, Jack finished with the hay about 1:00 in the afternoon. Though it was blistering hot and time for a break, Jack grabbed his picking bucket, some bushel baskets, and his twelve-foot, tripod ladder and loaded them into the pickup truck, heading for the orchard. Flies buzzed in the cab, and Jack angrily swatted them away. He was not in a good mood. Without a doubt, picking peaches was his least favorite chore. The peach fuzz would get in your eyes and down your neck, and on any exposed skin. Mixed with sweat, the fuzz created a thin, sticky paste that made your skin itch if it wasn't protected. To solve the problem, Jack wore a long-sleeve shirt over his T-shirt. But in spite of precautions, the fuzz always found a way in.

Already scratching his groin, Jack lined a bushel basket with newspaper, grabbed a picking bucket and climbed the ladder.

When he reached the top rung, Jack spotted Mick weaving his way toward the orchard. Like a field mouse aware that there was chicken hawk overhead, Mick dashed from the cover of Johnson-grass-lined ditch banks to the weed blind of the fence lines. Jack's bad mood melted. Smiling, he followed Mick's erratic progress. What the hell kind of a prank was he up to? With Mick, it was always something. Jack decided he might be hunting rabbits or mourning doves when he noticed Mick was carrying his Winchester pump-action .22 in his right hand. In the other hand, he had some kind of a leather pouch with a handle.

Suddenly Jack's mirth vanished like frogs in winter. Out of the corner of his eye, he saw Sheriff Meecham's patrol car rapidly approaching from the west on Vineyard Road.

As the patrol car barreled down the dirt road, dragging billowing clouds of dust behind it, Jack scrambled down and dashed across the orchard to intercept Mick. They met under an aging black-walnut tree in the southwest corner of the orchard.

"J.T.," Mick wheezed, out of breath. "I've got it! Goddamn, have I got it!"

"Got what?"

"I've got the goods on them," Mick said, patting a brown leather briefcase. "I've got the AEC papers! I'm goin' prove those friggin' bastards are lying."

"Are you out of your ever-lovin' mind, Mick? "Jack blurted. "This is insane. Stealing government documents is a federal crime. What the hell are you thinking? "

"We'll talk about it later. We gotta get out of here. Sheriff Meecham is on his way to arrest us."

"I saw his car from the ladder. What makes you think he's going to arrest us?" Jack demanded.

"You remember my cousin, Alice? She works for Judge Ballard. She called me this morning and said the judge had just issued warrants for our arrests on manslaughter charges. We've got to go!"

"Not so fast, Mick. We've got to think this through. If we run, that's another crime they'll charge us with. If we stay, they might show us leniency. Just give us probation. Hell, we're still kids—almost."

"Probation, my ass! One of their own was killed, and the police protect their own. They'll want revenge. Count on it, J.T., we'll do the maximum," Mick insisted.

"Running could change our whole lives."

"Tell me, J.T., what kinda of life you got now? If you think there's going to be a mission or medical school, or a life with Emily, your fucking kidding yourself. We gotta go!".

"Hey, you two!" Sheriff Meecham shouted.

"He's packing a gun, Sheriff," Deputy Fowler warned.

"J.T., I'm outta here," Mick snapped as he pivoted, jumped the fence and sprinted toward the thick willow cover of the creek bed.

"Halt!" Sheriff Meecham yelled."Goddamnit it Graff! Stop or I'll shoot."

"Sheriff," Deputy Fowler stammered, his face losing its color.

"Just a scare him a bit, Sheriff Meecham said as he unsnapped his holster.

Mick, oblivious, didn't look back. In a flash, Sheriff Meecham pulled his .357 magnum and jerked the trigger.

Jack heard the bullet crash through the leaves and shatter a branch. Deflected, the bullet abruptly changed course, rapidly losing velocity and altitude. It penetrated the soft cotton fabric of Mick's shirt, then pierced the leathery skin of his back. Instantly, a patch of blood appeared on his white T-shirt. Mick buckled to his knees and fell face first in the alfalfa stubble like he'd been tackled from the blind side.

"Good God, Sheriff! You've hit him," Deputy Fowler shouted , as the sheriff re-cocked the hammer.

"Fuck!" Sheriff Meecham fumed, as Fowler pinned his arms in a bear hug.

Appalled, Jack watched his friend stagger to his feet and with faltering steps, fight for the creek bed. Jack was over the fence in an instant. Reaching his friend, he circled an arm around his waist. Mick draped his left arm around Jack's shoulders as they limped into the river willows, vanishing in the thick undergrowth.

11

Upon entering the willow thicket, Jack quickly guided Mick upstream. This time of year with Pine Valley Mountain's snow pack gone and no summer rain, there was precious little flow in the Santa Clara River. Sloshing through the stream bed was easier than fighting the dense undergrowth of willows and sapling cottonwoods on the river bank.

They struggled along for about an hour, occasionally slipping on the slick, river-polished rocks. Blood was oozing from Mick's wound, and he finally begged for a rest. Jack eased him down in the shade of a water-faded outcropping of black lava boulders, then cautiously doubled back to see if they were being followed. He went as far as his father's alfalfa field, but saw no one. That was curious.

Either Sheriff Meecham didn't think they were worth chasing, which was unlikely, or he thought they might be dangerous. They did have Mick's .22 rifle. Perhaps, he thought, with a wounded man as baggage, they couldn't get far. Jack could picture that fat, smug sheriff confidently sitting back at his desk, drinking a Coke and waiting for them to just walk in and surrender. Still pondering the possibilities, Jack hastily returned to where he had left Mick.

Mick was sleeping when Jack returned. Concerned, he watched his friend for a moment. Mick's moans were punctuated by intermittent muscle spasms, making his left leg twitch. A trickle of blood had dried in the corner of his mouth.

"Mick." Jack gently shook him. "Roll over so I can look at that wound." Mick groaned, and slowly complied.

The wound was probably not as bad as it looked, Jack thought. The bleeding had pretty much stopped. A dull halo of a mottled purple had developed around the wound, and the lesion was caked with a dark red plug of clotted blood. Mick moaned as Jack gently brushed the clot away so he could inspect the wound cavity. The bullet must have been pretty much spent. Even though it punctured the skin, it had not gone much further. As Jack spread the skin apart with his fingers, he saw the butt of the bullet resting in the crimson-stained, yellow fat, but like trying to retrieve a cork that had been pushed too far in a wine bottle, he couldn't get his fingers far enough in to extract the bullet.

As best he could tell, Jack thought, there were three options. One, he could incise the wound with his knife and enlarge it enough to get his fingers in and pull out the bullet. Two, he could bandage the wound and leave well enough alone. Or three, if he could find a small instrument like a needle-nose pliers, he could extricate the bullet without cutting.

After few moments, Jack decided on option three. He doubted the wound would heal if he left the bullet and with an open wound, there was always a chance of infection. The problem was, he didn't have a needle-nose pliers.

On instinct, Jack climbed up the river bank and looked for something he could use as a surgical instrument. Instantly, his eyes landed on a barb-wire fence. This might do, he thought smiling. With his pocket-knife he pried loose a U-shaped fencing staple from a cedar post.

Jack sterilized his knife and the metal staple with a match. As Mick writhed in pain, Jack planted the tines of the staple into the wound so it cradled the bullet. Then with the knife blade, Jack pressed the bullet into the prongs of the staple and slowly pulled it out.

The wound started to ooze again, then hemorrhaged, bubbling out like water from a drinking fountain. Jack was now sweating heavily and his hand shook slightly as he ripped off his long-sleeved, peach-picking shirt. Swiftly, he tore off the sleeves, wadded them into a ball and pressed them into the wound. Then he tore the rest of the shirt into strips and tied them tightly around Mick's torso. Within a few minutes the bleeding stopped.

Mick was now wide awake and in misery. "Did you get it?" he groaned.

"Yeah," Jack said, showing Mick the bullet. "You should be okay. It's a pretty superficial wound, just under the skin. The only thing we have to worry about is infection."

Mick moaned, "Is the sheriff still tracking us? We'd better get out of here."

"No, I checked. There's no one coming. They're probably organizing a posse or something."

"J.T., thanks for taking care of me. I know you didn't want to come."

Jack sighed. "You are right. I thought they might go easy on us. We've got no criminal record. But from the looks of it, they're hell bent to get us anyway they can, even if it takes shooting us in the back."

Mick rolled to a more comfortable position. "J.T., you're mostly right in what you said, but we do have one prior. Remember last Halloween?"

"Yes, but that was a misdemeanor. We're not exactly hardened criminals," Jack replied then became quiet. After a moment he continued. "Mick, how the hell did you get that briefcase?"

"It was pretty easy. You remember Doris, Brenda's younger sister? Anyway, she works as a maid at the Big Hand Motel. While Rudy Popovich and his bunch were in the café eating lunch, I just had Doris open the door with her key, and the friggin' briefcase was sitting there on the bed, just beggin' to be taken." Mick's snickered.

"I swear sometimes you just don't think things through. How long do you think it will take them to figure out it was you? They'll interview anyone with access to that room. Probably not more than a handful of people. With the FBI grilling her, how long do you think Doris will hold out? My guess is about five minutes, or less."

"Well, I—I really don't care if she talks. I stole the papers to expose the cover-up, so the more people that know, the better," Mick argued, clenching his jaw muscles. Even his freckles glared in defiance.

"How do you know there's a cover-up? Have you even looked inside? Do you even know what you have? And if those papers are radiation data, do you have the training to make any sense of it?"

"Well—"

"And for the sake of argument, let's suppose you have caught the

127

AEC red-handed, who are you going to tell? Who would believe you? You're now a wanted man. Wanted for killing a deputy sheriff. You try taking those papers into the offices of the *Washington County News*, they'll have you arrested."

"I hear you, J.T., but I know we've been exposed to high levels of radiation. This is some serious shit. People have to know."

"Well, you can count on it. With you taking those papers, we'll not only have the sheriff after us, but the FBI as well. Where are we going? We've got to have a plan," Jack said, trying to keep the irritation out of his voice.

Mick was thoughtful. "First of all, we need to get out of here. We've still got about three or four hours of daylight. Let's try to make it to Boomer's Peak. From there, we can tell if they're coming. We can see them coming from any direction. They can't surprise us. We'll spend the night there and work on a plan for tomorrow. For now J.T., we just need to take it one day at a time."

"If you're up to it, let's go. The sheriff could be back at any moment."

Boomer's Peak was a remote, roadless, table-top island mesa about five miles southwest of Santa Clara. Jutting 800 feet from the desert floor, it stood like a lonely sentinel guarding the northeastern finger of the great Mojave wasteland. The crown was created by an uplifted layer of erosion-resistant limestone rock that formed a circular cliff around the entire mesa. From that craggy rimrock, the ground sloped steeply down in all directions to the desert valley floor below. Vegetation was sparse and consisted of a meager assortment of sage, greasewood, cactus and an occasional Utah juniper. There was no trace of surface water. But it had that one huge advantage, there was no way anyone could approach the mesa without being spotted for at least two miles in advance.

By the time the two friends crawled over the lip to the top, the sun was sinking in the west behind Utah Hill. They were exhausted, hungry and dirty, but most of all they were thirsty. The setting sun offered some relief from the brutal heat, but that was about all. At Mick's suggestion, Jack kicked over a barrel cactus and used a flat rock to flatten the razor-sharp needles. Then with his pocket-knife he cut two large chunks from the core and handed one to Mick. It wasn't like drinking a frosty glass of ice-water and it had a slight melon taste, but it was wet and helped quench their thirst.

As Mick rested on a slab of gray rock, Jack took the .22 and went rabbit hunting. He soon bagged two cottontails without much difficulty and quickly gutted and skinned them, finally impaling them on a spit. After ripping dead sagebrush from its roots, Jack quickly constructed a fire. He carefully placed the rabbits over the flames, periodically rotating them.

While the game was roasting, Jack took another look at Mick's wound.

"Looks pretty good. There's still a slight ooze, but not enough to get you into trouble. Mick, I think you just might live," Jack said cheerfully. But privately he worried about the trickle of blood and the continued exposure of the open wound to grime and sweat.

Mick then rolled over on his right side. "I must have bruised my stomach when that bullet knocked me down. I've sure got a tender spot on my left side. Right here." Mick pointed to the left upper quadrant of his abdomen.

Jack gently palpated the area.

"Shit Jack, go easy. That hurts like hell. What is it? My liver?" Mick winced.

Carefully, Jack probed a little deeper. There was a blunt, ovoid mass on the left side that seemed to be hanging down from the ribs, and extending almost to the pelvis. "I don't think that's the liver. The liver's on the right side. It's probably the pancreas or spleen. Yep, I think it's the spleen."

"Whatever it is, it's damn sore," Mick exclaimed.

"You probably did smack it with the fall. It's not too surprising if it's swollen and tender," Jack said with a confidence he did not feel. He was uneasy about his layman's diagnosis. "We really need to get you to a doctor, Mick."

"You're worse than my mother, Jack. Anyway, you're almost a doctor. I'll be okay in a couple days." Mick pushed Jack's hands aside and sat up. "Isn't that rabbit done yet?"

"You know damn well that's not true."

"About the rabbit?"

"No, about me being a doctor. I don't know what the hell I'm doing. You need to see Doc Hilton," Jack said as he checked on their meal.

Gingerly, Jack removed the hot, charcoal-blackened meat from the spit and yanked off a hind-quarter, offering it to Mick. Then he ripped off the other hindquarter for himself. It tasted like sage smoke and was a little gritty from the charcoal, but it was edible.

"You're getting to be a pretty good shot with that .22, J.T. Didn't take you long to get those rabbits," Mick said.

"I've always been pretty good but I wished to hell you hadn't brought that gun. It's going to get us in trouble. Probably, already has," Jack predicted, smiling slightly in the firelight. "Seems there's always trouble when the three of us get together, you, me, and a gun."

"You're not talking about that damn shoe thing again, are you?" Mick grinned, his freckles dancing. "I can't help it if you're so damn gullible."

"You did that on purpose, wearing your older cousin's shoes," Jack said as he remembered what had happened just after Christmas ten years ago. The two of them had arranged to go bird hunting with their new BB guns. Unknown to Jack, Mick had showed up wearing an older cousin's large shoes that left his toes at least an inch from the leather's inside rim. Mick had dared Jack to shoot his big toe with the BB gun, then goaded him on by demonstrating that it didn't hurt by blasting at his shoe, just beyond his toe, with his own gun, then grinned. "See, it doesn't hurt." Not to be outdone, Jack had then placed the barrel of his BB gun squarely on his shoe, directly above the great toenail and pulled the trigger. Instantly, the pain was excruciating. Jerking off his shoe, Jack stared in horror at the battered nail as a huge purple hematoma expanded right before his eyes. Within minutes, his toe looked like a careless carpenter's thumb. He eventually lost the toenail.

"Of course I did it on purpose," Mick said, chuckling with laughter. "I'd been planning that for a week. The only thing I regret is there wasn't anyone but me to see it. You were hopping around on one leg like a lovesick flamingo doin' a mating dance."

"Well, don't think I've forgotten about it. I'm still going to get you back for that one. Like General MacArthur in the Pacific, I pick my battles. I'm just waiting for the right time and place. I'll be back," Jack chuckled as he tossed a rabbit carcass into the fire. Feeling the warmth of the fire and their friendship, the two companions lapsed into silence as they ate.

After a while, Mick asked, "What do you think is going to happen, J.T.? We're kinda in a fix."

"I don't know. They've probably seen our fire by now. Maybe I shouldn't have started it, but I figured they could track us anyway without too much problem."

"Yeah, probably," Mick agreed. "But the fire was worth it. The rabbit sure tasted good."

"Anyway, I suspect tomorrow they'll be coming for us. We're definitely in a no-win predicament. There's no place for us to run. We're over a hundred miles from Vegas, and even if we did make it through the desert and heat, then what? The sheriff would assume that's where we'd gone and be there ahead of us. The only place we'd be safe is in Mexico, and with no money, I'm not sure how we'd get there," Jack said. "Anyway, I'm not sure I want to live the rest of my life in Mexico."

"Well, I damn sure don't want to spend the rest of my life in prison. How about we go north to Cedar City or Milford? We could hop a train in Milford."

"God Mick, that's still a hundred miles to Milford, and we'd have to hike over Pine Valley Mountain to get there. I doubt you're in any condition to do that. What we need to do is get you to a doctor."

"Nah, I'm fine. How about east to Kanab? That's right on the Arizona border. From Kanab, we could just stroll into Arizona, then hitch-hike to Mexico."

"That's a still eighty miles, and when we get there, we're still in Utah. It's hard to hide in a small town. You'd be about as conspicuous as Bishop Heinke in the Sun Bowl Club," Jack said with a glum look on his face.

"Well then, what do you suggest?" Mick snapped.

"I think we should turn ourselves in, not to Sheriff Meecham or the FBI, but to the Saint George City Police. Tomorrow, we should just work our way back to Saint George and then walk into the police station and say, 'Are you looking for us?'"

"I don't know J.T. I think their shooting me means they have no intention of going easy on us. They'll throw the book at us. Have you thought about what life would be like in prison?"

"Of course I have, and I hate the idea of it, but it's not like we have a bushel of options. You think about it tonight and we'll talk about it some more tomorrow. Tonight, we both need to get some sleep."

"J.T.," Mick said. "I don't want to turn these papers over to the police. Hell, they'll just give em back to the friggin' AEC. We've got to get them to a newspaper, a real paper like the *Salt Lake Tribune* or the *Deseret News* not the *Washington County News*.

"Let's sleep on it tonight. Tomorrow we'll decide. Need anything, Mick?"

"Well, I wouldn't mind some ice-cold Colt 45, and if you could get Brenda to come and snuggle up to me, that would be nice," Mick said with a smile. Then he groaned as he turned on his left side and pulled the briefcase under his head for a pillow.

Sleep did not come immediately to Jack. His mind would not unwind. His thoughts wandered to the bizarre way the sheriff shot Mick. It was totally incomprehensible. Why the hell would Sheriff Meecham do that? Sure, Mick was trying to escape, and he did have a gun, but even taking that into account, Mick had not made any threatening motions toward the sheriff. He had just turned and run. Maybe, it was as Mick had said all along. When it comes to avenging their own, the cops have no mercy.

Fleetingly, Jack's reflections turned to his father. He would be furious. Likely, he would be more angry that Jack hadn't finished picking the peaches and doing the chores than he would be concerned about the fact that Jack was a hunted fugitive on the run for his life or that he was trapped in the desert without food or water. With a sharp pang of remorse, Jack thought how disappointed his mother would be. His mission was now out of the question. Maybe, he could try to convert his fellow inmates. Of course, that would have to be in the idle moments when they weren't gang-banging him.

Trying to dispel that ugly image, Jack thought about Emily. What was she doing tonight? Was she thinking about him? By now, knowing how gossip travels in Santa Clara, she'd probably heard he was a wanted outlaw. That certainly would shock her, considering all the preaching he'd heaped on her. But what had Mick said about her hair falling out? Could that be true? Jack tried to picture her. In his mind, she was still beautiful, even if her hair was falling out. If she was going bald, it was his fault. He was the one who took her up on Utah Hill to see Shot Harry and got her doused with radiation fallout.

Jack unconsciously shook his head as he thought about Mick stealing Rudy Popovich's briefcase. What the hell was he thinking? This complicated things even further. Mick should let him do the planning. Whenever Mick freelanced, he always screwed things up.

Even if it were true that the AEC was involved in a cover up, who would believe them? Or for that matter, even care? The whole country was immersed in a kind of paranoid hysteria. They were far more concerned about the Russians and their bombs than they were about a few weird Mormon farmers in southern Utah. The rest of the country, Jack thought, would gladly sacrifice the whole of Washington County if it would save them from the Russians. Jack decided he would look at the AEC papers tomorrow.

But adding the FBI to the mix was troubling. They always got their man. Mick with his freckles and him with his crooked teeth. Jack could visualize their pictures plastered on every post office wall in the country. Escaping the clutches of the FBI would certainly be difficult, if not impossible.

Finally, Jack fell into a fitful sleep teeming with ghostly, technicolor images. There were magnificent, iridescent mushroom clouds. A bald Emily also appeared, losing her skin and flesh in huge ragged, necrotic chunks. And, there he was, running as fast as he could. But in spite of the distance he'd covered, he could still hear the crack of a gunshot and see a bloody, gaping hole expanding in his back. When he looked closely, he could see right through his body to blue sky on the other side. Through it all, Jack realized he was trying to wake up, but he could only continue to run from some faceless, nameless pursuer.

It was sometime after midnight when Jack was finally rescued from his nightmares by Mick's moaning. At first, Jack thought the groans were part of his dream, but slowly he realized they were from Mick. Opening his eyes, he struggled with a ticker-tape of rapid images as he quickly recalled the events of yesterday and fought to get himself oriented. Finally, Jack remembered he was on Boomer's Peak, and the reason Mick was moaning was that he was wounded.

Rolling to his left, Jack groped for Mick's forehead in the dark. He was hot and beaded with sweat. As Jack pondered these physical signs, Mick suddenly had an attack of rigors. His whole body trembled like a horse shaking off water after crossing the Virgin River. Sweating heavily, Mick quaked violently for a couple minutes, then began to shiver.

"J.—J.T., I'm cold. Turn up the heat," Mick mumbled, his teeth chattering.

Jack crawled to the fire and stirred the coals, then heaped on more sage brush. "I need to look at that wound, Mick. I think you've got an infection."

"Sure as hell feels like I have something. A minute ago I was burning up, now I'm freezing. And my back feels like it's got a watermelon stuck in it." Mick inched closer to the fire.

In the dim light, Jack fumbled with Mick's bandage. Instead of the deep purple, the wound was now a fiery red, and a coarse clot plugged the bullet hole. As gentle as he could, Jack loosened the clot, then plucked it from the crater. It was like popping the lid from a Coke bottle after shaking it a couple times. A thick, yellow-green exudate literally gushed from the wound and ran down Mick's flank. The smell was musty and nauseating. Without water, it was difficult to clean the wound, but Jack sopped it dry with a piece of shirt, then re-bandaged it. Within minutes, Mick ceased shivering and said he felt much better.

The crisis over, the two young men stared silently at the fire, each lost in his own thoughts. Mick whispered, "J.T., you really believe in the church?"

Without taking his eyes off the fire, Jack replied, "You know I do."

"You still believe in heaven and hell and all that stuff?"

"Of course I do, otherwise this existence makes no sense. We're rewarded or punished for our deeds here on earth. It's as simple as that."

"You think Greg and Easy went to heaven or hell? They certainly weren't perfect."

"Mick, you don't need to be perfect to go to heaven. You need to be trying, and have the proper ordinances done, like baptism and temple marriage. God knows what's in every man's heart," Jack said with assurance, though after the events of the last few days he didn't feel as certain about these things as he once had.

Mick murmured, "Doesn't the church teach some sins are not forgivable, that they are so bad there is no forgiveness?"

"Yes, basically two. One, blasphemy against the Holy Ghost, and two, murder. Mick, this is a strange conversation to be having in the middle of the night on Boomer's Peak." Jack raised his eyes from the fire and peered through the gloom at his friend.

"What's blasphemy against the Holy Ghost?"

"I'm not sure, but I think it's when you have gained a testimony of the truthfulness of the church, then turn against it."

"What about murder? There's all kinds. What about war or manslaughter? Deputy Saunders?"

"No. War and manslaughter are not murder. They're forgivable," Jack said.

"What's the difference? The person is just as dead."

"They're not premeditated. No intent. No malice."

"Oh," Mick said hollowly, as he stared into the fire. After a few moments he continued. "Seems like a fine line. What happens to them who commit unforgivable sins?"

"I don't know, I guess they become Sons of Perdition." Jack shivered. He did not like talking about this. "You know, they remain in limbo for eternity. They get no degree of glory. Why do you ask?"

Mick rolled over with his back to fire and mumbled to the darkness, "No reason, just curious. I'm tired, J.T., let's get some shut-eye."

However, sleep didn't seem possible right now for Jack. He glanced over at Mick. He appeared to be asleep already. That was certainly an odd conversation they had just had, he thought. The fever and everything must have put Mick in a contemplative mood, realized he was mortal after all. Staring back at the fire, Jack thought about their situation. This was not good. Mick's wound was infected, and though he had drained it, Jack had a feeling the pus would re-accumulate. What Mick needed was a real doctor and some penicillin, not some wannabe medical student with only dirty rags for bandages.

Tomorrow they could try to make a run for it, but to where? Without money, transportation, passports or connections, how far would they get? To get money and transportation, they might have to rob a service station, or steal a car, and maybe even injure or kill someone. Quickly, Jack glanced at the .22. That damn gun could get them into serious trouble.

But if they turned themselves in, the thought of spending five years or so in prison made Jack shiver. He seriously doubted he could survive a week in prison, let alone five years.

The more he ruminated, the more Jack was convinced there were no good answers, just bad consequences. To run or to go to prison, it was a hell of a choice.

12

As the sun broke over the coral-pink bulwarks and towering cathedral spires of Zion National Park, it hurled shafts of golden light some fifty miles through crisp morning air to Boomer's Peak where Jack awakened still groggy and, with a start, realized that he had been asleep. Not only had he slept, but he had over-slept. Clearing his mind, Jack glanced at Mick. He stirred slightly, rolling to the right and shifting his head from the briefcase pillow to his arm. Soon, he was snoring again.

Moving quietly so he would not wake Mick, Jack retrieved the briefcase, sat down on a flat rock and opened it. It was just about what he expected. There were a half-dozen manilla folders containing white papers with figures scrawled on them. Each folder seemed to represent an individual recording station and each sheet of paper was dated and broken into 24 sections, one section for each hour of the day. The data in the papers must be the number of rads recorded at that station for each hour of the day, Jack thought. He shuffled through the papers for a minute and found the day Shot Harry was detonated. Depending on which station, they had recorded figures ranging as high as 5.2 rads/hour for the Santa Clara station, to 8.6 rads/hour at the Coyote Springs station on the western slope of Utah Hill.

Jack had no idea what was considered a safe level, but certainly Mick had been convinced that the radiation levels were high. And perhaps they were. He remembered the conversation he and Mick had overheard at the carwash. What had the one official said? "We're blowing the safe limits all to hell. The people need to be warned to stay indoors."

Suddenly, Mick grunted and stirred. Jack quickly replaced the folders and eased the briefcase back beside Mick.

"How you feeling this morning?" Jack inquired.

"Fine. Just great. Except my tongue feels like a prickly pear cactus and my head aches like I spent the night boozing. Other than that, I'm fine. What's for breakfast? Eggs and pancakes?" Mick grinned.

"We have some leftover rabbit and I'll find another barrel cactus, but we need to find some real water today. How's the back doing?" Jack asked as he handed Mick the picked-over, cold rabbit carcass.

"What back?" Mick chuckled and tapped his flank for emphasis. "You got me totally fixed up last night, Dr. Kunz."

"I doubt that. We've still got to get you to a real doctor soon. Have you given any more thought to what we talked about last night?"

"I still think we could make it to Vegas, then hitch-hike to Mexico. We could survive in Mexico. We're smarter than the average wet-back, and I wouldn't mind being spoiled by a pretty señorita." Mick picked a morsel of meat from the rabbit's spine.

"You know that's nonsense, Mick. I doubt I could make it across the desert, let alone you with a hole in your back. We've got to go back and turn ourselves in."

"Like I said, I'm fine. You just pick a direction and I guarantee that I'll keep up with you. But not back to Saint George."

Sensing he was getting nowhere, Jack stomped off to search for a barrel cactus. After about five minutes, he found a plump one near the mesa's northern lip. As Jack kicked it, trying to dislodge its roots, he detected motion out of the corner of his eye.

About a mile away, four horsemen were just emerging from the mouth of an arroyo. Jack resisted his immediate instinct to flee, and took a few moments to evaluate the situation. There was no doubt about it. They were headed for Boomer's Peak. It had to be Sheriff Meecham, Deputy Fowler and a posse of two. Or, perhaps by now, the FBI had arrived and the other two horsemen were agents. There was no FBI office in Saint George, Jack reasoned, but how long would it take them to come from Salt Lake City or Las Vegas? Not long, Jack thought. They could very well be part of a posse by now.

Anyway, Jack had just about run out of time to think about it. He and Mick would have to decide right now what they were going to do. Dragging the cactus by the roots, Jack quickly trotted back to camp.

"They're coming," Jack declared. "Sheriff Meecham and three others on horseback."

"Well, at least they could show us the courtesy to wait until we've finished breakfast. That's friggin impolite." Mick was still in a good mood.

Hurriedly, Jack stomped in the cactus needles and cut out its heart. "We've got to go. They'll be here in twenty minutes. Where do you want to go? We've got to decide right now."

"Anywhere, except prison," Mick replied, sauntering over to accept a hunk of cactus.

"Okay, we'll head east toward Kanab, and if it looks like we can't make it, we'll just angle a little north and be back in Saint George. By heading east, we should run into the Virgin River in a few hours."

"Sounds good to me. Let's go off Boomer's south side before turning east. Posse'll never see us." Quickly chewing and swallowing the wet pulp, Mick spat out the woody residue as he headed to the rim.

Jack sprinted back to the other side to check on the posse. They were coming fast. There was no time to waste. They eased down the vertical slope and almost immediately ran into a shallow dry wash running east. Its banks were fringed with abundant willowy chaparral, offering some cover.

Though it was only 9:00 a.m., the already tepid air hinted at what kind of day it would be. Another scorcher. Within another five miles or so, Jack figured, they should reach the Virgin River just below the ghost town of Bloomington and just before the river entered the gorge that carried it well into Arizona.

As the sun arched higher, the temperature soared. Battling de-hydration as well as his wound, Mick's initial bravado slowly vanished and he started to lag behind. At first, Jack did not offer to help. Dammit, he thought, Mick had said he didn't need any help, that he could make it to Kanab. Jack figured another mile or so of this inferno would force Mick to recognize the futility of it all and he would agree to return to Saint George.

As they limped on, the sand fried their sneaker-clad feet. The sun burned every drop of water from them. Then without warning, Mick gasped and collapsed on the hot sand.

Now Jack was really worried. Mick looked like an over-ripe tomato bulging and cracking open in the sun. His face was scarlet and his lips cracked and swollen, his eyes puffy almost to the point of closing. If they didn't reach the river soon, they would both founder and perish right here in this god forsaken desert, Jack thought, as he sank into the hot sand. By his calculations, it couldn't be more than a mile or two, at the most, to the river.

Fortunately, there was no sign of the posse yet. Jack smiled at the thought of the fat sheriff huffing-and-puffing up Boomer's Peak only to discover they had gone. He would be pissed. But even Sheriff Meecham would be able to pick up their conspicuous trail in the sand and with horses, they'd cover ground fast. Jack shuddered. At any second he half expected to feel a bullet ripping through his flesh.

Struggling back to his feet, Jack dragged Mick with him. Using his hand as a tent for his eyes to shield the harsh sunlight, Jack surveyed the horizon. Still no posse, but no Virgin River either. Half-carrying, half-dragging Mick, he continued eastward, wading through ankle-deep sand. The sun continued to pound them.

An hour passed, maybe two. Time seemed inconsequential. Now Jack was mostly carrying Mick. With the extra weight, he rapidly tired and the two soon collapsed in the burning sand. Jack felt consciousness slipping.

His mind floated. He dreamed of cool water splashing on his face and trickling into his mouth, his tongue soaking up the water like a dried sponge. He felt more splashing of water on the face. This seemed real. Jack fought to open his eyes. There seemed to be a black reservation hat crowned with a silver conchos blocking the sun.

"*Yaa' eh t'eeh,* Jack."

Jack slowly rubbed the blur from his eyes and sat up. Smoky tossed him a canvas bag canteen.

"What you doing passing out in the desert?" he asked, peering at Jack. "Only a drunk Navajo or some cowardly mountain In'dan like those horse thieve'n Utes would pass out in the middle of the desert. Bad night?"

Jack gently cradled Mick's head in his lap and sloshed water on his face. The smell of wet canvas tickled his nostrils. "I guess you haven't heard."

"Hurd what?"

"There's a posse chasing us. Sheriff Meecham." Jack pried Mick's lips open, forcing him to drink.

"From the volcano thing. I hurd about that volcano." Smoky smiled a rare smile, displaying teeth in various stages of decay, then turned more serious. "What'cha gonna do?"

"I don't know. Right now were headed to Kanab."

"Kanab, a long ways, Jack. It's hard to outrun a *biligaana* posse when you're on foot. It's hard to live in the desert. 'Specially, when you don't have no desert know how. You're not a coyote, Jack." Smoky stood up, walked over to the paint, rummaged through his saddle bag and returned, tossing Jack a leather pouch.

"Have some deer jerky, Jack. Salt will help."

Jack gnawed off a piece. Mick was more alert and guzzling water.

"God—odamn that's good. Better'n Colt 45," Mick gasped between gulps.

"Sometimes." Smoky squatted on his boot heels and fished his shirt pocket for smokes. "But not always." He lit his cigarette. "You boys is in a mess."

"What would you do?" Jack asked, feeling a sting of embarrassment at asking an Indian for advice even if this Indian was his cousin.

"It's your life, Jack. How can one Ind'an tell another Ind'an what to do with his life?" The smell of cigarette smoke hung in the windless air.

I'm not an Indian, Jack wanted say, but he bit his lip. "How far is it to the Virgin?" he asked instead, still exasperated with Smoky. Even when you asked an Indian for advice you never got it, Jack thought. They loved to speak in parables. There was something sneaky about people who couldn't come right out and say what they mean.

"Not far, 'bout a half hour walk." Smoky pointed east.

"I suppose that depends on how fast you walk," Jack said coldly.

"Just follow my tracks." Smoky smiled, mounting the paint.

"Thanks," Jack sighed, shaking his head.

"Jack, you keep the canteen and jerky. I got another one." Smoky gently nudged the paint in the flanks and headed east.

Jack had trouble focusing on the paint's tracks as they trudged after Smoky. Mick was getting weaker by the minute. Ironically, Jack thought, they might die within a few hundred yards of water.

Suddenly, on the eastern horizon, Jack thought he saw a break in the monotonous gray desert terrain. That break just might be where the Virgin cut through the desert floor, slowly deepening its channel before it entered the gorge. Jack readjusted Mick's weight as he leaned on his shoulder. Then, with one arm wrapped around his waist for support, the two friends limped forward. Mick dragged the briefcase and Jack carried the .22.

As they topped the bank, their hopes were fulfilled. Below was the muddy stream, flanked on both banks by dense tamarisk stands. Charged with adrenalin, they ran-hobbled down the bank and flopped head first into the cool river. Totally oblivious to its disgusting color and consistency, Mick and Jack splashed their faces, gulping down the gritty water.

A thick dirty red, the river looked more like it should be chewed, rather than sipped and, superficially at least, it appeared to be anything but a virgin. Jack recalled once talking to an old timer who pointed to its snow-capped mountain headwaters and exclaimed, "It might be a virgin up there, but it's a dirty damn whore down here." Jack had no previous experience with whores, but he figured if they all felt as good as this one, he might just consider it.

As the coolness cleared his senses, Jack turned to Mick. "This is no good. It's still over seventy miles to Kanab. There's no way we'll make it. If we turn north and follow the Virgin upstream we could be in Saint George by dark."

This time Jack got little argument. "J.T., if you leave me and strike out on your own, by yourself, you might make it."

"You know damn well I'd never go off and leave you in this condition. Let's head to Saint George. We'll go see Police Chief Callahan and let him sort this whole mess out."

"Seems we got no friggin' choice. Lead on, J.T. Let's get out of here." Mick sighed, shaking his head. "I know Coach—ah, Chief Callahan. Maybe he'll help us out."

"What about the briefcase?" Jack asked. "I've given it some thought and I can't see how that damn thing's going to help us. Even if the data proves the AEC has been lying, who are you going to give the information to? Do you honestly think any newspaper will publish stolen data without checking it out with the AEC? I doubt it. The AEC will then reclaim the papers and that will be that."

"But J.T.," Mick protested. "I know the friggin' AEC has been lying to us. They're treating us like dumb animals. Like white rats."

"Maybe. I don't know," Jack said, as he cupped a handful of water over his head.

The wound, the heat and physical exhaustion had pretty much taken the fight out of Mick. "Well then, what do you think we should do?"

"This briefcase is going to be nothing but trouble. If the posse catches us with it, they'll probably charge us with stealing federal property in addition to everything else. I think we should throw the damn thing in the river."

Mick thought for a minute. "Ah, what the hell, J.T. Go ahead. I'm tired of lugging it around anyway."

Like a boy launching a model boat, Jack gently set it afloat. As he watched it disappear around the bend, Jack glanced over at Mick and suspected that they had vastly different emotions. He, however, was glad to see it gone.

"Let's get out of here. If we don't get a move on it, that posse'll overtake us before we get to Saint George."

"If they do, they do. We'll worry about that if and when it happens," Jack answered. "You start out up the river and I'll take a minute to cover our trail."

Jack stood up, then crashed through the tamarisks and clamored up the opposite bank, leaving plenty of sign. He trudged another fifty yards eastward in the sand, then returned by hopping from one rock to another. Mostly, he was successful, slipping onto the ground only once. Then, he quickly jogged over the damp river sand toward the gorge leaving soggy footprints in his wake as he headed south. As the gorge narrowed, his path was blocked by a jutting wall of limestone, so he entered the river and backtracked.

The ruse completed, Jack soon caught up with Mick and they laboriously waded upstream, often slipping on the polished river rocks.

But they hadn't gone more than a hundred yards, two bends in the river, when Jack heard the sounds of hooves pounding on the desert floor. The posse had reached the river. Jack quickly helped Mick over to the shade of a sand hollow carved in the four-foot high river bank, then crept back. By half-slithering, half-crawling, Jack hid himself in a thicket of tamarisks. He was only about twenty feet from the riders but shielded from sight. After picking the feathery tamarisk-needles from his mouth and eyes and easing forward a bit, Jack had a good view of the posse between limbs.

"There's no doubt about it," boomed Sheriff Meecham. "They entered the river here."

"Looks like they left here." Deputy Fowler's high-pitched voice came from over by the east bank.

"I don't know," a third voice that Jack did not recognize, chimed in. "I've got tracks heading down the river too."

After a moment of silence, Sheriff Meecham said, "'Pears to me, they're trying to confuse us. We've got tracks heading every-goddamn-where. Anyways, forget the tracks for a minute. Which way do you think they're most likely to go?"

"Well, from here, there's not too many places you can go," another unrecognizable voice joined in. "You can either go back to Saint George or head east to Kanab."

"I kinda doubt they'd head back to Saint George knowing what's waiting for them there, and the tracks heading down the gorge make no sense at all. Anyways, let's assume for now, they're headed east to Kanab. We'll take a ten-minute break, and rest and water the horses," Sheriff Meecham ordered, then shouted, "Ralph, you got any drinking water left in that canteen of yours?"

"Yeah, Sheriff, but we're going to have to find some more fresh water if we don't catch them by nightfall," Ralph said, tossing the canteen to Sheriff Meecham.

Sheriff Meecham laughed. "You're standing in fresh water, Ralph."

"Nobody drinks this shit, Sheriff. You just as well pour sorghum in a sand dune, then scoop it up in you hands and try to drink it. Like I said, we'll need fresh water if'n we don't catch em by dark."

"Oh, we'll catch them and real soon. Nobody," Meecham paused in mid-sentence and Jack could hear the gurgling of water from the canteen, "kills one of my deputies and gets away with it."

"How about giving me a swig. My canteen's dry," the fourth voice asked. Then after more gurgling sounds, he continued. "Those little bastards stole government secrets. God only knows what they're planning on doing with them. Maybe sell them to the Russians, they're that valuable. We need to catch them, and soon. It's for their own good. They could get themselves killed if they start dealing in international espionage. They're way in over their heads."

"Don't worry Rudy, we'll get them," Sheriff Meecham said. "They can't be more'n fifteen or twenty minutes ahead of us right now."

Jack slowly started working his way back, but could still hear snatches of conversation. "Goddamn kids, it'll be dark in about four hours," the sheriff said. "That Mick Graff must not be hit very hard. They're covering ground faster than a prospector's jackass in heat."

"Shit, I'm surprised they made it this far. Those kids have some grit," Deputy Fowler added.

"Grit my ass. They know damn well what they did to Deputy Saunders, and they know damn well the consequences. That's not grit, they're just running scared," Sheriff Meecham said. "Anybody got any sandwiches left?"

"They're just a couple of punks, and probably traitors to their country, too," Rudy said, ignoring the sheriff's question.

"Yeah—yeah, they're all of that," Meecham said brusquely. "I asked if anyone had a goddamn sandwich?"

Rudy Popovich! Jack thought. Why was Rudy Popovich with the posse? Why not the FBI? Jack could not think of a good reason, unless Rudy hadn't called in the FBI. And if not, why not? Maybe he didn't want them involved. He wants to get the documents back himself without involving a lot of people. A lot of people seeing and handling the evidence, if they were arrested and brought to trial, might result in some explaining. The AEC and Rudy Popovich may be trying to hide something after all.

Not wanting to get into a long discussion, Jack did not tell Mick about Rudy Popovich when he got back to the sand hollow. "It's the sheriff all right. We've got a little time. They think we're headed to Kanab. You ready to go?"

"Yep, let's get the hell out of here before that son-of-a-bitch has a chance to put another bullet in our backs," Mick said gamely.

Jack insisted that they stay in the river as difficult as it was. Not only did it conceal their tracks, but it kept them cool from the brutal afternoon heat. The water seemed to revive Mick for a while, but after an hour of stumbling on unseen rocks, he was ready for a rest. They headed up a feeder gully with a protruding ledge of limestone for shade, then collapsed in the sand.

After taking a minute to catch his breath, Jack cocked his ears for sounds of horses. There was only the cawing of a raven somewhere to his left. Mick had already nodded off and Jack was left with only silence and the faint fragrance of the tamarisks blended with the scent of muddy water. Overhead, an enormous cloudbank bluffed and boiled, creating gnarled and threatening shapes, but it was all pretense. There was no rain. For a moment, Jack imagined he saw a mushroom-shaped cloud that looked a little like Shot Harry. But the image rapidly scrambled and in its place, the face of a radiation ravished Emily appeared briefly in the shifting clouds.

Jack fell into a fitful sleep punctuated with bizarre visions and random vignettes that raced around the attic of his mind. Everything seemed real, even the neighing of that damn horse.

Instantly, Jack was awake. There it was again, close, just down the wash sloshing in the river. A quick glance confirmed that Mick was still asleep. Inching down the gully, Jack spotted a horse and rider. Deputy Fowler had now dismounted and was examining their tracks where they turned up the gully. Jack surmised that the posse must have split up, deciding they were not going to Kanab after all.

Formulating a plan as he went, Jack quickly worked his way back up the wash, then climbed the towering bank that stood just above Fowler. He darted into the open and crouched behind a car-sized boulder on the lip of the bank. Had the deputy seen him? Did he have his gun drawn? No way to know for sure. Cautiously, Jack peeked around the boulder. Fowler had remounted his horse and was unsnapping his holster. Was he going to shoot him on sight? Just the same way they did Mick? Jack instantly reached down and grabbed a baseball-sized rock in his right hand. Then he jumped.

The blow caught Deputy Fowler completely unaware. Jack's flying body, like a perfect blind-side football tackle, exploded into Fowler's ribs just below and behind his left shoulder, throwing him from his horse. Both of them crashed to the ground, stuck together in a heap of entwined appendages. The horse reared and danced in and out of the melee, crushing arms, legs and fingers beneath his iron-shod hooves. Through it all, Jack maintained his grip on the rock. After struggling for a moment to free his right arm, Jack swung it above his head, smashing Fowler's skull. The deputy groaned, rolled over, unconscious.

Terror gripped Jack. Had he killed him? Crawling over, Jack placed an ear on his chest and groped his neck with his right hand to feel for the carotid artery. Thank God! He was still alive. Jack quickly struggled to his feet and grabbed a loop of rope from the saddle. Using his best Boy Scout knots, Jack lashed the deputy's feet together, his hands behind his back, then secured the rope to a tamarisk trunk. He would eventually be able to wriggle out of the knots, Jack thought, but it would take him a while. Jack leaned over and checked the deputy's vital signs one more time. Satisfied, he scurried back up to the arroyo.

Jack woke Mick, explained what had happened, collected the .22, and they started out, retracing their steps back down to the river. Deputy Fowler's horse had wandered down the river about twenty yards, but he was easy to catch. To Jack's way of thinking, there was no need of walking when they could ride. Anyway, it didn't look like Mick had much walk left in him. Jack helped Mick up, then swung himself over the horse's rump, settling in behind his friend.

The sun was just dipping behind Utah Hill when Jack spotted the tattered ruins of the old ghost town, Bloomington. From there, an old wagon track would take them directly to Saint George. In the gloom of the gathering night and in silence, Mick and Jack headed into a future that looked as murky as the coming darkness.

On the outskirts of the city, they turned the dun loose in a fenced pasture, then trudged up 100 West. The street lights popped on, deceptively glowing a welcome light. Like truant schoolboys plodding home to face their punishment, they were in no hurry now. At 700 South the two friends turned east onto Main, then continued slowly north toward downtown and the police station. .

Jack broke the silence. "You ready for this, Mick?"

"I guess so. My back's killing me. My feet are caked in blisters and I'm so damn tired I feel like I'm already dead. I'm beginning to think prison won't be all that bad."

"Well, if it's any consolation, you'll probably get out before me. I don't know how much more time they'll add for assaulting a police officer," Jack sighed.

"Police officer, my ass," Mick spewed. "Those bastards were trying to kill us. All you did was act in self-defense. The son-of-bitch was drawing a gun on you."

"I sure hope Chief Callahan sees it that way. You know him very well?" Jack asked.

"Don't you remember? He was my coach in Little League with the Cubs. Maybe, you don't remember him because you were with the Dodgers that year. He lives just about a block from here."

"Did he like you?" Jack asked.

"Yeah, he thought I was the best. I was his star player that year. Remember, that was the year we won the championship and I led the league in home runs." Mick's freckles bunched as he smiled thinking about his glory days.

"Why the hell should we walk another ten blocks to the police station? It makes more sense to just go around the block to Callahan's house, knock on the door and turn ourselves in," Jack said.

"Shit, J.T. About once a year you come up with a good idea."

13

Jack tried to picture Chief Callahan in his mind. It had been a long time since he had seen him.

Chief Wade Callahan was a likeable man. In his uniform, he looked like the typical policeman, tall and muscular. However, Jack recalled he limped badly, the result of polio when he was a teenager. Through years of rehabilitation and sheer will, he had re-learned to walk and could even run in a wounded dog sort of way. But Chief Callahan had never conquered the hitch in his gait, and he still wore a hinged ankle brace.

Callahan liked almost everybody, that is everyone except Sheriff Meecham. It was rumored that there was an ongoing feud between the two. Apparently, it was deeper than just professional jealously, It seeped into the personal level as well. Meecham was a little too authoritative, too self-righteous, and a little too pushy with his badge. Regardless of the facts, he would never sit down with an open mind to discuss things.

Abrupt and unyielding, the sheriff never tried to understand young people, just insisted they toe the line. He was always preaching that if the youth of the county would live the principles of the gospel as taught by the church, there would be no youth problem. Idealistically, Jack knew the sheriff was probably right, but realistically, Sheriff Meecham never seemed to grasp the concept that rebellion was a natural part of growing up or, at least it had been in Jack's life.

Chief Callahan was just the opposite. Even though he had none of his own, he liked kids and realized there would be a certain amount of civil disobedience and as long as it didn't get out of hand, he mostly looked the other way.

This feud between Callahan and Meecham, Jack realized, might just play to their advantage.

As they approached, Jack noted that almost every light was on in the house and the chief's patrol car was in the driveway. At the porch, Jack motioned to Mick to go first. "You know him better than I do." Mick rang the doorbell and waited.

"Hi, boys." Wade greeted them warmly, with his customary grin. "Kinda been halfway expecting you. How you been, Mick?"

"Well, Coach, I haven't been hitting many home runs lately," Mick replied, fidgeting on the threshold.

"You boys look like you could use a cold Coke and some fried chicken. Come on in." Wade hobbled ahead of them to the kitchen. "Martha, we have two more for dinner."

The dining room was small but cheerful. Mrs. Callahan was a heavy-set woman who tried to hide her figure with floral-print sun dresses. She smiled and offered them a seat. The table was wooden, stained to look like oak but was probably pine. On the walls were dozens of pictures of the little league teams the chief had coached, even the one of the championship year with Mick. The scent of fried chicken made Jack's stomach churn.

After guzzling down two Cokes each and almost inhaling Mrs. Callahan's chicken with steaming mashed potatoes and gravy, the boys were feeling more relaxed. The Cokes, Jack thought, sure beat drinking Virgin River water and the was no contest between Mrs. Callahan's fried chicken and Smoky's jerky.

"Mick, how's the back? I heard about Sheriff Meecham's trying to do a Wyatt Earp impersonation. I don't know what the hell he was thinking," Wade said, his eyes narrow with concern.

"Hurts a little but I'm okay. Jack says the wound's superficial and that I'll probably live."

"It's shallow, but it's infected. I drained a lot of pus last night. Mick needs a doctor. And no, I did not say he would live," Jack said with a laugh.

"Let me see it." Chief Callahan unwound the now filthy bandage still damp with river water. The chief frowned and turned to his wife. "Martha, would you get some rubbing alcohol and clean bandages from the first-aid kit?"

As Martha left the room, Chief Wade turned to the boys. "Through my own sources, I've heard almost everything that's happened. I know all about the volcano and Deputy Saunders and the manslaughter charges. And, I know what happened when Sheriff Meecham tried to arrest you and about his shooting Mick. Incidentally, he says that was an accident. That he was only trying to fire a warning shot, but the bullet deflected off a tree limb and struck you."

"When Deputy Saunders was killed," Mick muttered. "That was an accident. This was no accident. He pointed a gun at me and pulled the trigger."

Martha returned with the first-aid kit and Chief Callahan quickly poured the alcohol on a cotton ball, then pressed it against the wound.

"Yow!" Mick winced in pain.

"What do you think, Chief?" Jack asked. "What we got facing us?"

"Well, boys, I'm not a lawyer, but I'll tell you what I think. It appears Sheriff Meecham has only a fair case for manslaughter. While it's technically true, a police officer was killed while you two were committing a crime, it's not like you two planned his death. Perhaps it could be argued that Earl and Greg were responsible, but you two were more of an accessory to the death, accessory to manslaughter, if there is such a crime."

Chief Callahan rummaged in the first-aid kit for bandages. "Furthermore, it's not like the crime you were involved in when Deputy Saunders died was a major felony, like armed robbery or murder. It was a prank, a misdemeanor—criminal mischief. Technically, it's still manslaughter, but in reality, the whole thing was just a colossal mistake. With a good lawyer, I think the whole thing might get plea-bargained down to almost nothing. But if the sheriff and the county attorney refuse, and knowing them they probably will, then I'm pretty sure a jury would be sympathetic to that argument I just gave." Wade carefully applied the gauze dressing to Mick's wound.

"What about us running, resisting arrest?" Jack asked.

"Well, you did do that. But under the circumstances, a jury might think that a reasonable and even a rational thing to do. With shots being

151

fired and Mick wounded, it could be argued you were just trying to save your own lives. Hell, if it had been me, I would have run, too." Wade finished applying the tape to the dressing.

"Chief, there's one other thing you don't know. Today, while we were running from the posse, I hit Deputy Fowler in the head with a rock, knocked him cold. Might have fractured his skull. He was trying to draw his gun on me," Jack said, as he stacked his dishes by the sink. "Then I tied him up and we took his horse."

"What did you do with the horse?"

"Left him in Foremaster's pasture, just south of town."

"I kinda wish you hadn't done that. I mean hitting Deputy Fowler," Callahan said thoughtfully, "but still, I think it could be seen as self-defense. Taking everything into account, especially since you two have no priors, you might just get probation and a fine."

Abruptly, Mick coughed, winching in pain, as he grabbed a napkin. "But, Coach, we do have a prior."

The Chief's smile faded. " Santa Clara falls under the jurisdiction of the sheriff's department, so I guess I hadn't heard. Tell me about it."

Mick grabbed another chicken wing before Mrs. Callahan cleared the table, then launched into the story.

"It was last Halloween night. We made a dummy. You know, we sewed a long sleeve shirt to some Levis, then stitched some old sneakers onto the pant legs. Then we stuffed the clothes with straw and fastened a ball cap on the head. As a final touch, we poured catsup on the dummy's chest. In the dark, it looked almost real, like an actual body. Anyway, you know how in Santa Clara those old sycamore trees form almost a perfect arch over Highway 91?"

Wade nodded.

"Well, after dark, we climbed up on those old trees with the dummy and crawled out over the road. When a car would pass under us, we'd drop the dummy right in front of the car. They would smack right into it, and sometimes run over it. Coach Wade, it was the damnest thing. You'd never believe the reactions we got, especially from those prune-pickers from California. What would you say, Jack? Two or three hit-and-runs that night?" Mick's eyes and freckles were dancing with devilment.

Jack smiled widely, momentarily forgetting about his ugly teeth. "I think it was three. Some cars would hit the dummy, slam on their brakes, roll down their window and glance back at the crumpled body, then punch their accelerator and race out of town. Even to this day, I bet there are several Californians who think they are wanted for hit-and-run in Utah. Then there was the other extreme. Some people would stop, back up, and even get out of the car. When they realized it was a dummy, they would get furious. Mick and I learned a whole new vocabulary that Halloween, didn't we, Mick?"

"I had to look up some of those fancy words in my Uncle Pete's Navy handbook," Mick laughed. "Never heard them in Santa Clara before."

"Anyway, some prune-picker went on into Saint George and called the sheriff's office. Sheriff Meecham, and Deputies Fowler and Saunders all drove over and arrested us. We pled guilty to criminal mischief and got a $25 dollar fine and a year's probation."

Chief Callahan was chuckling. "You guys sure know how to pull a prank. That one is a classic. If you guys ever find something constructive to channel all that energy and imagination into, there's no telling how far you can go."

"Anyway," Jack said, "The year's not up yet. We're still on probation."

"Without a doubt," Chief Callahan said smiling, "you've violated your parole and for the same offense, more criminal mischief. This is a real disturbing pattern—like hardened criminals." Wade chuckled.

"There's one more thing," Mick said reluctantly. "I stole an AEC briefcase from their room at the Big Hand Motel. By now, I suspect they know it was me. Doris Frei, a maid at the motel, let me into the room and she's probably told them."

"Why the hell would you want to go and do that, Mick?" Callahan asked.

"It's a long story Coach, but I know the AEC is lying to us about this fallout stuff. The levels we're getting here are not safe and the AEC knows it. I guess, I was just trying to make them be honest about it."

"This is not good," Chief Callahan exclaimed. "Did Doris actually see you take the briefcase?"

"No, she just opened the door, then left. I don't think she saw anything."

"Where is it now?"

" J.T. convinced me it would do us no good, so we just put it in the Virgin River. It's probably somewhere in Arizona or Nevada by now."

"The strange thing is," Jack piped in, "the FBI wasn't with the posse chasing us, but Rudy Popovich of the AEC was."

"I didn't know that," Mick mumbled, but Jack waved him off.

"Well anyway," Callahan said. "I'm glad you got rid of the briefcase. Maybe the AEC hasn't involved the FBI yet, though I can't imagine why."

"I'll tell you why," Mick fumed. "The AEC wants to keep this low key. It's because they don't want anyone to see what's in that briefcase."

"Well if that's true, and I'm not saying it is," Chief Callahan reasoned. "Then, I doubt any formal charges will be filed. My guess is they just want the briefcase back with as little publicity as possible. Let's just wait and see what happens."

"Chief, can we surrender to you?" Jack asked.

"No, I don't think so. The volcano and the road to Veyo where Deputy Saunders died, are out of my jurisdiction. As you know, that's out of the city limits, so that makes it Meecham's territory. I'm afraid I'll have to turn you over to him, but believe me boys, I'll be looking over his shoulder. I know all the attorneys in town, so I will try to find a good lawyer for you. I don't think it's going to be as bad as you think."

"Coach, I don't trust that man," Mick said. "How do I know he's not going to shoot me again?"

"You don't. But, with me now personally involved, I sincerely doubt he'll try anything. He'll just concentrate on beefing up his legal case against you."

"We appreciate your help and advice, Chief. And Mrs. Callahan, the chicken was great," Jack said as he stood up. "Mick, we might as well get going and get this over with."

Chief Callahan pushed his chair back and reached for his hat, grinning. "You boys look beat. I'll give you a ride down to Meecham's place. I want to talk to Evan about this case anyway. See what all he's going to charge you with and make sure he gets medical attention for

Mick. Before we go, let me give the good sheriff a call and let him know we're coming. I don't want to surprise anybody, and I especially don't want anybody making any snap decisions with a gun."

Reaching for the phone, Callahan turned to Mick. "Speaking of guns, I think you'd better leave that .22 here with me."

"Geez, coach. I forgot I had it."

It took two calls for Chief Wade to locate Sheriff Meecham. As it turned out he was still at the office. He'd just returned from the desert. Wade told the sheriff they would be there shortly, then the three piled into the patrol car like friends cruising Main and drove to the sheriff's office.

Evan Meecham was draped over the top of his desk stretching out the muscles in his back as they entered. He looked grimy and fatigued and it took only one glance to tell he was in an exceptionally foul mood. He slowly got up with a grunt and flopped into the arm-chair behind his desk.

"Well aren't you two regular Lawrences of Arabia? I'm honored you will finally grace me with an audience. To what do I owe this rare honor?"

"Evan, Mick and Jack want to surrender peaceably," Callahan said. "And, Mick needs some medical attention."

"Anyways, now you want peace." The Sheriff arched his back over the top of the chair, working his sore muscles. "After killing one of my deputies and cracking the other one's head like a ripe melon, you now want us all to sit down and talk this out like a family quarrel? Like it's all just a big misunderstanding? Hell, you two have wiped out half my department!"

"How, how is Deputy Fowler? When I left—"

Chief Wade nudged Jack in the side. "Be careful what you say Jack. Anyway, Evan, how is Fowler?"

"How do you suppose he is after having his head caved in with a rock? I left him at the hospital with Dr. Hilton. He's got a skull fracture. Might need to go to Salt Lake for surgery to lift the bone and drain the blood."

"But he is awake? Able to walk and talk?" Jack asked.

"Yes, and he had to ride my horse back," Meecham said, scowling. "It was me who had to walk back to town."

"What are your plans for these boys, Evan?" Callahan asked. "Should we just chalk this whole thing up to an unfortunate run of bad luck, to a shitty hand of cards?" Wade grinned.

"It's a shitty hand of cards all right. Jack and Mick drew the cards, but they didn't have to play them. They could have folded at any time. Instead, they insisted on running the game to the finish. We started off with criminal mischief and manslaughter, now we can add resisting arrest, flight from justice, assaulting a police officer, and maybe attempted murder."

"You forgot about horse stealing." Chief Callahan smiled

"You think this is funny, Wade? All in all, I think we have about ten to twenty years for these boys. Then there's probably federal charges for stealing classified government documents, maybe even espionage. I suspect the feds will want them for at least another five to ten. Anyways, they'll be old men before we see em again on the streets of Saint George."

"Espi-a-what?" Mick asked.

"Espionage. Spying," Sheriff Meecham answered, a smug look on his face.

"Come on, Evan, you can't be serious. Hell, these boys don't know what the word means. And, as for the other stuff, it was just a prank that snowballed out of control," Wade argued. "You definitely have some criminal mischief. But the manslaughter charge is a bit of a stretch. Mick and Jack were not directly responsible for Deputy Saunders's death. The rest of it was just an unfortunate sequence of events that resulted from you shooting Mick in the back. Hell, these kids thought you were trying to kill them. And there is no proof they took any federal documents. Anyhow, that's out of our jurisdiction. That's up to the feds."

"That shooting was an accident," Sheriff Meecham said, his voice rising. "The son-of-a-bitch was already running. I just fired a warning shot, but the bullet was deflected. Anyways, he looks okay to me. Couldn't be too bad. He romped around in the desert for more'n two days in 110 degree temperature."

"Evan, these are good kids, two of our own. You talk to the county attorney and see what he thinks. I suspect he'll think that your case is a little thin. Anyway, Mick needs some doctoring. He's got an infected wound."

"Okay," the sheriff relented, "but he looks fine to me. I'll have Doc Hilton check him tomorrow. Tonight, I'm going to book them and jail them."

Wade turned to Mick and Jack. "In the morning, I'll hire a lawyer for you and after the arraignment, he should be able to get you out on bail. I'll see you tomorrow." Wade smiled at the boys, then added, "Evan, I know you would never let anything happen to these boys, not while they are in your custody. It just wouldn't look good."

Callahan then gave Meecham a long stare before he limped away.

With Deputy Fowler in the hospital and Deputy Saunders deceased, Sheriff Meecham had to do the booking himself. First he wrote down their vital statistics, then photographed them, a frontal exposure followed by a profile. Having already gotten their finger-prints, Meecham herded the boys into the vacant cells. After locking the cell doors, he sighed, sat down at his typewriter and laboriously pecked out the arrest report with his index finger. Occasionally, he would groan, and the chair would creak as he tried to stretch out a muscle spasm.

After about an hour, Jack noticed the typewriter had fallen silent.

"Operator, give me the Big Hand Motel. No, I don't know the goddamn number. Look it up." There was a pause, then the sheriff continued. "Rudy Popovich's room please." Another pause, then he bellowed, "Goddamit, he's with the government."

"Rudy. Sheriff Meecham here. You still awake?" Jack heard the Sheriff shift his weight in his chair and groan.

"I've got em. They're right here in my jail." There was another pause. "They just walked in."

"Yes, you can interrogate them tomorrow, and no, they don't have no briefcase." The chair groaned again. "Yes, I'm sure. Search them? Shit, they're just wearing T-shirts. What's to search? Tomorrow at nine will be fine." Meecham slammed the phone down mumbling, "That little Jew bastard. Who does he think he's talking to, some green rookie? Search them, my ass."

The cells were bleak and depressing. With three walls made of flat steel bars, the boys were in full view of the booking-receiving room. The only furniture was an army surplus cot and thin, khaki wool blankets. Though a single, shadeless ceiling light could be switched off, the cells were never really dark. Also, to add to the lack of privacy, there were no plumbing or toilet facilities.

When an inmate had to relieve himself, he was escorted from the cell to a windowless commode in the back of the main room. At night, with only one jailor on duty, the cells were locked down and prisoners were issued metal urinals.

Exhausted physically and emotionally, Jack flopped on the cot. It seemed like years since he'd slept in a bed and to Jack, even this army cot seemed comfortable. The sheriff had offered him a phone call, but Jack had refused. Whom would he call? Chief Wade had promised to get them a lawyer, and he certainly didn't feel like talking to his father, at least not tonight. Briefly, Jack thought about calling Emily, but what would he say? Em, I'm in jail, just thought you might want to know, and yes, I'm still planning to go on a mission.

Mick had not been anxious to talk to his family either. He had called Brenda, and she was going to notify his mother. Knowing what a gossip Brenda was, she would probably call Emily as well. This was just plain embarrassing. What would she think? Would she be concerned, or would this just reinforce her growing disgust for him and his religion? Jack the hypocrite. On the one hand literally forcing religion down her throat, and on the other, living a life that was certainly not Christian.

He felt like alfalfa leaves blown about by every puff of wind. Without any motion of their own, they had no control over their route or final destination. He seemed to have no control of his life either and the road—well, the route lately had been pure hell.

Perhaps this was a character flaw on his part and through no fault of his own, he was not in control of his circumstances. Maybe a virus had invaded his genes, his constitution, sometime after birth, Jack thought, and was now manifesting itself as this character flaw. Maybe none of this was his fault. Maybe he had some kind of disease.

But did he really have to let life dominate him? It was time that he gained some mastery of his life instead of floating like the alfalfa leaves in the breeze.

With growing despair, Jack silently prayed to God. Then to his chagrin, he caught himself wondering, was anyone listening?

Jack could hear the discordant, sounds of Mick's breathing in the next cell. At times, Jack envied Mick. He surely didn't have any trouble getting to sleep. Part of Mick's ease at falling asleep was sheer exhaustion from their desert ordeal and the wound. But it was more than that. Mick always seemed to have a clear conscience. He wasn't hounded by gnawing ghosts of guilt or the shame of promises unkept. Or at least, he didn't seem to be. It wasn't that Mick lived a better life than Jack. They had broken the same rules. He just seemed to live by a different code of ethics, a separate set of moral standards. They no longer shared the same religious values. Mick had certainly made that clear. He was not going on a mission and had even hinted that he doubted God's existence. And strangely, Emily seemed to share his same attitude.

Jack sighed with the heaviness of it all. Maybe he should adopt Mick's philosophy. There was no question about it, Mick wasn't losing any sleep over what was happening and he was.

Around midnight, Jack heard the night watchman come in and exchange some brief, muffled words with Sheriff Meecham. After a couple of minutes the front door closed and Jack assumed the sheriff had gone home. Being shorthanded, he had been working long hours. Jack tried to feel some sympathy, but that emotion was hard coming.

Jack restlessly toyed with his broken hand. He'd almost forgotten about it the last two days. He got up and tested his grip on the steel bars. It must be healing. The grip was good and pain was almost gone.

Unable to sleep, Jack thought about Smoky. They could have died if it hadn't been for him. Jack hated to admit it, but Smoky saved their lives. And in retrospect, he had always been nothing but kind. So why did he find Smoky so irritating? With that on his mind, Jack drifted off into an uneasy sleep.

It was still dark when Jack heard his name being called. "Yeah, what'a you what?" he mumbled

"J.T., I'm real sick," Mick moaned.

Jack was instantly awake and stumbled to his feet. "Mick, I'm here. What's wrong?"

"One minute I'm burning up, the next I'm so freezing cold I'm shaking," Mick said, his teeth chattering.

"How's the back?"

"Throbbing like a son-of-a-bitch, and my belly's aching again," Mick's replied, coughing hoarsely.

"You bring anything up?"

"Just phlegm with a little blood. God, I'm sick, J.T."

"Doc Hilton's supposed to see you first thing in the morning."

"I can't wait til morning," Mick moaned weakly.

This was the only time in their twenty years together that Jack could recall Mick complaining, even once, about his health. He never whined for sympathy. That was just not his way. He was always just fine. This is what alarmed Jack. For Mick to complain or ask for help was alarming.

Jack quickly grabbed his metal urinal and banged on the bars. There was no response. He banged louder and shouted. Finally, the night watchman appeared.

"Goddamnit Jack! What's all the fuss?"

"Dan, this man is sick. He needs help right now."

"Can't it wait til morning? It's almost four. I hate to wake Doc Hilton at this hour."

"It can't wait!" Jack shouted. "This man may be dead by morning."

Dan glanced over at Mick. "How do I know this isn't some plan you two have to escape?"

"Cuff him, tie him up, I don't care. But get him to the hospital!"

Reluctantly, the night watchman shuffled over and made a call. Twenty minutes later the ambulance arrived. As they were hauling a cuffed Mick out on the stretcher, he turned to Jack and whispered. "J.T., am I going to die?"

"You damn well better not die Michael Graff. I still owe you for that toe incident," Jack replied, fear rising in his chest.

"J.T., there's something I need to tell you."

"We've got to go!" the ambulance driver commanded. "This man is real sick. Every minute counts."

14

Rudy Popovich did not show for his 9:00 a.m. interrogation. Jack thought that was strange, but then everything was a little strange right now. However, this gave him a little more time to think before the 11:00 a.m. arraignment. Around 10:00, Brian Bugsby, the attorney Chief Callahan had lined up, sauntered into the jail.

"Sheriff, I hear you're holding a client, probably without probable cause."

"I might have known it would be you," Sheriff Meecham growled, nodding toward Jack. "In the back."

"We'll need a conference room and some privacy. Maybe, your office?" Attorney Bugsby peered at the sheriff through Mason jar thick glass lenses.

"You see any damn conference room? You can talk to him down at his cell and as for privacy, I don't give a shit what you two talk about," Sheriff Meecham responded.

"Well, at least open the cell," Mr. Bugsby demanded, "so I don't have to talk through bars."

"You got forty-five minutes, then I got to get him to the court-house." Meecham said as he grabbed the keys and waddled over to the cell. Bugsby followed, grabbing a folding chair from the fingerprinting table as he passed by.

After the sheriff had locked them in the cell and left, Mr. Bugsby grinned. "How you been, Jack? Haven't seen you since that Snow Canyon sand dunes party."

Brian Bugsby had been in practice for just a little over a year and was still single. Almost all other twenty-seven-year-old men in Washington County were married, so Brian tended to hang around with the younger crowd, sometimes even the same crowd as Jack and Mick.

"Yeah, I had to leave early. Had an irrigation turn to tend to."

"You missed the best part. Sally Kratz got drunk and took off her blouse. Man, does she have big ones." Brian cupped his hands. "Anyway, we've got an arraignment at eleven," he said, turning serious. "Chief Callahan has filled me in on most of the details."

"What do you think? Do they have a case?" Jack asked, frowning as he stared into Bug's huge eyes.

"In my opinion, you shouldn't be in jail at all. The biggest problem with the youth in Washington County, " Bugs said, adjusting his glasses, "is Sheriff Meecham."

"So, you think our chances are pretty good?"

"Jack, I'll bet they drop it before it ever comes to trial. I've made a fool of the county attorney on more than one occasion, and I doubt he'd risk tangling with me again on such a flimsy case as this."

"What about, Mick? You know he's in the hospital."

"Don't worry about Mick. I'll represent him in absentia. If it ever comes to trial, the fact that the sheriff shot him and that he's in the hospital might play well to a jury. Anyhow, it's about time to head on over to the courthouse for the arraignment."

"What do I do?"

"Nothing. Let me do the talking. Just try to look sincere and innocent."

"How do I do that?"

"Just look like yourself, but don't try too hard or you'll look guilty," the attorney explained.

Jack groaned. He hoped he was in the right hands. Brian was not even a native of Washington County, nor was he a Mormon, and consequently, he was not well accepted, virtually a social outcast. But in spite of his social exile, he tried hard to be cool. He drove an almost new 1953 Corvette, liked the current rock-and-roll sounds of Bill Haley and Chuck Berry, and drank malt liquor by the case (which was almost taboo in Saint George, and almost unheard of with professional men). But Chief Callahan, Jack thought, must think he is the man for the job.

"What should I say when they ask how I plead?" Jack asked, bringing his mind back to business.

"They won't ask. This is an arraignment, not a hearing. We don't have to plead today. All that happens today, is Judge Ballard will make sure you understand the charges against you. He will see if there is enough evidence, in his opinion, to bind you over to trial. Then, bail will be set."

Regardless of his juvenile life-style, Jack had heard Bugs was smart, graduating second in his law class at the University of Utah.

"Do you have any idea how much bail will be?"

"You're such a notorious desperado, it could be as high as ten thousand dollars," Bugs laughed. "I don't know for sure," he said, getting serious, "but I suspect it will be somewhere in the five hundred to seven hundred fifty range."

"What happens if I can't come up with the money?" Jack asked, swallowing hard.

"What about your father? Surely, he can raise $500."

"Yeah, he has the money, but I'm not real sure he will spend it on me," Jack answered weakly. "We're not exactly on the best of terms right now."

"Well, if he won't make bail, I will," Bugs replied, "You can pay me back when you show up for the trial, and you can add a case of Colt 45 for the interest."

"A deal," Jack said, shaking Brian's hand while glancing in his eyes. They were hideously magnified by his glass lenses and though Jack had seen this spectacle before, it never failed to startle him. Indeed, Jack thought, he did look like an arachnid, a bug. From his zoology classes, Jack knew the theory was nonsense, but Brian lent new credence to the now debunked hypothesis: People grow to resemble their names. Brian was aware of this uncanny resemblance and took it all in stride. In fact, he almost seemed proud to be called Bugs.

The arraignment went just as predicted. Judge Ballard went over each charge with Jack, making sure he understood the implication of each, then he had County Attorney Epson present what evidence he had to support the charges. With the criminal mischief, flight from justice, and assault of a police officer, Judge Ballard seemed satisfied with the evidence, but the manslaughter charge seemed to trouble him.

The county attorney read the legal definition from the Utah Criminal Code. After reminding County Attorney Epson that he was thoroughly familiar with the law, a reluctant Judge Ballard let the charge stand, but only after asking him, "Are you sure you want to do this?"

Bail was set at $600, since the judge felt that Jack was not really a threat to society, but conceded that in light of recent history, there might be a slight risk he would run. Though Jack felt guilty about not calling his father, he decided it was a blessing that his father was not there. He probably would have grudgingly come up with the money, but it would have been at a price. The cost would have been high. A tedious tirade about how big a disappointment Jack had been and that his mother would not be pleased. Jack was more than happy to take Bugs up on his offer.

Jack left the courthouse at 2:00 p.m. then quickly walked the four blocks to Dixie Pioneer Memorial Hospital. He realized his stomach was growling as he crossed the foyer and headed for the hall leading to the patient's ward . Rounding the corner, he collided with Dr. Hilton, sending his stethoscope clattering to the floor.

"Geez, I'm sorry, Doc," Jack said, as he picked up the scope and handed it back.

"They need to paint white lines and make it two-way traffic in these halls," Doc Hilton said, stuffing the scope in his pocket. "How's the hand?"

"Huh? Oh the hand's fine," Jack said sheepishly, glancing down at the filthy tape on his hand. "How's Mick doing?"

Dr. Hilton studied Jack for a moment. "You and Mick are best friends, aren't you?"

"Yes, we're like brothers," Jack said, wondering why he asked.

"Were you with him when he was shot?"

"I'm the one who took the bullet out." Jack looked embarrassed. "I didn't use sterile technique and the wound got infected."

"How's Mick been, the last month or so? I mean, as far as his health is concerned?"

"Well," Jack thought for a moment. "He's had a cough for a month or more. Sometimes he coughs up a little blood."

"Does he get fatigued easily?" the doctor asked.

"Yes, I have noticed that," Jack answered. "Is he okay?"

"His mother just left, so I'll tell you what I told her. To be frankly honest with you Jack, he's a bit of a puzzle for me. There's no question his wound is infected, and that may be all it is, but—" Dr. Hilton paused as he noticed Jack's downcast eyes. "Jack, I'm not saying the infection is your fault. I'm sure under similar circumstances, it would have gotten infected if I'd been the one to remove the bullet—" Dr. Hilton's voice trailed off.

"You were talking about how Mick's case is a puzzle."

"Oh. It just doesn't quite all add up. There are certain lab tests that are hard to explain away by just a wound infection."

"What tests, Dr. Hilton?"

"You probably wouldn't understand," Doc Hilton said doubtfully.

"I've taken a lot of biology in school and am majoring in pre-med. I'd like to try to understand."

"Well, for starters Jack, the white count is extremely high, over sixty thousand. The normal is from five thousand to ten thousand, and with bad infections it can go as high as eighteen to twenty thousand, but sixty thousand is exceptionally high."

"Maybe Mick just has a really bad infection," Jack said.

"Maybe," Dr. Hilton continued, "but another troubling thing is the differential count."

"The differential?" Jack said, looking puzzled.

"The differential count of the white cells," Doctor Hilton replied. "As you know, white cells fight infection, among other things. There are several kinds of white cells: granulocytes, lymphocytes, monocytes, basophils and eosinophils. For instance, granulocytes fight acute bacterial infections, lymphocytes viral infections, eosinophils parasitic infections and so on. With Mick, his granulocytes are high, which is what you'd expect with a wound infection." Dr. Hilton paused, staring intently at Jack.

"I'm following you so far," Jack said.

"The unsettling thing is though," Dr. Hilton continued, "Mick seems to have used up all his good granulocytes and now the bone marrow is sending extremely immature granulocytes, we call stem cells, into the blood stream.

"I'm not quite sure I understand."

"Well, let me explain it another way," Doc Hilton said. "It's kinda like the Germans did at the end of World War II. When they ran out of men at the front lines, they sent boys."

"Could all this still be a bad infection?" Jack asked, as he tugged nervously at his chin.

"Anything's possible. Medicine is not an exact science. But the fact that the granulocytes are so terribly immature, so precocious, makes one think this has been going on for some time. Certainly, longer than that three-day-old gunshot wound. And another thing that bothers me is Mick's huge spleen."

"What about that?" Jack asked. He'd been right about the spleen all along.

"It could be from infection also, but there are other things that can cause an enlarged spleen," Dr. Hilton replied.

"What things?"

"I'd rather not say right now. I'd just be speculating."

"How long is Mick going to be in the hospital?" Jack asked, hoping for some good news.

"Hard to say. It depends on a number of factors including how fast the infection responds to the antibiotics, how much reserve he has, and if there is anything else going on." Dr. Hilton squinted at his watch. "I've gotta go Jack. I'm already forty-five minutes late for the clinic."

"Before you go, can you tell me what you really think?" Jack asked.

"At the risk of sounding like a politician, I'm just going to have to say, it's too early to say. I'll run more tests later on today, including a bone marrow biopsy. Maybe we'll get some answers there. I'll let you know." Dr. Hilton smiled at Jack, then headed for the door.

"Oh, Doc!" Jack said, his voice rising. "Doc, you ever heard of people's hair falling out for no reason?"

The doctor stopped with his hand on the door. "Men go bald all the time. It's genetic."

"No, I mean women and suddenly, all at once."

"Yes it happens, sometimes with extreme stress, sometimes with chemotherapy, sometimes with malnutrition."

"How bout radiation?"

"Yes, I've seen patients lose their hair when they've been irradiated for brain tumors."

"Does it grow back?"

"Most of the time, but it could take several months. Jack, I've really got to go."

"Thanks a lot," Jack said as the door closed behind the doctor.

Jack asked to see Mick at the information desk but was told that visiting hours were from 5:00 p.m. to 8:00 p.m. No matter how much he argued, the receptionist refused to make an exception. Even "it's an emergency" didn't work.

Not to be put off, Jack left the lobby, circled around back to the receiving dock and quietly entered the hospital through the central supply door.

As it turned out, Mick was in the same wing, even the very same bed Easy Earl had been in. Jack did not believe in omens or even coincidences, but this was a bit unnerving. Seeing Mick lying in the same bed that Easy had died in, rattled Jack. It was downright eerie. Particularly when Mick looked almost as bad as Easy Earl had.

Jack eased in, closed the curtains behind him and leaned over the bed. Mick's breathing was rapid, shallow and wheezy, his face colorless, his skin a faded, pale-lemon color and there was just too much of it. It was loose and seemed to fit like old hand-me-down clothes. Until now, Jack hadn't been aware of how much weight Mick had lost.

Ever curious when it involved medicine, Jack inspected the IV and noted they were running in normal saline mixed with 2.4 million units of penicillin G and 10 milliequivalents of potassium chloride. To dissipate excess body heat from the fever, the sheet had been turned down, exposing Mick's abdomen. Chief Callahan's bandage had been removed and replaced with a professional white one wrapped around Mick's torso. Jack noticed it appeared to be clean. Perhaps that meant Mick's wound had quit draining.

In a few minutes, Mick stirred. Jack gently placed a hand on his shoulder. Mick's eyes fluttered open and he whispered, "Is that you, J.T.?"

"Yeah, it's me. How you doing?"

"I'm just fine," he answered with his ususal line. "How'd you get out of jail? Fake an illness too?"

"Nah, I'm out on bail. Actually, you are too. I think your mother posted your bond. Brian Bugsby, you know the attorney we met at the sand dunes party? He's going to defend us."

"Who?"

"You know, the guy with the big glasses that looks like a bug," Jack said. "They call him Bugs. Anyway, he thinks this is, to quote him, 'much ado about nothing.'"

"Shakespeare?"

"Yeah," Jack said, surprised that Mick was up on his literature.

"He thinks eventually the county attorney will plea-bargain this down to a misdemeanor."

"My back sure doesn't feel like it was a misdemeanor. Anyway, that's good. But I sure hope Bugs is a better at legal than he is at chasing women. It's just a little odd to have a drinking buddy defend us."

"He's never lost a case yet. At least that's what they say."

"He looks like he's never tried one," Mick said, smiling weakly.

"Well, he's the one the chief got for us," Jack said, then changed the subject. "Doc Hilton says he's going to fill you full of penicillin and you'll be out of here in a few days."

"I guess so. Doc said he wanted to run some more tests. Going to stab a needle in my breast bone sometime today. Get some bone marrow. God that sounds fun. I can hardly wait."

"I'm sure it's just routine—" Jack's voice trailed off. They sat in silence for a few moments.

"Kinda ironic, don't you think, me being in the same bed as Easy?" Mick said softly.

"Yeah, I was just thinking about that."

"Maybe, it's only fitting—"

"Young man!" A stern faced, white-frocked nurse yelled. "What are you doing in here? You know very well it's not visiting hours. I'm asking you to leave, and right now! Before I call security."

"Yes, Nurse, I was just leaving," Jack said, even though he knew there was no security department at Dixie Pioneer Hospital. "I'll see you tomorrow, buddy. Get better."

15

After leaving the hospital, Jack hitched a ride to Santa Clara with Fritz Reber. Before they got their drivers' licenses, Jack recalled, hitchhiking was how they often got to and from Saint George. Now, it was a little embarrassing. Fritz had asked where his car was. Not wanting to go into details, Jack had said it was broke down.

The sun was still high in the western sky when Jack got to the farm. The heat was stifling and the orchard smelled of rotting peaches. Normally, Jack wouldn't work this time of day, but today he had no choice, even after what he had been through the last two days. Better to face the fierce afternoon sun than his father's fury. That was being optimistic, Jack thought bitterly. His father would be furious anyway, but a few lugs of peaches might help.

At a furious pace, Jack picked five lugs, fed and milked the Guernsey, grained the chickens, gathered the eggs and slopped the hogs. He then headed for the house, dreading the confrontation with his father. Quietly entering the kitchen, Jack poured the milk through a strainer into two half-gallon Mason jars, placed the eggs in a straw basket, and stored the milk and eggs in the refrigerator. He could hear his father and sister in the dining room as he mechanically washed the grime from his hands. He took a deep breath and joined them as if nothing had happened.

Mr. Kunz carefully cut his pork chop, ignoring Jack. Mary looked down at her plate, rearranging the piles of food. Jack reached for a plate and served himself.

"Nice of you to join us, Jack," his father said after a few moments of raw silence. "Shall we plan on you every third night now? Or perhaps we should just keep a place set for you in hopes that you might occasionally favor us with your presence."

"I'm sorry. There were things beyond my control."

"Perhaps you'd enlighten us. What could possibly be so important that it would justify letting ripe peaches fall to the ground, cows go un-milked til their bags dry-up and animals go unfed?"

"I suppose you know the answer," Jack replied, looking at Mary.

"I want to hear it from you," his father said, his eyes hard as flint.

"Well," Jack replied, pausing briefly. "The sheriff found our fingerprints, mine and Mick's, on the flashlight and those match books. When he came to arrest us, Mick and I were down in the peach orchard. Mick panicked and ran. Sheriff Meecham shot him in the back. I thought the sheriff was trying to kill Mick and I was probably going to be next. Without thinking, I ran to help him, and we just kept on running." Jack took a breath. "We hid from the posse for a couple days in the desert but yesterday we'd had enough. We turned ourselves into Chief Callahan. I spent last night in the county jail and I'm out on bail. Mick is in the hospital and not doing real well. Got an infection or something from that bullet."

Jack hurriedly added, "But this afternoon, I did pick five lugs of peaches. You can take them with you on the truck tomorrow."

"If it were up to me, I was going to let you rot in jail. Give you some time to think about what a mess you've made of your life. Who paid the bail?"

"Chief Callahan got Mr. Bugsby to represent us. He loaned me the money."

"How much?"

"Six hundred dollars. I'll pay him back."

"I don't know how you're going to do that. With the amount of work you've been doing around here, it'll take you about twenty or thirty years to earn that."

"I'll use the money I've saved for my mission," Jack said as he poked at his food. "Probably not going to need it anyway."

"And just whose idea was it to hire that beatnik Bugsby?" Mr. Kunz shouted. "That's like having a hooker preach a sermon in church on morality. And who's going to pay him?"

"Don't worry. I'll figure out a way."

"You'd better. I'm sure as hell not going to. What does that skirt-chasin' lawyer think of your chances?" his father asked, calming down.

"He's pretty optimistic we can plea-bargain this down to criminal mischief, a misdemeanor."

"Lawyers are always optimistic, they can afford to be, cause they're playing with someone else's dollar." Feeling he'd made his point, Mr. Kunz resumed eating.

"Did I get any calls while I was gone?" Jack asked Mary, hoping to change the subject. "Did Emily call?"

"No, she didn't call. The only call was from that AEC man, Rudy Popovich." Mary replied reluctantly, knowing what her father thought of him.

"What did that son-of-a-bitch want?" Mr. Kunz asked, putting down his fork.

"I should have told you," she said to her father. "I'm sorry. He said the tests showed the cows died from malnutrition. But he did say he wanted to buy a couple cows from you."

"He wants to buy my cows? Who wants to buy starving cows? They're not any damn good to eat. Those connivin' bastards probably want to run some tests on the living animals and don't want me to know. I'll bet they'll shoot em to see what radiation fallout does to the innards of a cow. I'm not selling them one damn cow til they pay me for the ones that have already died."

"Dad, they're not going to reimburse you for cows that have starved to death." Jack said, immediately wishing he'd kept his mouth shut.

"Goddamnit Jack, you don't have the sense God gave a lizard. How may times do I have to tell you? They did not die from starvation. This is all bullshit."

Jack felt his face flush with anger. With his fists clenched at his side, Jack stood up from the table. "I may be wrong about the fallout. But I'm not going to take any more insults from you."

His father's jaw dropped in disbelief, then he bolted from his seat. "Don't talk to me that way young man," he shouted. "Not after all I've done for you. You think you can take me? Let's go outside and we'll find out."

"Outside, hell!" Jack shouted back as he swung a furious right hook that packed with it all his years of accumulated frustration. The blow struck his father full in the left jaw, and instantly, Jack felt fire in his hand. He'd forgotten about his broken bone. But the punch had worked and Mr. Kunz's knees buckled. He staggered sideways, grabbing at the table. It skidded under his weight and plates of food crashed to the floor.

"Not mother's china!" Mary screamed.

Recovering quickly, Mr. Kunz viciously rabbit-punched Jack in the stomach, the blow leaving him doubled over and gasping for air.

"You two are not going to fight in here!" Mary shouted. "This is crazy." She instantly wedged herself between them.

Jack slowly lowered his fists. "You'd better hire someone else to help you on your precious damn farm," he said, turning away. "I'm outta here."

"Don't let the door hit you in the ass on the way out."

Jack gritted his teeth and stomped away to his bedroom, slamming the door. In a few moments, he heard the kitchen door bang shut and his father start the pickup. I've got to get out of this house, Jack thought, and permanently. Since his mother had died, it hadn't really been a home anyway. I'm just a hired hand, except I don't get paid like one. It's time to make my own way in life, Jack thought.

But Jack felt sorry for Mary. She seldom dated and would probably spend her entire life taking care of an unappreciative father, being his maid, cook, laundress, and now, probably even his farmhand. That cantankerous old bastard!

He didn't regret the fight with his father. It had been coming for a long time. But, he did feel bad about the china. How his mother had loved that china and Mary had been almost obsessive about it. It was about the only thing left that they had to remember her by. Now, like everything else in his life it was smashed—gone.

As his anger subsided, Jack became more aware of the throbbing pain in his hand. He took a look at it. It didn't seem as bad as before. At least the bone fragments were not displaced. He went to the bathroom and carefully re-taped it, then returned to the bedroom.

To distract himself, Jack sat on the bed and went through the motions of filling out his mission papers. Probably just an exercise in futility, he thought. It was becoming quite unlikely he would go. If he was convicted of a felony, he wouldn't be called, and if he was called, he probably couldn't pay for it.

Jack then rummaged through his dresser and finally found the application papers for admission to the University of Utah. He might as well explore that option also. Lastly, he pulled out his savings passbook from the same drawer. With dismay, he stared at the total, $657.87. That didn't include this month's interest, and he had two $25 Savings Bond booklets that were completed with a stamp on every square. They hadn't matured yet but he could cash them in for at least the $17.50 he had paid for the stamps, probably more.

To pay Bugs back for the bail bond would chew up almost his entire savings. But of course, Jack thought, that money would be returned when he showed up for court. So depending on what Bugs charged him for legal services, he might have enough money for one year in the mission field or one year at college, then he would have to improvise. Something would work out, even if it was what Chris had done, enlisting in the army and going to Korea. He was not going to starve and anything was better than here. He'd just have to play it one day at a time.

"Jack, there's someone here to see you," Mary said, appearing quietly in the doorway.

"Mary, I'm just not in the mood," he snapped.

"It's Rudy Popovich. I told him Father wasn't in, but he said he's here to see you."

Jack looked sullenly at his watch: 9:00 p.m. Actually, he had expected a confrontation with Rudy Popovich long before now. He might just as well get it over with. Jack put away the passbook and with a mixture of apprehension and irritation headed into the living room.

"Hi, Mr. Popovich. What can I do for you?" Jack said sharply.

"Hello, Jack." Rudy smiled. "You've been a mighty hard man to track down. The sheriff didn't tell me you were back in town til late last night."

"I've been around. I've had a busy day."

"Sounds like the last three or four days have been very busy for you." Rudy grinned.

"What do you want Mr. Popovich? It's late and I've got to get up early."

"Well now, Jack. I know you, or Mick Graff, have those papers. They're important research documents and they're classified. After I finally found out Mick was in the hospital, I tried to talk to him. Wasn't visiting hours. Jack, you two are in serious trouble. Stealing government property is a federal offense. Why don't you just hand over the briefcase?"

"I don't know what the hell you're talking about, Mr. Popovich," Jack said calmly.

"Come on, Jack. I know Mick took the briefcase. I've talked to Doris Frei. I'm just trying to be nice here, but if you want to play hardball, I can get the FBI involved. I just thought it would save us all a lot of trouble if you just handed over the documents and we forget the whole thing," Rudy said, crossing his arms over his chest.

"I don't understand why the FBI isn't already involved if these documents are as important as you say. Why don't you just have the FBI arrest us? Something doesn't smell right about this whole thing."

"Well now, Jack. I'm just trying to be nice. You've got enough problems without federal charges. Just give the briefcase back and we'll call it even."

"You know what I think, Mr. Popovich? I think you don't want the FBI involved because you don't want anybody to see those papers. And I'm wondering why," Jack said, pausing for a moment. "I will tell you this much. If I did have those papers, I might want a newspaper, maybe the *Salt Lake Tribune*, to help me look them over and tell me what they all meant."

Beads of sweat had gathered on Rudy's forehead and he was no longer smiling. "You don't want to do that, Jack. That would not be in your best interest."

"In that case, if I did have those papers and I don't, I would probably throw them into the river. Yep, that's what I'd do, I'd throw them into the Virgin River," Jack said as his eyes met Rudy's.

"I think I hear what you're saying, and I think we do have an understanding. Those papers are replaceable. But, Jack, if those originals turn up in anyone's hands but mine, I'll throw the book at you." Rudy looked hard at Jack, then turned and quickly left.

With a sigh, Jack returned to his bedroom, turned off the light and climbed into bed. He hated to admit it, but it looked like his father and Mick were right about the AEC after all. Maybe, if he'd talked to Rudy before tonight that whole messy fight with his father could have been avoided. Probably not. There was a hell of a lot more going on between him and his father than just the AEC. Anyway, it looked like he and Mick were finished with the AEC. If only the county charges would go away that easy.

Jack slowly closed his eyes. Even then, they continued to burn and itch. Fatigue suddenly flooded over him like a warm bath and his mind started to wander. His thoughts soon turned to Emily. What was she going to do with her life now that her mother was gone? Would she get a job and continue to live with her grandparents? Certainly, she was smart enough to go to college. Either way, with her good looks, intelligence and personality, it would not be long before she met someone. Not someone like me, Jack thought. I'm definitely a small-town hick, depressed, moody, a blatant hypocrite, and not going anywhere in life.

Then his thoughts drifted to Mick. In the hospital today, Jack thought, he really didn't look good. He had understood what Doc Hilton had said about the leukocytes, but then he had also said Mick was a puzzle. When it came to questions of health, puzzles were generally not good. Tomorrow, he would drop by the library and see if he could figure it out for himself.

Finally, Jack began surfing on sweet waves of oblivion. He saw a small army of leukocytes patrolling like vacuum cleaners, looking for particles to eat. When they found anything that glittered, like radioactive particles, they would ruthlessly gobble them up. Eventually with all that eating, they ballooned to enormous proportions. Then without explanation, they turned on Jack. He had to run for his life. The huge, bloated white cells chased him, snapping at him with enormous jaws. Jack ran until his chest was on fire, but he still could not shake his pursuers. Physically spent, he turned to face them.

Suddenly, the leukocytes took form and Jack could see them clearly. It was Sheriff Meecham, his father, Rudy Popovich and Mick! Jack forced himself awake. He was shaking and covered in a cold sweat.

16

The next two days passed in shaky peace. Jack and his father had pretty much managed to avoid each other and both had ignored Jack's threat to leave. Every evening Jack went to visit Mick, and while in Saint George, he stopped at the Polar Bear for dinner. Though he thought it would never happen, Jack was beginning to get tired of burgers, shakes and fries. He had to admit, Mary cooked a better meal.

His father would tape a list of chores that needed to be done each day by the phone in the kitchen before he left on his truck-produce route every morning. This was fine by Jack, he really didn't have anything to say to him anyway.

Grudgingly, Jack had to admit, he was thankful for the work. It kept him busy and gave him less time to think about things. He soon finished harvesting the peaches, picked the first crop of rattlesnake striped watermelons, and went through the tomatoes again, gleaning the ripe and pink ones for his father's daily produce run.

Also, another irrigation turn had come around. With no rain and the winter snowpack gone, the stream had dwindled to half flow, requiring constant vigilance to cover the fields. But the heat and shortage of water had stunted the alfalfa's growth. The next cut would be smaller.

Jack also found some time to send his college admissions application to the University of Utah and he personally delivered his mission papers to Bishop Heinke. After giving a long, silent look of disappointment, the bishop confirmed that Jack was still eligible for a mission, providing he was not convicted of any felony. But Bishop Heinke firmly stated that he would not forward the papers to church headquarters in Salt Lake City until the volcano matter had been resolved.

Meanwhile, Mick had rallied some. He had less rigors and fever at night and his wound was looking better. Results of the bone marrow biopsy had not come back yet, but somehow that seemed less important now that Mick was getting better. Dr. Hilton hinted that after a couple of more days of intravenous penicillin, Mick might be ready to go home.

Several times in the last two days, Jack had considered trying to call Emily. But if he did, what would he say? Nothing had changed. It was still hard for Jack to visualize a future without her. And he continued to worry about her hair falling out. Jack wondered if his hair would fall out as well. Doc Hilton had assured him that her hair would grow back, but that didn't make him feel less guilty. If he did talk to her, she would probably ask questions. Questions about things he really didn't want to talk about. In the end, he did not phone her, nor did she contact him.

It was in the middle of the afternoon while Jack was picking peaches that Bugs dropped by for a strategy conference. After cursing the dust of the Vineyard Road, he swore he would never again make house calls. That's why he had an office, he said. When Jack reminded him he had not asked him to come, he cussed again and threatened to leave.

Jack apologized, though he was not sure why, and Bugs calmed down.

"The hearing is set for Monday," he said, squatting on his heels.

"I get hearings and arraignments confused." Jack sat on the ground next to Bugs. "What do we do?"

"No big deal. This is when we enter a plea."

"How are we going to plead?" Jack asked, worry lines creasing his forehead.

"Not guilty to all charges."

"But I am guilty," Jack softly protested, as he eased his back against a peach tree.

"Come on Jack, don't be a putz. I've gone over the police report and I'm telling you, they've got nothing."

"They have my fingerprints."

"They may have your prints, but what they don't have is an

eyewitness. At least they don't if Curly and Alan keep their mouths shut." Bugs joined Jack on the ground. "Without witnesses, they can't establish time. The county attorney can prove those are your fingerprints on the flashlight, but he can't prove when you dropped it there."

"I hate to lie," Jack said, shaking his head. "It grates on me. How about I confess and throw myself on the mercy of the court. That would be the Christian thing to do."

"That would be really stupid," Bugs said, pushing his thick glasses back further on his nose. "Confessions in court are totally different from religion. You can't just promise the judge you'll never do it again and be forgiven. A confession is tantamount to a conviction. And a conviction mandates a penalty."

"How much of a penalty?"

"Depends. But if they got everything, and if you confess they will, about ten to twenty years."

"Twenty years," Jack said slowly. "Bugs, I guess we'd better do it your way."

"See ya on Monday." Bugs grinned, then stood up and climbed into the Corvette. "We'll give em hell."

After finishing with the peaches, Jack walked over to the tomato patch. Six lugs of tomatoes had been on his father's list. By working through the afternoon heat, Jack finished picking the tomatoes by 5:00. Carefully, he placed them in the receiving hamper of the wooden sorter. Then he still had to separate them by size into four separate bins, and hand-pack them into lugs.

It was the packing that was the most time consuming. First, Jack spread newspaper on the bottom slats of the lug to protect the tomatoes from bruising. He then set the first layer of tomatoes neatly in rows, trying to keep the size equal. A cardboard divider was placed on top of the first layer, followed by another uniform layer of tomatoes. Each row had to be carefully packed so the tomatoes would not jiggle loose, but at the same time, not so tight to cause bruising. It was a slow process.

When he finished, he had five and a half impeccably packed lugs. But his father's morning note had indicated he needed six to fill his orders. Oh, what the hell, Jack thought, shrugging his shoulders. This would only serve as another source of irritation for his father. He had picked all the tomatoes that were ready, that was all he could do. Glancing at his watch, Jack noted it was now nearly 6:30. He was going to have to hurry if he was going to get to the hospital during visiting hours.

As Jack parked his car, Mick's mother was just leaving. He waited until she was gone before getting out. Jack had the impression that Mick's mother disapproved of him and held him at least partly responsible for Mick's troubles. After the hospital scene with Easy's mother, he didn't want to chance another.

As Jack parted the drapes to Mick's cubicle, he could feel something was wrong. Melancholy hung in the air like wet-wash on a clothesline. The air was stale and reeked of musty sheets, rubbing alcohol, urine and depression. Mick's face was drawn and he was staring at the ceiling.

"Hi, Mick. How's it going?"

Mick managed a weak smile, his freckles glittering like a rash on his pale skin. "Just fine."

"Come on Mick." Jack sat in the bedside chair. "I'm not blind."

"Actually, if you want the truth. Not worth a shit, J.T."

"What's wrong, Mick? Did the fever come back?"

"No, no more fever, and the pain's almost gone. The bone marrow test came back today."

"What did Doc Hilton say?" Jack asked, his throat raspy.

After a few moments, Mick reached for a piece of paper on the metal night stand beside his bed. "Dr. Hilton says I've got friggin' acute myeloblastic leukemia."

Jack was stunned. Leukemia struck the fear of God into everyone, just as polio had done a few years ago before Jonas Salk. "Surely, there's treatment, a cure?" Jack said, trying to sound optimistic. "After all, this is the fifties, not the dark ages. There's got to be a lot of research going on."

"Says here, we could use nitrogen mustard, potassium arsenite or even cobalt radiation, but as long as I am feeling okay, the doc doesn't recommend any of those things. The treatments can make you real sick and may or may not help."

"Well, what did he recommend?"

"Basically, he suggested we do nothing. Let the friggin' disease run its course. If I develop complications, like bleeding from a tumor, then we could start treatments."

"What about Salt Lake City? They have specialists up there."

"Doc Hilton called Salt Lake and talked to a hematologist. What I just told you, is what he suggested."

"Well hell, Mick. He's recommending nothing."

"I know, J.T. That's what I said."

"But—" Jack stammered. "We've got to do something."

"Don't you get it, J.T.? There is no cure for leukemia. Those treatments don't even prolong life. They just make you goddamn sick. Jack, it's obvious, I'm going to die."

"Is that what Dr. Hilton said?" Jack asked quietly.

"He didn't want to tell me, but I insisted. It's my goddamn life and I have a right to know how much of it is left."

"What did he say?" Jack whispered.

"Somewhere between one and four months. Then, that's it, no more Michael J. Graff. It's kinda scary J.T."

"I could get the elders from the ward to come and give you a priesthood blessing. I know you don't believe in healing prayers, but there have been some miraculous cures with the power of the priesthood. Anyway, what would it hurt?" Jack asked earnestly.

"I've been giving that some thought. It sure wouldn't hurt to cover all my bases. Yeah, why not?"

Jack nodded, wiping the tears from his eyes, and agreed to make the necessary arrangements.

"J.T., honestly, do you think there's a life hereafter?" Mick asked after a few minutes.

"Yes, Mick, I'm sure there is."

"Do you think they'll take me? I'm not really the best candidate."

"Mick, they take everyone, especially you."

"But, what about the degrees of glory? You know the different kingdoms of heaven, the celestial, terrestrial and telestial. If they put me in the telestial, which I assume is like hell, I'm not sure I want to go."

"Mick, you haven't lived a bad life. God will be forgiving of even your most serious transgressions," Jack said quietly.

"J.T., you don't know everything. There's stuff I haven't told you. I haven't lived a very good life, no matter what you think." Mick's voice trailed off. He stared vacantly at Jack for a moment. "What about repentance? When can that be done?"

"Anytime. It's never too late to repent," Jack said, wondering what Mick had done that was so serious. A few pranks and some weekend drinking. Big deal.

"But, didn't you tell me some sins can't be forgiven?" Mick's hand played nervously with the loose skin under his chin.

"Yeah, you're talking about blasphemy against the Holy Ghost and murder. Neither of those apply to you. You really have to work hard in this life to get eternal damnation."

Mick forced a smile. "So, you think there's hope for me then, Jack?"

Yes, I know there is, Mick."

Jack reached for Mick's hand and the two friends sat in silence. Finally, Mick turned to Jack and smiled thinly. "Looks like I'm going to beat this manslaughter rap after all," he snickered. "But my mother may lose her bail money if I don't show up for the trial. Think Judge Ballard will make an exception in my case, J.T.?"

Biting his lower lip, Jack fought back the tears. Suddenly, the hard-faced nurse appeared. Visiting hours were over.

On his way home to Santa Clara, Jack stopped by the Washington County Library. It was just after 8:00, and the library was open for another hour. Jack browsed through the medical biology section and settled on a large brown book entitled, *Clinical Hematology* by Maxwell M. Wintrobe, M.D., PhD.

According to Wintrobe, leukemia was first recognized as a disease of the white cells in 1845 by Virchow and he had coined the term leukemia. Life insurance statistics indicated there were approximately 3,000 deaths a year in the United States, with the highest incidence in young white males between the age of 15 and 40. There was no known cause of leukemia, but in humans, there was a puzzling ten-fold increase in leukemia in radiation workers and handlers. Other possible causes included, infections, toxins, drugs and trauma. The latest research seemed to indicate there was a distinct similarity between leukemia and cancer, with some investigators even proposing that leukemia was a cancer of the blood.

There were two major types of leukemia, acute and chronic, then there were several sub-types depending on which white cell was involved, i.e. lymphocytic leukemia (from lymphocytes), monocytic leukemia (from monocytes) and myeloblastic leukemia (from immature leukocytes). In chronic leukemia, the average survival after diagnosis was 3.28 years, but in the acute variety, almost all were dead within six months. Death was almost always the result of infection, hemorrhage or the leukemic infiltration of vital organs.

Over the years, there had been several reported cases of cure, but in retrospect these were hard to document, and may have been a missed diagnosis from the beginning. In other words, the "cures" may not have had leukemia to begin with. Dr. Wintrobe made a point of saying, "the easiest disease to cure is non-disease." Statistically speaking, none of the standard treatments had increased longevity. Therefore, treatment was relegated to the treating of complications from leukemia, such as leukemic masses, hemorrhage from leukemic infiltration, and of course, serious infections. In spite of their dismal track record, the treatments currently being used in this fashion were cobalt radiation, nitrogen mustard, the arsenicals, and Benzol, all of which had significant and often debilitating side effects.

Jack slowly closed the book and wiped the moisture from his eyes. It appeared what Dr. Hilton had told Mick was correct after all. According to Dr. Hilton and now Dr. Wintrobe, Mick would get weaker from progressive anemia and malnutrition and he would probably have a series of infections due to his impaired immune system and experience repeated hemorrhages from leukemic infiltrations of mucous membranes. The bleeding could come from almost any organ, but the most likely sites would be the respiratory or gastrointestinal tracts. Also, he could develop huge leukemic masses almost anywhere, including superficial lymph nodes, the brain and almost any other of the internal organs, especially the spleen. That meant, Jack thought, Mick's already large spleen would continue to grow. Then within two to six months Mick would be dead. A fine, vibrant, young life, no more.

This was all a nightmare, Jack thought. Surely, he would wake up and this whole bizarre thing would have vanished like his recent, ghastly dreams.

What purpose would Mick's death serve? Surely, God didn't need Mick nearly as much as I do, Jack thought. What urgent mission could God possibly have for Mick in the hereafter? Even the word urgent now seemed inappropriate. In God's realm, time was insignificant. God lived in eternity, so what possible difference could it make to God to delay Mick's return for a measly fifty or sixty years? How could that make a difference in the grand scheme of things?

Jack closed his eyes and bowed his head. "Oh God, he prayed, I know I am unworthy to come to you for favors, but over the years, I haven't asked for very much. God, I know I don't fully understand your eternal plan, but I can't see what difference it would make to let Mick tarry here on earth for a few more years. If you will grant me this favor, I promise I will devote the next two years to preaching your gospel, and the rest of my life to your service. Personally, I think it's a good deal for both of us. I ask this humbly, in the name of Jesus Christ, Amen."

Jack felt much better. Mormon lore and legend were full of examples of curing the sick, and even raising the dead with the laying on of hands by members of the priesthood and by personal prayer. Silently, Jack chastised himself for recent doubts about the church. For Mick's sake, he had to keep the faith, remain strong in the church. It was now in God's hands and that was good enough for Jack.

A calm feeling seemed to settle over him, like the first dusting of winter snow. Deep in his soul, Jack had the feeling that Mick would be all right. It was just a matter of faith.

Suddenly, the lights dimmed twice in rapid succession. It was closing time at the library. Jack looked at his watch. It was 9:00 and he still hadn't done his evening chores. Oh well, it wouldn't be the first time he'd milked the cow in the dark. Hopefully, Jack thought, his father would still be ignoring him.

Then Jack remembered that he needed to call Bishop Heinke before it got too late and arrange for the elders to give Mick a blessing. Between the power of the priesthood and his personal prayers, surely God would cure the leukemia. Of this, Jack had no doubt.

Jack quickly returned Dr. Wintrobe's book to the shelf, then his eye caught another title, *Origin of the Species* by Charles Darwin. Jack pulled the book from the shelf and thumbed through it. In his biology class, Professor Watkin in a hushed voice like he was revealing a conspiracy, had briefly mentioned the book as a possible alternate theory, but said it was controversial. Of course, Bishop Heinke had denounced the book as ludicrous and the work of Satan. Jack couldn't help but wonder what all the fuss was about. He hesitated, then put the book under his arm and pulled out his library card.

17

August was now pretty much over but the brutal heat continued. Jack had just finished with the fourth crop of hay and unless there was rain, there wouldn't be a fifth. With the Santa Clara River now reduced to a trickle, the water company had cut the irrigation turns to a half-hour per share and even then with the meager stream in the ditches, Jack had barely enough water to keep the tomato patch, the watermelons and orchard trees alive. The alfalfa fields browned and went dry.

Bishop Heinke had dedicated an entire sacrament meeting to an appeal, pleading for God to intercede in the drought. But even that did not seem to help. Jack wondered if Smoky Grayman could do any better with his rain dance, though nobody asked him. The only benefit of the drought to Jack was that his workload had lessened considerably as the crops withered in the unrelenting heat. With his right hand still sore, Jack appreciated the slack time, and it gave him more time to spend with Mick.

Meanwhile, Jack had arranged to have the elders administer to Mick. He was to stand in the circle prayer for the laying on of hands. Elder John Tobler, Jack's uncle, along with Elder Franklin Ence, performed the ordinance for Mick. After putting a few drops of consecrated oil on Mick's head, they placed their hands on his head and Uncle John offered the prayer. First he invoked God's presence through Jesus Christ and by the power of the holy Melchizedek Priesthood. Then Elder Ence asked God to intercede on Mick's behalf, to make him whole and well again, if it were God's will. Elder Ence closed the supplication in the name of Jesus Christ. Jack was convinced that he had felt God's presence in the hospital room. It had been a powerful scene, and Jack had left the hospital convinced more than ever that God would intervene. It was only a matter of time.

Mick was now at home and for a time he seemed to rally. In spite of the apparent recovery, Dr. Hilton suggested that he stay indoors, basically to conserve his strength and lessen the likelihood of exposure to some communicable disease. In his condition, any infection could be devastating.

Jack visited Mick almost every day but as time went on, he found the visits were becoming increasingly awkward and uncomfortable. There was very little they could do in Mick's bedroom but talk, and Jack purposefully tried to keep the conversation light. He deliberately danced around the subject of Mick's health. Mick had approached the topic on a couple occasions, but Jack just didn't want to deal with it.

It had now been over a month since Jack had talked to Emily, but time had not diminished his longing for her. She hadn't been to church and Jack had not seen her around town either. Through Santa Clara's grapevine, he had heard she had indeed lost all her hair, but that it was now starting to grow back. That might explain her absence from church and her not socializing with friends although Jack had a feeling it was more than that. She was probably trying to avoid him. It would be nice to have a friend to share the burden of Mick's illness with, and the fears of his upcoming manslaughter trial, Jack thought.

On a couple of occasions, Jack had talked to Curley and Alan about Mick, but they seemed less affected by Mick's illness. He really couldn't open up with them anyway. They were more concerned with girls, a weekend party at the sand dunes, or the upcoming football season, things that now seemed inconsequential to Jack.

And Jack's relationship with his father was no better. When they met face to face, they were cordial and words were used cautiously and sparingly, but mainly they just tried to avoid each other. Their primary method of communication continued to be the daily work lists. Even those memos were now shorter and more infrequent because of the drought.

As far as Jack's legal problems were concerned, the initial hearing two weeks ago had been uneventful. As Bugs had counseled, Jack had pled not guilty to all charges. Morally, Jack still felt this was wrong, after all he was guilty, but practically, he had to agree that Bugs might be right.

The trial date had been set and today was the day. The prosecuting attorney, Mr. Epson, after consulting with Dr. Hilton, indefinitely deferred the charges against Mick, but steadfastly refused to plea-bargain with Jack. This was inconceivable to Bugs, and seemed to make him crazy. He unwaveringly maintained that the prosecution's case was thin as Pine Valley Mountain air and that if the bastards wouldn't play ball, then by God, he would stuff the damn ball down their throats. Rumor had it around town that the prosecution was out to get Bugs with this case but, of course, Sheriff Meecham wanted Jack.

The crucial point of the trial, according to Bugs, would be the time factor with the flashlight. With verified fingerprints, there was no doubt the prosecution could prove that the flashlight found at the volcano had been handled by Jack, but could they establish when the flashlight was discarded at the volcano, and by whom? For that they needed an eyewitness.

Bugs had interviewed all the officers involved that night, and none of them could positively identify any of the perpetrators though, of course, they had their suspicions. Easy Earl and Greg, two possible eye-witnesses were dead, and according to Bugs, not likely to talk. So, that left only Alan and Curley as potential witnesses.

At Bug's insistence, Jack had talked to Alan and Curley. They had been subpoenaed to appear at the trial as witnesses for the prosecution. However, both had assured Jack that they had told the county attorney nothing. This seemed to satisfy Bugs, but it bothered Jack. It was one thing to tell a lie to an irritating, badgering lawyer trying to scrounge up a witness, but quite another to take an oath on the Bible to God, then tell the same falsehood to the court. Not only was it morally wrong, it was also a crime. The crime was called perjury and it was a felony.

Hurriedly, Jack finished combing the sides of his flat top, sweeping his hair to the back forming a perfect ducktail. The Brylcream had pretty much greased his hair so it would stay in place. Jack examined himself in the mirror. Bugs had told him to look presentable, not like he'd just climbed off a tractor. Unfortunately, Jack concluded, this was just about as presentable as he could get. Put a stalk of straw between his crooked teeth and he would look just like a farmer.

Jack met Bugs at his office. Brian quickly gulped down his

breakfast of black coffee and two glazed doughnuts, raked a comb through his straw-thick, rooster-red hair and adjusted his powerful glasses.

"Well, let's go kick some butt," Bug's said. "This ought'a be fun."

The Washington County Courthouse was a two-story square building constructed of slabs of native red Navajo sandstone. There were four windows to a side, each trimmed with pine board painted ivory white. The bannisters on the entrance steps were painted the same color. The courtroom and foyer occupied the first floor; the second floor housed the county agencies and administrative offices. The courtroom was spacious with abundant natural light from large windows in the three outside walls. Its white walls contrasted with the stained walnut desks, trim and railings. Once deep and rich in color, the stain was now faded with varnish peeling in patches like scabs from a road rash.

When Jack and Bugs entered the courtroom, it was already hot, even with all the windows open. There was no breeze, and the air was stale and smelled of perspiration. County Attorney Blaine Epson was already at his table shuffling papers. The gallery was noisy and surprisingly full. Apparently a trial for manslaughter bordered on the sensational. Out of the corner of his eye, Jack spotted Howard Trumbull, reporter for the *Washington County News* . He was already jotting down notes.

Jack quickly scanned the gallery for Emily. She was nowhere to be seen. It was just as well, Jack thought. He really didn't want her seeing this. But there in the back row, holding his reservation hat in his lap, his long grey-black hair slicked back on his head, sat Smoky Grayman. The seats on either side of him were vacant.

Why did that Indian seem to always be around? He was a constant irritation and embarrassment. Jack didn't want everyone in town to know they were related. He hoped Smoky didn't try to talk to him after the trial.

Soon everything settled down and the bailiff barked, "All rise." Judge Ballard entered and quickly marched to the bench in his ink-black, magisterial robe. He immediately wiped the sweat from his brow, removed the robe and draped it over the back of his chair.

Selecting and seating a jury took an hour and a half. All potential jurors had heard of the case and Bugs complained to Judge Ballard that a fair trial was not possible in Saint George. He motioned the court for a change of venue which the judge quickly denied. In the end, however, Bugs seemed satisfied with the jury. He had allowed almost every potential juror to the box except the very old and those he perceived to have a problem with the younger generation.

After a brief recess, Judge Ballard arched his bushy eyebrows, then stated he wanted to get the trial wrapped up today. Not waiting for a rebuttal, he ordered the prosecution to proceed with its opening statement, to keep it brief and to the point.

Prosecuting attorney Blaine Epson immediately rose from his chair, nodded to the judge, then bowed to the jury, trying to establish eye contact with each member.

"Your Honor, ladies and gentlemen of the jury, and my esteemed," he paused and swallowed hard, "colleague Mr. Bugsby. I will be brief, because this is a simple, uncomplicated case. Unfortunately, it is also a sad case. Not only is it a case of death, it is a case of unnecessary death. It is also a regrettable tale of youth gone bad. It's a story about how bad deeds can snowball into more bad deeds, and eventually things get out of control. You have an avalanche, and somebody gets killed. This is exactly what happened. On the night of July third of this year, Jack Kunz and five friends dragged a bunch of tires up to the cone of the Snow Canyon volcano, doused them with gasoline and set them on fire. Apparently, they were trying to simulate a volcanic eruption.

"This, as you know, is a violation of the law. One cannot endanger public safety by creating a panic. Plus, this is obviously an illegal use of public lands. When the officers tried to arrest them, the boys fled, first on foot, then in three automobiles. Now comes the unfortunate part of the story. As they sped north toward Veyo, one automobile driven by Earl Jaussi failed to negotiate the turn at the Veyo bridge, hit the guard rail and spun around in the middle of the road. With no time to react, a swiftly-pursuing Deputy Saunders slammed into the car, pushing both cars off the bridge to the canyon floor below. In this tragic accident, Deputy Saunders was killed along with Gregory Hafen, one of the perpetrators. Earl Jaussi suffered a grave head injury and later died as well. Whenever a police officer is killed in the commission of a crime, it qualifies as murder or manslaughter. In this case, it is manslaughter, as it appears there was no intent to kill Deputy Saunders."

Epson paused and took a few steps toward the jury before continuing.

"Following this catastrophe, do you think the other boys stopped to offer aid and assistance? Not on your life, or for that matter, on the lives of Deputy Saunders, Greg Hafen or Earl Jaussi. They just kept going, concerned only with their own escape from justice, and not giving a damn about the dead and injured.

"Fortunately for us, in their haste to flee from the volcano, the young men left behind a jacket, a flashlight and a book of matches. From these articles, the police were able to obtain two sets of fingerprints: those of Jack Kunz and Michael Graff."

"Hummm." Judge Ballard raked his fingers through his gray, unruly hair and loudly cleared his throat, plainly signaling that prosecutor Epson was taking too much time.

Taking the hint, the county attorney dabbed his forehead with a handkerchief, then quickly continued.

"When Sheriff Meecham tried to arrest Jack Kunz and Mick Graff, they ran. For two days Sheriff Meecham and a posse courageously chased those two fugitives across the scorching desert before they were finally arrested. During their flight from justice, Jack Kunz had a violent encounter with Deputy Fowler. Rather than surrender to him, Jack ambushed and bashed Deputy Fowler in the head with a rock fracturing his skull, then continued his lawless flight. Needless to say, Deputy Fowler sustained serious and substantial head injuries and spent several days in the hospital.

"In summary, Jack Kunz has committed serious crimes against Washington County and the State of Utah. Many innocent people have been injured or killed. When you see all the evidence and hear all the testimony, I know you will feel, as I do, that Jack Kunz is guilty and should be punished for the following crimes: criminal mischief, manslaughter, resisting arrest, flight from justice and assault on a police officer. Thank you for your patience and attention."

Epson nodded to the jury and sat down.

Jack was feeling depressed. Mr. Epson had done a good job with his opening statement. He even had Jack believing that he was a hardened criminal and should be jailed.

Judge Ballard turned to Bugsby. "The defense may deliver its opening statement now," muttering under his breath, "Don't they teach you lawyers to summarize in law school?"

Bugsby slowly rose, adjusted his glasses and peered at the jury." Your Honor, ladies and gentlemen of the jury. I, for one, will be brief. The prosecution can speculate, tell a good yarn, but they can't prove a goddamn—"

"Mr. Bugsby!" Judge Ballard interrupted. "You will not use that kind of language in my court."

"Yes, Your Honor," he replied smiling. "We'll admit the finger-prints on the flashlight are Jack's, but he lost the flashlight a full two weeks before this unfortunate episode and was not involved in the volcano incident at all. Yes, he did run from Sheriff Meecham, but only after seeing the good sheriff gun down his friend, Michael Graff, by shooting him in the back. What does that tell you? A man being shot in the back? Do you blame Jack for running? Also, that's why he hit Deputy Fowler in the head. Deputy Fowler was drawing his gun, and in the light of recent past events, Jack thought Deputy Fowler was going to shoot him as well. In his mind and in mine, Jack was only defending his own life, which by law, he has a right to do.

"Just to keep the record straight, Sheriff Meecham did not arrest Jack and Mick. The boys successfully evaded the intrepid sheriff and his fearless posse for two days in the desert, then voluntarily turned themselves in to Chief Callahan."

Judge Ballard scowled at that last remark.

"In summary, listen closely to the evidence and see if one speck of that evidence directly implicates Jack Kunz. There are no eyewitnesses, only a ton of speculation. No one can say, 'We saw Jack Kunz at the volcano, or speeding away from the volcano.' Not even Deputy Fowler can say for sure he saw who hit him. We admit some crimes were committed, but we think the county would be better served if the sheriff's department and prosecution spent their valuable time protecting the county from real criminals. I suppose, I could best illustrate the prosecution's shaky case by comparing it to Cervantes' blind *Don Quixote*. They, the prosecution and Sheriff Meecham, are indiscriminately charging at windmills in hopes their lances will hit something. It appears my job is much the same as the Don's Squire, Sanchez, to make sure innocent people are not injured in this madness." Bugs stared long and hard at the jury, and they were mesmerized by his magnified eyes.

Following this, Judge Ballard announced that they would immediately proceed with the evidentiary portion of the trial. He directed Mr. Epson to proceed and present what evidence he had to corroborate the county's case, and substantiate the charges against Mr. Jack Kunz.

Mr. Epson then examined a parade of witnesses including Sheriff Meecham, Deputy Fowler, the officer that found the flashlight at the volcano, and the fingerprinting expert from the Utah State Crime Lab in Salt Lake City. In cross examination, Bugs showed that while each witness could testify that a crime had been committed, none of them could say absolutely for sure it was Jack Kunz that committed any of those crimes.

The fingerprint expert had to admit that even though the prints on the flashlight were Jack's, he had no way of knowing how long they had been on the flashlight, or how long the light had been at the volcano. On sharp cross-examination, even Deputy Fowler, as Bugs had predicted, could not positively identify who it was that assaulted him. When the deputy volunteered that he felt certain it was Jack, Bugs objected that it was speculation, and Judge Ballard agreed.

Sheriff Meecham, though he admitted shooting Mick, maintained that it was an accident. Regardless of that, he insisted that Jack Kunz resisted a lawful arrest by running, and even though he turned himself in, was also guilty of flight from justice. After all, he ran around in the desert for two days like a damn Arab.

So far, about the only thing the prosecution had absolutely proved, was that Jack had fled from Sheriff Meecham after the Sheriff had shot Mick in the back. At 1:00 p.m., Judge Ballard granted an hour recess for lunch, but warned the participants the court would resume at 2:00 p.m. sharp, and if they were late, that would qualify as contempt.

Jack and Bugs quickly headed across Tabernacle street to the

Polar Bear. Brenda Frei bounced over to wait on them.

"Hi, Jack. Haven't seen you in a while. Who's your friend?"

"Hello, Brenda. You know Brian. Brian Bugsby. He's been to some of our parties."

Why did they have to run into Brenda? Jack thought.

"What ya doing in town in the middle of the day? You already got all your hay thrashed?" Brenda bubbled.

"You don't thrash hay, Brenda," Jack said through clenched teeth.

"Today's Jack's trial. I'm his lawyer." Bugs butted in.

"Oh yah, the murder thing," Brenda blurted out.

"It's not a murder trial, it's manslaughter. There's a big difference," Jack growled.

"You don't need to get so testy," Brenda said as she bent over to wipe the table, exposing her ample cleavage.

She quickly finished, took their order of hamburgers, onion rings and french fries, then disappeared in the back. Fifteen minutes later she returned with their food, placing it in the middle of the table. Then she smiled at Bugs, bending lower than she needed to. "Now I know you. You're the one with the Corvette. I've always wanted to ride in a Corvette."

"Anytime you want, sweetie," he replied, staring at her open blouse.

"Uh, Brenda," Jack asked. "How's Emily doing? Haven't seen much of her."

"Oh, she's fine," Brenda said as pulled out her pad. "Let's see. Two burgers at thirty-five cents each, and one order of fries and onion rings at twenty-five cents each. Come on guys, help me out here."

"One dollar and twenty cents," Jack said. "She ever ask about me?"

"Nope," Brenda said, as she smiled at Bugs, slapped the ticket on the table and left.

When he wasn't eyeing Brenda, Bugs talked about how satisfied he was with how the morning had gone. As predicted, he said, the prosecution had proved there were crimes committed, but had failed to convincingly prove it was Jack who had committed them. He theorized that the ticklish part of the trial would be this afternoon. Curley Reber and Alan Leavitt were scheduled to appear as witnesses. If they didn't crack, the case was in the bag.

Still wiping onion ring grease from their faces, Bugs and Jack returned to an even hotter courtroom at 2:05 p.m. and to an impatient Judge Ballard, who was staring at his wristwatch. Seemingly unconcerned, Bugs sat down at his table and opened his briefcase while Jack scanned the courtroom for Curley and Alan.

There was that damn Indian cousin, Smoky Grayman, sitting in the very same seat and gnawing on a piece of jerky. Probably didn't have enough money to go to lunch, Jack thought, but surely he had taken a break to have a smoke and a swig of whisky. Thinking about it, Jack had to grudgingly admit, Smoky did seem more interested in his welfare than his own father did.

There they were. On the opposite side of the gallery, looking washed and scrubbed, were Curley and Alan. They appeared nervous, their heads crammed together in conversation.

Judge Ballard suddenly banged his gavel. "If we're not infringing on the counsel for the defense's lunch time, we'll proceed."

"Not in the least, Your Honor. Please do," Bugsby replied without a blink.

Judge Ballard glared at Bugs for a moment, then turned to Epson, "Counselor, please call your next witness."

The county attorney nodded to the bailiff. "The court now calls Charles G. Reber."

Looking like an orphaned kitten, Curley slunk to the witness stand, staring straight ahead. "Do you promise to tell the truth, the whole truth, so help you God?" the bailiff asked.

Jack cringed as Curley answered with a shaky, "I do."

Curley eased down in the witness box, trying to find a comfortable position as he tugged at his collar. He stared out at the gallery with glassy eyes, seemingly distracted. When Mr. Epson asked him to state his full name, Curley started to come alive and jerked his head to face the county attorney.

"What?"

"I said, state your full name."

"Curley Reber."

Consulting his notes, Epson said, "It says here your name is Charles G. Reber."

"Who? Oh, yeah, I never use the name Charles."

"What is your present occupation?"

Curley answered nervously, "I ain't got none."

"You must do something?" the county attorney persisted.

"Oh, yeah, I forgot. I go part-time to college and farm for my dad the rest."

"So do you consider yourself a student or a farmer?" Epson asked, shaking his head.

Curley was getting flustered. "I ain't very good at neither."

"Pick one."

"Pick one, what?"

Epson threw his arms up in frustration, revealing sweat-stained rings under his arms. "If it will please the court and in order to conserve time, I will answer these questions for the witness."

"Please do," Judge Ballard said, then added, "This one would be a good candidate for law school."

Ignoring this comment, Mr. Epson continued. "The witness's name is Charles G. Reber and, for the record, let's call him a verbally challenged student, in need of more schooling."

"That's fine, Mr. Epson. Proceed with your questioning," Judge Ballard concurred.

"Mr. Reber, are you acquainted with the defendant, Mr. Kunz?" Epson drummed his fingers on his table waiting for an answer.

Finally Curley blurted out, "You talking to me? When you said Mr. Reber, I wasn't sure you were asking me. Nobody calls me Mr. Reber. And, I wasn't sure which Mr. Kunz you were talkin' about neither. Could you repeat the question?"

Epson was now beside himself. "Curley! Do you know Jack?"

Now on more secure footing, Curley grinned nervously. "Sure, we're friends."

"Were you with Jack on the night in question, July third?"

"Yeah," Curley said, now confident he was getting the answers right.

Bugs turned to Jack, covered his mouth and whispered, "I

thought you'd talked to him. Our whole case rests on this imbecile. You said he wouldn't fink."

Before Jack could answer, Epson continued. "So, you were with him at the volcano?"

Curley hesitated.

"Remember your oath, young man."

With his voice cracking and rivers of perspiration running down the sides of his face, Curley stuttered, "N-a-h, no me, Alan, Mick and Jack were in Cedar City chasin' women. Didn't do no good. None of us was at the volcano that night!" Curley grinned.

Bugs slapped Jack on the back as Judge Ballard pounded his gavel.

When order was restored, Epson said, "I have no further questions of this wit—" He paused and gritted his teeth. "This witness."

"Neither do I, Your Honor," Bugsby said, almost cutting into Epson's statement.

Alan Leavitt's testimony, though not quite as colorful as Curley's, was more of the same. After Alan was excused from the witness stand, Judge Ballard turned to Bugsby and declared, "If you're not too incapacitated with glee, let's proceed with the defense witnesses."

Pulling himself up to his full height, Bugs announced, "Your Honor, I would like to make a motion."

"Go ahead, counselor," Judge Ballard said wearily.

"In the interest of time, it's now 4:00 p.m., and because the prosecution has offered absolutely no evidence linking my client with any of these crimes, I would like to move for dismissal on the grounds of lack of evidence."

Judge Ballard sat quietly for a minute, then replied. "I tend to agree with you, counselor. There is no direct evidence implicating Mr. Kunz to the volcano incident. And without a criminal mischief conviction, there is no manslaughter. One is predicated on the other. The rest is a chain of unfortunate events, actions and reactions."

Standing, Judge Ballard replaced his robe, then continued. "That said, I will offer my personal thoughts. There is little doubt in my mind that the defendant is guilty, but the prosecution has failed to prove it. I hope both parties have learned from this little exercise in futility.

Specifically, I hope Mr. Kunz has learned it's a lot cheaper, and a lot less headache, to stay aligned with the proper side of the law. And I hope Mr. Epson has learned that cases should be tried on the evidence, not by personal grudges or vendettas. Case dismissed!"

18

His father's note was concise and contained one item: *Jack, start rounding up the cattle on Utah Hill and hauling them back to the Vineyard Farm. Put them in the Loren Webber piece. You'll need to leave the gate open so they can water in the creek.*

Normally, their cows grazed on the summer range until early October, but with the drought and nothing left to eat and little to drink, it was necessary to move them back to the Santa Clara Valley. There, the cattle could graze on un-cut, withered alfalfa fields. After that, they would feed on the hay Jack had stored throughout the summer. The drought had reduced the summer's yield to only three and a half cuts this year, so there was a good possibility the hay would not last until spring. In that event, the Kunz's would have to haul their cattle to Cedar City to sell at the auction.

All the other ranchers would be doing the same. With a glut of cattle flooding the market, the prices would be down. The only thing that might prevent this from happening was that they didn't have as many cattle to feed this winter. With fifteen-head dying of malnutrition or radiation sickness this summer, depending on whose story you believed, there would be fewer mouths to feed this winter. Jack hoped he would be gone by spring and wouldn't have to listen to his father complain about cattle prices.

It was still early as Jack jammed the stock racks into the metal slots of the flatbed truck. Then he saddled Ginger, leaving the cinch loose for traveling, and loaded her into the flatbed. Jack had briefly thought about taking A.C. instead, but quickly abandoned that idea. He was not in the mood for a rodeo, and anyway, Ginger was a better cutting horse.

Jack donned his dusty, sweat-faded, black Stetson and spent the next hour and forty-five minutes bouncing over the rutted road to the summer pasture.

This gave him plenty of time to think.

The pretense of justice in the courtroom yesterday had left him a little hollow. On the one hand, Jack was grateful for the acquittal. Obviously, he did not want to go to prison, and without that verdict, he would not have been eligible for a mission. But on the other hand, he and Mick were guilty, guilty of most of the things Mr. Epson said they were. It rankled Jack that his vindication had been achieved through a blatant lie, perjury. Without question, the perjury seemed to bother him more than it did Bugs or Curley or Alan. And this was no ordinary fabrication, this was lying after taking an oath to God to tell the truth. So in essence, this lie involved not only the telling of a falsehood to the state, but also lying to God. Why did this seem to bother no one but him? Everyone else had celebrated with Colt 45.

It went against his grain, against all the teachings of his youth, and was definitely in direct opposition to the tenets of the church. In the final analysis, Jack guessed what troubled him was that in the rigid eyes of the church, everything was either black or white, good or bad, Godly or Satanic, but in real life, pragmatism seemed to be fundamental. Sure, there were some solid blacks and some pure whites, but lately there seemed to be a whole hell of a lot of grays mixed in. It seemed to Jack nowadays that everything looked gray whereas, just a few short months ago, he was not even aware that gray existed.

Jack had talked to Bishop Heinke just after the acquittal and he had decided to send his mission papers on to church headquarters in Salt Lake City. He should have his answer in a week or two, but Bishop Heinke assured him there wouldn't be a problem. Jack knew he should be excited. He was twenty-one and going out into the world alone for the first time. This was a major step in his life, and the realization of a lifetime dream, not to mention the fulfillment of his promise to his mother. But somehow, at this moment, the prospect of a mission seemed to lose some of its luster, its urgency, and Jack had to admit, it was not his paramount concern. He was worried about Mick.

Lately, Mick had seemed a little better. His gunshot wound had pretty much healed, though there was still a small raw crater in the skin that had not bridged. The penicillin had killed the bacteria and with the receding infection, Mick's appetite had improved, as had his strength.

The antibiotics, of course, were mostly responsible for Mick's recovery, but Jack figured that his constant prayers and the Elders' blessing for the sick certainly hadn't hurt. He knew it was wishful thinking, but at times he allowed himself to believe Mick might even beat this thing. With God backing him, anything was possible.

Emily was still absent from his life and he thought about her all the time. He wondered if she had heard about his acquittal, or if she even cared. In a town the size of Santa Clara, undoubtedly she'd heard. But Jack doubted she cared, if she did, she sure wasn't showing it.

The flatbed suddenly jolted to a stop at the barb-wire gate and was immediately engulfed in swirling billows of dust clouds that had been dogging the truck for several miles, just waiting for this opportunity to catch up. Jack swatted the dust from his face and eyes, sneezed twice, then trudged over to open the gate.

For the next hour, Jack and Ginger crisscrossed the BLM land gathering cows. They were all alive, and the hide-burns on the sick ones had scabbed over, healed and scarred, leaving barely a trace of the horror he had witnessed earlier in the summer.

Jack and Ginger patiently herded the cows into a cedar-post holding pen that looked like a miniature log stockade of the old west. After he had corralled fifteen, a full load for the flatbed, Jack forced them through a funnel gate, up the fenced board-ramp to the loading dock and onto the flatbed truck. Then he crammed Ginger into the bawling bovine melee, replaced the gate rack and started for home.

With any luck, he would get back to Santa Clara, unload the cows, and get over to see Mick before it got too late. Mrs. Graff had become increasingly rigid about Mick's visiting schedule.

Hours later with displeasure showing like a tear in new Levis, Mrs. Graff escorted Jack up the stairs to Mick's room.

Through the years, it seemed that whenever he and Mick got together, they were in trouble. What one couldn't dream up, concoct or fabricate, the other one would. Usually it was not vicious, criminal stuff, just creative mischief. But Jack had the feeling Mrs. Graff had always blamed him for Mick's roguish activities, and always hoped he would find a better class of friends. Though it was probably his imagination, Jack sometimes had the feeling Mrs. Graff blamed him for the leukemia as well.

Mick was down the hall in the bathroom when Jack entered. His bedroom certainly looked like it was occupied by a sick person. The shades and curtains were drawn and the overall impression was dim, dreary and depressing. Without ventilation from an open window, which Mrs. Graff did not allow for the fear of germs, the air was stale and reeked of body sweat, lard and turpentine. The lard and turpentine meant Mrs. Graff had been applying her vile chest poultice, trying to cure Mick's cough. There was a half-empty water glass on the night stand and a brown bottle of pills. He picked up the bottle and read the label: Demerol. So Mick was on pain killers. That was definitely not a good sign. If he was getting better, why would he still be needing pain killers?

"Hi, J.T., You want to try some Demerol?" Mick said, hobbling into the room and flopping on the bed. "Go ahead, take one. It'll make you feel good."

"I didn't realize you were still in that much pain." Jack frowned.

"It comes and goes. Some days are not too bad, then other days it seems to get to me. Mainly, my stomach in the area of that big spleen." Mick rubbed his abdomen, winced, then continued. "But I'll tell you one thing, the Demerol certainly does help. The world's a better place because of Demerol."

"You seem to be feeling a little better today," Jack said.

"Yeah, I am. Most days all I want to do is sleep, but today I'm bored. Damn Doc Hilton and my mother won't let me leave the house. Afraid I'll get an infection or something."

"What do you want to do?"

"Today, I think I'll drive to Saint George, stop at the Polar Bear for a burger, cruise Main, kick the shit out of Wit, pick up Brenda and go parking on the Red Hill. What you going to do?" Mick grinned, his freckles bouncing and for a moment seeming like his old self.

"You mean I'm not invited?"

"When it comes to parking on the Red Hill, three's a crowd."

"Well, before you go, could I talk you into a game of chess?" Jack said, going along with the joke. "And when I beat you, you can say shit and nobody will care."

"Okay, I'll let you have a half-hour, then I gotta go. I'm a busy man."

"A half-hour is all I need." Jack grinned.

"And then, only if you let me win. Just once before I die, I'd like to whip your ass but good."

In awkward silence, Jack pulled the chessboard down from the dresser and began to set up the pieces. "You want white or black?" he asked, his mood darkening.

"I'll take white. I need every advantage I can get." Mick forced a laugh. "You know, J.T. I am going to die. Only a miracle could save me. Over the years, I haven't deposited much in God's savings and loan, and I'm pretty sure there's not enough in my account," he said moving his queen pawn to B-2.

"I've been praying for you, Mick," Jack said quietly, making his opening move.

"I appreciate that, J.T. You probably don't believe it, but I really do. And, I've had a good life, a short one, but a good one. We've had some good times."

"Sounds like you have no regrets." Jack stared at his friend, forgetting the game.

"Come on, J.T, pay attention. It's your move. Yeah, I've got some regrets," he continued. "I'm starting to regret some of the friggin shit we pulled in the past. I do feel bad about the way I've treated my mother and —" Mick's voice trailed off.

"I know what you mean," Jack said, thinking about his father.

"But, J.T., you know what I regret the most?"

"The sorry way you treated me?" Jack tried to smile.

"I only regret that I couldn't have made your life more miserable," Mick said smiling, then drifting into silence. After a moment, he continued. "But, seriously, what I do regret the very most about my life is that I have never made love to a woman."

"What about Brenda?"

"We've done a lot of touching and feeling, but we've never actually done it. You and Emily?"

"Nah, we came close that night on Utah Hill, but I broke it off. Didn't want to jeopardize my chances for a mission. Now, I kinda wish I had," Jack said, a trace of remorse in his voice.

"If you believe the books and movies, it's supposed to be the ultimate pleasure in life. Hell, it is life, and I have never done it. And from the looks of things, I never will," Mick said. In silence, they moved their chess pieces.

After several minutes, Jack brightened. "Well, what about Brenda? I'll bet she would do it. Why don't I ask her for you?"

"You can't be serious?" Mick said, looking at Jack in amazement. "By God, you are serious. But, I can't even leave the house."

"When does your mother do her grocery shopping?"

"Tomorrow, Wednesdays. She goes to Saint George about one and doesn't return til five. But, Brenda works at the Polar Bear on Wednesdays."

"Well, it won't hurt to ask. I'll give her a call tonight."

"Checkmate!" Mick shouted.

"Shit!" Jack replied, knowing he had not been paying attention.

On his way home Jack was surprised with himself. The morality question of arranging a premarital affair did not bother him. A few months ago he would not have considered such a thing. Had he changed that much in just a couple of months? What seemed like a mortal sin three months ago, now seemed like the right thing to do. It was almost a compassionate service, almost humanitarian.

The more he thought about it, the more Jack felt this was not the kind of favor one asked of a friend over the phone. Abruptly, he slammed on the brakes, made a sharp U-turn, and headed for Brenda's house. As he got out of the car, Jack was amazed at how calm he was. If he were asking for himself, he was sure he'd never be able to get the words out, but asking for Mick was different. He rang the doorbell.

Brenda's father answered the door with a napkin tucked in his belt-line. "Oh Hi, Jack. Haven't seen you in a while."

"Hello, Mr. Frei. How's business at the Merc?" Jack said.

"Business is fine. With all these AEC workers in town, things are hopping. I heard about the trial. Sounds like Sheriff Meecham was just trying to pin the blame on someone and you happened to be his target. Won't you come in?"

"No, I'm filthy. Just got done hauling the cattle off the mountain. Is Brenda in? I need to talk to her for a minute."

"Sure, I'll get her."

As Mr. Frei disappeared into the house, Jack thought he might not be so friendly if he knew why Jack was here. A minute later Brenda appeared, wearing a transparent white cotton blouse that showed her bra, figure-tight, orange-print pedal-pushers and white sneakers.

"Hi ya, Jack. Heard you beat that murder charge yesterday." Brenda had big breasts, but other than that, Jack never could see what Mick saw in her.

"Like I told you, it was manslaughter, not murder. There's a big difference. Anyway, I'm glad that's over." Jack took a deep breath, then asked. "How's Emily doing? Thought I might see her at the trial."

"She's the same as when you asked yesterday. Her hair is starting to come back. Looks kinda like yours." Brenda playfully patted Jack's flat-top. "She lost a lot more hair than me. I just lost a couple of clumps."

"She ever talk about me?" Jack asked, though he was not sure he wanted to hear the answer.

"Yeah, once in a while. She say's you're a nice guy, but that mission thing kinda has her bummed out. How's Mick? I need to get over to see him, but I've been really busy and sick people make me so nervous."

"I know he would be happy to see you."

"What's he got? Anemia or something?"

"No Brenda, he has leukemia." Jack gritted his teeth. "And, he's not doing well. There's no cure for it."

"Really?"

"Really, and he misses you Brenda."

"I miss him too. I like Mick a lot. He's a lot of fun," Brenda said, fiddling with her cardboard-stiff hair.

"Brenda, I'm going to be straight with you," Jack said confidentially. "Mick's dying, he could go at any time. And you know, he's twenty-one and still a virgin."

"Really?"

"I was talking to him today, and he says he has only one wish. He wants to make love just once before he dies. And of all the women in the world, do you know who he would choose?"

"Who?"

"You Brenda, just you and no one else."

"Me?" Brenda giggled.

"Yes." Jack said, trying not to wonder why.

"I don't know, Jack," Brenda said. "You make it sound like an honor, or something, to be chosen."

"Yes, it is an honor Brenda. Think about it. Of all the women he could pick, and Mick has dozens of women to choose from, he chose you. Why? Because he thinks you're special, Brenda. Told me that himself. More than once, he's told me that someday he would like to marry you."

This was turning out to be harder than Jack had imagined.

Brenda frowned. "I just don't want to get pregnant. You know, that can happen."

"Men with leukemia are not capable of having kids," Jack quickly declared, not knowing whether that was true or not.

"And you know there's the church thing. I'd have to confess it to the bishop if he asked. You know how hard that is."

Instinctively, Jack took a chance. "Come on Brenda, it's not like this is your first time."

"Oh, so you heard about Frank! Who told you, Emily?" Brenda shot back, her eyes firing darts.

"No, it wasn't Emily. How about it Brenda? Mick loves you and really, when you think about it, this is compassionate service."

"Could he give me something, I mean a disease, with his anemia and everything?"

Jack masked his thoughts with a tight smile. "Brenda, I assure you, there is nothing communicable about leukemia."

Brenda thought about it for a minute. "Oh, all right," she said. "But only if you tell me who told you about me and Frank."

"Nobody, I just guessed. After all, you dated him for three months."

"Two months. He turned out to be a creep."

"So, you are going to do it?"

"Yes, but only for Mick, cause he's sick and dying." She seemed excited now that she had made her decision. "When and where?"

"Tomorrow at one p.m. at Mick's house. You'll have the whole house to yourself til five."

"But, I've got to work tomorrow." Brenda frowned, then suddenly brightened. "I guess I could call in sick. Everybody else does."

"What a good idea," Jack replied, as he patted Brenda on the arm, said goodnight and headed on home.

Before going to bed, he phoned Mick but was told by his mother that he was sleeping. Jack asked her to tell Mick that everything was arranged for their chest match tomorrow. He knew Mrs. Graff would think he was talking about chess. Reluctantly, she agreed to give Mick the message.

Smiling at how clever he was, Jack went straight to his room, avoiding both Mary and his father who were in the living room watching television. He collapsed on Chris's bed, then rolled over and turned on the radio.

The KSUB disc jockey was in the middle of a public service announcement. "The AEC has announced another test firing for tomorrow. Shot Climax is the last of the eleven shots in the Upshot-Knothole series. Weather permitting, Shot Climax is due to be detonated at five a.m. at the test site in Yucca Flats, Nevada. This may be the last one for a few months. So folks, if you're going to watch this one, you'll have to get up with the chickens," he laughed. "Now, for your listening pleasure, here's a brand new one that's exploding up the charts. You're going to like this one, Chuck Berry with *Maybellene*."

For a moment, Jack thought about going. He had to pick up another load of cows anyway. Why not get up a couple hours early and see the test? But instantly images of sick and dying cows, a bald Emily, and an emaciated Mick waiting to die raced through his mind. There was no way he was going out of his way to see Shot Climax. In fact, Jack decided, he would leave a couple hours later than usual, in case there was another one of those fallout storms. Furious, he slapped the off button on the radio. Did the AEC think they were all fools? Or, did they just not care?

Jack left for Utah Hill around 10:00 the next morning. The more he thought about it, the more upset he got. Goddamn those AEC officials! They had been lying all along. The government knew how dangerous those tests were. That's why they only set them off when the wind was blowing east, he reasoned. It was simply a numbers game. If the wind was blowing south, Las Vegas was at risk. If the wind shifted to the north, then there was Salt Lake City. And God forbid a wind from the east. That would put the fallout in Los Angeles. But not to worry about a wind from the west. To the east of Yucca Flats there was just southern Utah along with a few dumb, patriotic, Mormon farmers and their livestock that were in harm's way.

Jack knew very well how the AEC workers, and the world at large, felt about the Mormons. Most of the country still thought they had a stable full of wives, and dressed in the old Amish style. Surely, they had long flowing beards with no concept of modern technology. The way the workers acted and talked down to the locals, you'd think they were talking to some wild tribesmen who wore bones through their noses, or ate their young. Who would miss a few dumb Mormons?

And if there was no risk, why was the AEC always prowling around with those damn radiation monitors, or pinning radiation badges on the school kids, or trying to buy cows from his father, or covertly buying samples of milk? Perhaps, the milk was just as deadly as the initial fallout.

There was no question, the AEC knew they were doing harm. The other night Rudy Popovich as much as admitted it when he said it was okay that the papers had been thrown in the river, but they better not show up in the wrong hands.

By the time Jack got to the summer range, he was fuming. This was an outrage. He would write a protest letter to his congressman and senators, he decided. But in the likelihood his congressmen did nothing, he should warn the citizens of Washington County. Jack decided he would write a letter to the editor of the *Washington County News* warning about the dangers of radiation. That was the least he could do.

As he gathered the cows, Jack penned the letter word by word in his head. When he got home, he would type it up and send it off. He clenched his jaw with resolve, as he crammed fifteen more cows in the flatbed. He'd have to hurry. With his late start, it would be dark before he got the cows unloaded, and he still wanted to go over and see how Mick's day with Brenda had gone.

It was after 9:00 that evening when Jack knocked on the door. Mrs. Graff scowled and looked at her mantle clock, then let him in, making him promise to make the visit short. Taking the steps two at a time, he bounded into Mick's bedroom.

"Well?"

"Well, what?" Mick said with a grin.

"Whaddyaa mean, well what? I want to hear all about it!"

"Well, I don't think I'll tell you."

"Come on, Mick."

"It was wonderful. Indescribable. I highly recommend it."

"I have never been down that road before. You know that I need details."

For the next fifteen minutes, Mick meted out the juicy details to an astonished and envious Jack.

Finally, it was time to call it a night, Jack stood up and stretched.

"Oh, J.T.," Mick said, as Jack was leaving. "Thanks for today. I know this was hard for you, with the church and everything. You don't know how much it meant to me. J.T., I think you know this already, but I do love you, buddy."

Jack swallowed hard. "Me, too."

19

A week had passed since Jack had brokered Mick's rendezvous. He had seen Brenda at the Polar Bear while getting his usual evening meal. When he asked Brenda about the afternoon with Mick, she just giggled and called him a pimp. Jack guessed that meant she had enjoyed it as much as Mick. However, it still surprised him that he had no pangs of conscience about his part in the affair.

Meanwhile, the *Washington County News* had printed Jack's letter in the same issue that had blazoned headlines: *Saint George Gets Publicity From Atomic Detonations*. His letter was tucked away on the third page and was titled: *An Open Letter To The Citizens Of Washingtion County*. Jack was satisfied with what he had written and felt his letter was succinct, informative, and honest. He had hoped Emily would read the letter and find it polished and educated, like it was written by a college student.

Jack picked up the paper and read it again:

I'm wondering if the citzens of southern Utah have any idea of the possible consequences associated with the recent nuclear tests? I feel morally obligated to warn the people of the irreparable damage that may have occurred or may still be occurring from those tests.

There are several questions the AEC has not satisfactorily answered. 1) What are the long term effects of inhaling air or drinking milk or water contaminated with plutonium? 2) Is there a correlation between exposure to fallout radiation and leukemia? 3) What are the effects of radiation on the mutation rate in humans? In cattle we have seen a bizarre rash of mutations and stillborns since the tests were started. 4) Why is the hair of some of the county citizens falling out? This is a well-known complication of medical cobalt treatments. Is it also a side effect of fallout radiation? 5) What happened to cause the recent highway incident where the AEC felt compelled to wash cars? There is every indication that those cars and their occupants were exposed to many times the safe dose of radiation, yet the AEC steadfastly maintains there was no danger.

In my opinion, the AEC has not been entirely honest or forthcoming with us. We as loyal citizens of the United States of America deserve better. We deserve some answers.

Respectfully,
Jack Tobler Kunz, Santa Clara, Utah

Jack's letter had barely a caused a ripple. Everyone seemed more concerned with the continuing drought, the opening fall football season at Dixie College, and the recent announcement that RKO pictures was going to film a movie, *The Conqueror*, starring John Wayne and Rita Hayworth in nearby Snow Canyon, than they were about some invisible, intangible and highly speculative radiation fallout.

One woman had even asked Jack if he were a communist. Certainly, he was not very patriotic writing such things, she said. It was a good thing his mother wasn't here to see this. One man had vented his irritation by informing Jack that what he needed was two years in Korea. That would certainly straighten out his thinking. In Korea men were not whining about their country, they were dying for it. But mostly, people ignored the letter and assumed he was just another young malcontent.

With the continuing drought and the coming of fall, the farm season was pretty much winding down. A couple of days ago, Jack had brought the last truckload of cows back from Utah Hill. The tomato vines were still producing, though not as heavily, and the apples were almost ready to pick. This year, it seemed, they were ripening early, probably due to the lack of water.

Jack's father wanted him to plow under the alfalfa on the Loren Webber piece. The field had been in hay for too many years and it was not producing well. It was time to rotate the field to barley but with the drought, the clay soil was like concrete, too hard to plow. Yesterday, trying to obey his father's wishes, Jack had snapped the point off the plow. He had left a note informing his father, but he hadn't gotten a note back yet.

Nothing had changed between them and when Jack was honest with himself, he knew this was partly his fault. He had made no efforts to resolve the problem, but then again, neither had his father. For weeks Jack had avoided his family and continued to take his meals at the Polar Bear. Though he hated to admit it, he actually missed their dinner conversations.

Jack had the feeling that his father was just as anxious as he for his mission call to arrive. Not so much now because of the glorious work, but because he simply wanted Jack out of the house. And Jack was doing his best to oblige him. The call should be arriving in the mail any day.

For two or three weeks Mick had seemed to rally, and Jack was convinced that God was responding to the elders' blessing. Unfortunately, that did not last. Lately, Mick had been looking a lot worse. With muscle wasting from malnutrition, the lack of exercise, and the pallor from no sunlight, Mick was beginning to look like a cadaver.

His skin was an anemic grey color, loose and shapeless. It drooped over his bones like a tent after being whipped in a violent wind storm.

Though he continued to pray for Mick, Jack had become discouraged by God's apparent lack of interest. Bitterly, he thought, maybe God has more important things to do, such as the calling of missionaries, like him, to preach the gospel. It appeared that in God's eternal plan, his gospel, it was more important to recruit new members than care for the old ones. In a way, it reminded Jack of the dealership where he had bought his Ford Fairlane. All they cared about was making the sale, but after the transaction was completed, service was almost non-existent.

Jack still visited Mick every day, even though their time together was difficult and depressing. Weakened, Mick often just slept through the visits and only occasionally had much to say. To fill the silent time, Jack often brought something to read. First, he had tried to get through the *Book of Mormon* to prepare for his mission. But somehow that all seemed inconsequential now and he lost interest. He started reading Darwin's *Origin of the Species*. It was way overdue now at the library, so in order to get his money's worth, now that the fine was over five dollars, he had decided to read the damn thing. To his surprise, Jack found that it was not filled with the Simian absurdities that were advertised from the pulpit, but rather, it proved to be a thoughtful and intelligent work.

On one visit, Jack had inadvertently left his copy of the *Book of Mormon* on Mick's night stand, and with some amazement, he noted that his bookmark had been advancing. Obviously, Mick had been reading.

Jack was thinking about that as he listlessly drove down the dusty vineyard road to the farm. Today he had to brand, castrate and de-horn this spring's crop of calves. Unfortunately or fortunately, depending on how you looked at it, that would not be too big of a job this year. With half the calves dead from radiation fallout, there were only about fifteen to do. But six-month-old calves were hard to handle and tried one's physical strength, as well as one's patience.

His father insisted that they wait until the calves were big enough so all three tasks could be performed at the same time. The advantage, you only had to wrestle with the calves once. The disadvantage was at six-months, they were almost too big to handle.

One at a time Jack forced an obstinate, bawling calf into the squeeze-chute. Then he tripped the lever and the side rails closed tight, trapping and immobilizing the calf. Jack quickly pulled a sizzling branding iron from the hot coals and plunged it onto his right rump, burning a charcoal black K. The air was instantly shattered with frantic bellowing and the pungent stench of burning hair and flesh. Bitterly, Jack remembered that right after Chris's death, his father had told him the Bar K Ranch would be his someday. Now, he seriously doubted that would happen. He'd give it to Mary or just sell the damn thing. What the hell, it really didn't matter. He wasn't much of a rancher and he'd be leaving anyway.

After he had completed the branding, Jack pinched off the two horn nubbins with a Barnes dehorner. Quickly, he smothered the bleeding with a thick black-tar unguent and wiped the excess salve on his Levis.

Lastly, with the male calves, Jack took out his pocket knife and made a two-inch incision in the scrotum. Then he popped out the testicle and severed the chord. There was a gush of blood from the spermatic artery but the vessel soon contracted and clotted, and the bleeding slowed to a trickle.

After spending some time in different cow camps, Jack had learned you could get both testicles with one, well-placed, transverse incision. The key was to realize that each testicle was housed in its own separate compartment. The scrotal incision was not sutured and would continue to drain for a couple of days. Jack had heard stories of how the old-timers had castrated using only their teeth, but they certainly had not done this with six-month-old calves.

When he had finished, Jack was spattered with blood, smeared with black-tar unguent, and soiled with fresh manure. He looked more like he'd finished a ten hour shift in a slaughter house than like he had been fixing calves. To stop all the bawling, Jack fed the cows early, then rushed home to clean up. If he hurried, he could finish his evening chores and get over to Mick's before dark. Not only would Mrs. Graff be pleased but he could get out of the house before his father got home.

In less than two hours, Jack pulled up at Mick's and climbed the stairs.

"Hi, Mick. How you feeling?" Jack asked as his friend looked up from his reading.

"Hello, J.T. Thought it was about time for you to show up. Actually, I'm feeling some better. This book kinda lifts my spirits. You know, even though I've been a member of the church all my life, I haven't actually read the *Book of Mormon* before."

Jack was somewhat encouraged by Mick's renewed interest in something. "I'm glad you're feeling better," he replied, happy that Mick wasn't sleeping. "What part are you reading?"

"I've been reading the chapter about Alma the Younger. You know J.T., I really identify with that guy. He was a rebel and a sinner in his youth but when he finally found God, Alma the Younger became a real force for good in ancient America. In those early days, he did some amazing things for God and the church." Mick spoke with more enthusiasm than he had shown in weeks.

"Yeah Mick, I'm familiar with that passage," Jack replied, not sharing his friend's excitement.

"Anyway, I see some real parallels comparing Alma the Younger's life to mine. In his youth, Alma the Younger was a real scoundrel, and so was I. It literally took an act of God to convert him, and it has with me as well," Mick said as he was seized with a fit of coughing.

"An act of God?"

"Yeah, I think me getting leukemia was an act of God. For years, God tried everything else to get my attention and finally he just had to club me over the head."

Jack turned his head and stared at the curtained window. He could not see the logic. It was like trying to make horses out of horse shit. But if this was Mick's way of making sense of the insensible, then he was not going to argue. He bit his tongue and said, "As He did with Alma, perhaps God has a mission, a task for you here on earth. Surely, if God can give you leukemia, He can take it away."

"No, J.T. I'm going to die," Mick replied calmly. "My mission is not here on earth, but up there." Mick pointed upward, then quickly added, "If God can forgive me, that is."

This was too much for Jack, and he exploded into tears. Mick quietly reached over and gently grasped his hand. "Come on, J.T. It's not that bad. You take care of things on earth. I'll do whatever God has planned for me up there, and in a few years we'll see each other again. It'll be okay, time will go by fast."

Jack could think of nothing to say as he sat quietly holding Mick's hand.

"You know what I'd like to do one more time before I die, J.T.?"

"No, I'm not going to ask Brenda again." Jack forced a smile as he wiped his tears. "You're already one up on me."

"Nah, not Brenda. Once was enough. Anyway, now, I'm not so sure God would approve. But, one more time, I'd like to go back to Boy's Pond. We had some good times there, didn't we J.T.?"

"But, Doc Hilton said you should stay indoors." Jack protested.

"Ah, hell, J.T. What difference does it make? Let's go back one more time. Just you and me."

"What about your mother? "

"I'll take care of her. Over the years, I've learned how to do that." Mick smiled as he shifted his shriveled body in the tangled bed.

"If we do, you'd better not get sick."

"I'm already sick, J.T."

Reluctantly, Jack agreed and promised Mick they would go tomorrow. He got up and left, feeling woozy from the suffocating emotion that had flooded Mick's bedroom. It reminded him of an incident years ago when his brother Chris had locked him in the old granary cellar. He had panicked in the dark and frantically tried to claw his way out. He felt the same way in Mick's bedroom. He had to get out of there.

Arriving home, Jack heard the television in the living room blaring the familiar sounds of the *I Love Lucy Show*. Somehow the audience laughter mixed with his father's coarse cackles seemed out of tune for his melancholic mood. After quietly fixing a roast beef sandwich from Mary's dinner leftovers, Jack smuggled the sandwich and a glass of milk to his bedroom and tightly shut the door without being seen. He quickly downed the sandwich, gulped the milk and undressed. Though he felt exhausted as he tumbled into bed, Jack figured this night would be no different from all the others. Sleep, like a disgruntled lover, and like Emily, would pass him by. To divert his mind from a dying Mick, Jack tried to concentrate on Emily. But tonight, to his dismay, she seemed far away and it was difficult to visualize. Her face was fuzzy and indistinct.

As he finally drifted off, Jack saw the God of Michelangelo's Sistine Chapel reaching down to him. But it was Mick's face on God's body that was extending a muscular arm to him. At that same moment, Jack found himself in the middle of a flooded and raging Santa Clara River. Stretching with all his might, God kept reaching out for him, but just as their fingers touched, a torrent of water swept Jack away into a vast unknown. In a panic, Jack forced himself to wake up. Unnerved and perspiring, he stayed awake for the rest of the night trying to figure out what it all meant.

The next morning his father's note stated coldly that he needed at least five lugs of tomatoes, the Jonathan's were ready to pick, and that Jack was to take the plow over to MacGregor welding to be fixed.

Fuming when he read it, Jack knew the apples were ready to pick. Hell, he spent a lot more time in that orchard than his father. And what was the rush to fix the plow? You couldn't plow the Loren Webber field. That ground would just break the plow again.

Anyway, Jack rationalized, in this life surely some things take precedence over tomatoes and apples. He was going to take today off. He and Mick were going to Boy's Pond.

Jack quickly finished the morning chores. He used the rest of Mary's roast beef to make sandwiches, then drove to get Mick.

Mrs. Graff, frustrated, watched from the window as Jack helped Mick to the car. He smiled broadly and waved cheerfully to his mother as they drove off.

The two friends drove down Highway 91 through the canopy of sycamore trees to the center of town, and turned right at Hafen Lane, then followed it to the end. From there, they would walk. With Jack supporting Mick like a drunken friend from a college dance, the two fought their way through the familiar thickets of squaw-bushes and sagebrush. Mick had to rest a couple of times, but they were in no hurry.

When they reached the bank, Mick took off his shoes and socks, then grunted as he sat down heavily and dangled his feet in the tepid water. Jack followed suit. It felt good. The day was hot, the water was cool and the air had the slight fishy smell of drying moss. In comfortable silence, they soaked their feet.

"You know what I was thinking, J.T.?" Mick said, breaking the silence. "I was thinking we should go skinny-dipping like we used to."

"You can't be serious?" Jack replied.

"Yup, I am. The water's warm, and that's exactly what I'm going to do." Mick quickly shed his clothes and slipped bare into the water. After recovering from the shock of seeing Mick's bony, emaciated butt sliding into the water, Jack managed a grin and did the same. Like two pieces of driftwood in a whirlpool, they bobbed around the pond. Once when Jack bumped into Mick, a water fight erupted, but it did not last long. After a short time, Mick was exhausted and dragged himself up on shore and flopped out on the bank spread-eagle, like a turtle sunning on a rock. Jack dunked his head one last time, then joined him.

"How you feeling? You want a roast beef sandwich?" Jack asked anxiously.

"Nope, no sandwich, maybe later. J.T., I feel fine. Just fine." Mick smiled and closed his eyes.

For a fleeting moment, Jack thought this might be it, but Mick's eyes fluttered open. "Too bad we don't have any watermelons. Maybe we ought to sneak upstream and float some down from old man Gubler's patch, like we used to."

"If you want, I'll go do just that. There should be some ripe ones this time of year."

"J.T., I was only joking. But, we sure did have some good times in this pond."

"Remember the time we were playing cowboys and Indians with Greg and Earl? You talked them into hiding in old man Gubler's rabbit pens, cause it was a good place to ambush cowboys. After Greg and Earl crawled into the pens to hide, we latched the pen gates, then came down here to swim. I can still see the shocked look on their faces."

Mick grinned. "Yeah, I can still hear Earl and Greg bellowin' like weaner calves. They got so mad, I was afraid to let them out."

The two friends then fell into a thoughtful silence. Jack suspected they were both thinking of how much they missed their friends.

"Don't forget that time in the sixth grade," Mick said, breaking the silence. "As I recollect, we had a substitute teacher, Miss Stout. I'd imagine she was just out of college. Remember how timid and unsure of herself she was?" Mick smiled weakly and took a deep breath.

"I remember her. It must have been late spring because it was hot and she had all the windows open. The way I remember it, during recess she had refused to come outside with us to play kick-ball. She just turned us loose and sat quietly at her desk reading. Mick, you had some cherry-bombs that day. Don't remember where you got them."

"Stole em from my cousin Rex." Mick chuckled.

"So you sold one to each of the six of us, me, you, Curley, Alan, Greg and Earl for a dime each, when they didn't cost you anything," Jack said, laughing. "Then we took our positions outside a window. On your signal, we lit the fuses and tossed them at poor Miss Stout."

Mick grinned. "I can still hear that explosion. It was deafening.

Miss Stout must have thought the world was coming to an end. She ran out of the school screaming something about how we were trying to kill her. I don't think she ever came back."

"We ran too, afraid Principal Bracken would catch us. Remember, we came down here and hid out all day, swimming and eating old man Gubler's cherries."

"I guess we deserved what the Relief Society sisters called us," Mick said.

Jack snickered."Maybe we are the two worst kids to ever come out of Santa Clara."

"Yeah, we were awful in those days, but we sure had some good times." Mick grinned. "Now, looking back at some of those shenanigans, makes me feel a little ashamed. I hope God will forgive us," he said, his face suddenly serious.

"For that? Those were just kids' pranks."

"No, not just for that. There were other things." Mick closed his eyes and a frown settled on his face.

What's to forgive? Jack thought. It was all innocent fun. Surely, if there is a God, he has a sense of humor.

"Mick, if you're talking about the volcano incident, I still think God will forgive us. We had no intention of hurting anyone."

"No, not the volcano," Mick mumbled and closed his eyes for a moment. "J.T., I'm real tired. Maybe, we'd better head on back."

"Yeah, we should get going. In a few days, after you rest up, maybe we'll do it again."

"Sure, Jack. Real soon. Next time, maybe I'll feel more like eating your dry sandwiches."

"They'll keep. I'll just leave them right here," Jack chuckled. "They should be ripe by then."

"They smell pretty ripe right now."

"Too bad Easy's not here." Jack laughed. "He would eat anything."

Mick struggled to get to his feet. "J.T, give me a hand. I'm beat."

Jack helped with his clothes, then pretty much carried him back to the car. When they got back, Jack lugged him upstairs and gently eased him into bed under the reproachful eyes of his mother.

Mick smiled, patted Jack's hand, thanked him for the day and was asleep within a minute. Jack watched his bony chest heave with each breath, and listened as the air whistled through his vocal chords. His face was drawn and cheek bones protruded, but his freckles still playfully peppered his pale skin. God, how he would miss him. But he didn't want to think about that now. What the hell was he thinking anyway? Mick could go on like this for months. Right now, he just needed some rest.

20

It was 4:00 in the morning when the telephone woke Jack up. He staggered out of bed and collided with his father in the hallway.

"It's for you. Mrs. Graff wants to talk to you," his father said, slapping the phone into Jack's hand. "And I want to talk to you too."

"Hello," Jack mumbled

"Jack, this is Ethel Graff. Mick's real bad," she said, her voice high-pitched and strained. "About midnight he took a turn for the worse. He's got a high fever, shaking chills, and just started bleeding from the bowels. There's a lot of blood. And he won't go to the hospital. He's talking crazy, Jack, says he's ready to die."

"Have you called Dr. Hilton?" Jack said quickly.

"Won't let me," Mrs. Graff said, "Says there's nothing he can do."

"That's not true. He could give him some antibiotics. Do something about the bleeding. Maybe give him a transfusion."

"He won't go. I don't know what to do," Mrs. Graff sobbed.

"I'll be right over," Jack replied, his heart beating rapidly.

"God, I wish you two hadn't gone out yesterday," Mrs. Graff added as phone went dead.

"What's that all about?" his father demanded.

Without answering him, Jack raced to his bedroom, pulled on some clothes, and sprinted for the door.

"Goddamnit, Jack! Don't you dare ignore me. We are going to talk," his father said, blocking the door.

"Mick's in trouble. He needs me. You can move or I'll go through you, makes no difference to me."

They glared at each other for a moment, and then Mr. Kunz stepped aside. As Jack raced for the Fairlane, Mr. Kunz shouted at his back, "I still need yesterday's order. Apples and tomatoes."

Right now, Jack fumed, he didn't have time for his father's shit. Apples and tomatoes, my ass. At a time like this!

What had Mrs. Graff said? Mick was bleeding from the bowels and running a high fever. This time she was probably right. They shouldn't have gone to Boy's Pond. The exertion had not been good for Mick, and God only knew what kind of bacteria he might have picked up in that pond. Cattle drank there and probably shit in it as well.

Also Mrs. Graff had said that Mick was ready to go. Maybe so, but Jack was not ready for that. It was impossible to think of life without Mick. Jack shuddered as he remembered the day his mother died. This couldn't be happening again.

Jack clenched his teeth as he stomped the accelerator. He would convince Mick to go to the hospital. Dr. Hilton could stop the bleeding, give him antibiotics, and maybe a couple pints of blood. Then everything would be all right again.

Jack slammed on the brakes, the Fairlane clipping Mrs. Graff's favorite lilac bush. He bolted out of the car, raced through the front door, and up the stairs. Mrs. Graff was removing Mick's pajamas as Jack entered. They were soggy and stained with blood. Jack went straight to his friend.

"Mick, how are you doing?" Jack asked, as he stared down at the emaciated shell of a human being that was his friend. He touched Mick's forehead. It felt like a furnace. In horror, Jack noticed the pile of blood under Mick's buttocks. The clots were thick and curdled and on the ivory-white sheet they looked like black-current jelly smeared on white bread. The odor coming from the bed was pungent, almost nauseating.

It was odd, Jack thought, that in spite of these desperate circumstances, Mick was tightly clutching a wad of notepaper in his right hand.

"I'm fine J.T., just fine. But, I'm glad you came anyway," Mick whispered.

"Mick, we've got to get you to the hospital. Doc Hilton will know what to do."

"Nah, Jack. There's nothing he can do. I hate hospitals. Kinda like my own bed." Mick smiled weakly.

"Doc Hilton said they could treat the complications. You're probably bleeding from a spot in the colon," Jack said urgently. "They could radiate it or something, and stop the bleeding."

"I've had enough radiation. I don't want to keep going through this week after week"

"Mick, we've got to do something."

"No, we don't. I'm ready. I've made my peace. I just want to die in my own bed surrounded by my family and friends. And, that is exactly what I've got now. No hospital, J.T.," Mick groaned, forcing more black clots from his bowels.

This amount of bleeding had Jack worried. Mick was already anemic. At this rate, he wouldn't last long.

"Mick, there's no need to do this. Even the church tells us, God helps those who help themselves. Let's get you to the hospital, get an IV in you, transfuse some blood, and then Doc Hilton can work on you. Let's do everything we can. Then we'll leave the rest to God," Jack pleaded, though nowadays he was reluctant to leave anything to God.

"No, J.T. It's like us running around in the desert. You knew when to quit."

"But that was different."

"No, it's the same. Anyway, I've been talking with God, and I know this is for the best. He's got plans for me."

"Mick, don't do this to me!"

"J.T., this not about you. It's my time to move on." Mick moaned as his colon contracted again. "It's not like we're never going to see each other again. Jesus said to his disciples, 'I go to prepare a place for you.' I'll be there when you come." Mick smiled feebly and groped the air, searching for Jack's hand.

"Mick," Jack pleaded, tears running down his cheeks. "Mick, I don't know what to say."

"Don't say anything. Your friendship has said it all." Mick's voice was barely a whisper.

"God gave me a rare gift when he allowed me to be your mother," Mrs. Graff said, bending over to kiss him.

"I love you, Mother," Mick murmured.

Mick peacefully closed his eyes and Jack felt his throat tighten. After a moment he gasped and opened his eyes again. "Jack, promise me, you'll go on your mission. You'll have to go for both of us."

Why were his loved ones always dying, Jack thought, and when they died, why did they always make him promise things? Especially, about that damn mission. Did they think without some kind of deathbed oath, he would go astray? Quickly, Jack contained his frustration. This was not the time or place. As Mick had just said, this was not about him.

Jack leaned over. "I promise, Mick. I'll go for both of us."

"And go to medical school. You're meant to be a doctor." Mick paused, his chest hardly moving. "And call Emily. I think she's right for you."

"I'll try, Mick."

"J.T.," Mick said, his voice barely audible. "I hate to do this to you, but I've got to tell someone." Then he thrust the crumpled piece of paper that he had been clutching into Jack's hand.

"I love you, J.T. See you in a few years," Mick mumbled, his eyes glazing over.

Jack kissed him on the forehead as a serene smile spread across his face. Then Mick closed his eyes.

Mick's respirations became progressively more shallow and more irregular. It was difficult to tell when his breathing actually stopped. It just seemed to slowly fade away with longer and longer gaps between gasps of air. The tranquil smile, however, did not fade. Through his tears, Jack was scarcely able to see his wristwatch. Michael Graff died somewhere around 5:30 a.m. on September the 14th.

Jack suddenly panicked. The walls were caving in. He dropped Mick's already cold hand and without saying a word to Mrs. Graff, bolted from the bedroom. He craved some fresh air and to be alone.

In a daze he stumbled into his car and roared out of the driveway. Oh, God, Mick was dead. This was unbelievable. One minute you're alive, talking, arguing and the next minute you're nothing. Gone! How is this possible?

Was nothing permanent? Was there no constant in this chaotic universe? God was supposed to be eternal. He was the only thing in the universe that was. And even at that, it was difficult to use him for an anchor. God seemed to enjoy toying with humans, giving and taking life on a whim, using people like pawns in some sick cosmic chess game. It was impossible to trust someone so capricious.

The problem with God is you never knew what to expect. The only certainty with God, was that regardless of what happened, it was always for your own good. Floods, drought, famine, wars all serve a purpose. Even if the only purpose was to teach humility and dependence on God. That was some racket! It was no wonder the church preached that we couldn't understand the workings of God.

On his deathbed, Mick was convinced he was going to a better life. But was he? It made a great story, and it certainly helped ease the sorrow of death. Maybe that was the very reason the idea of life after death was invented. Man just could not deal with the thought of his own demise. It was eerie, Jack had to admit.

But to contemplate life without Mick was a frightening thing. His life would be empty. Without Mick, he had no companion, no confidant. Jack had been closer to him than any other human being. No one could fill that void. Certainly, not his own family, or even Curley or Alan. For a time, Jack had thought he might achieve that kind of relationship with Emily, but obviously that wasn't going to happen.

Startled from his thoughts by a looming barb-wire gate, Jack slammed on the brakes. He missed the gate by inches. From habit he had driven down the Vineyard Road to the farm. While I'm here, Jack thought, I might just as well pick those goddamn tomatoes for dad. It would be therapy. He needed something to occupy his hands and divert his mind.

Jack got out of the car to unfasten the wire loop around the gate, then realized with surprise that he still had Mick's paper clutched in his hand. Mechanically, he started unfolding the note. Deep down, Jack knew this was probably a farewell. Things Mick wanted to say, but could not put into words. Tears welled in his eyes again. His emotions just could not handle another goodbye.

What had Mick said when he gave him the note? "I hate to do it to you, but I had to tell someone." Whatever the hell that meant. After smoothing out the wrinkles against the Fairlane's fender, Jack took a deep breath.

Dear J.T.,

I hate to burden you with this, but I feel I must confess it to someone. Sorry about the note, I tried to tell you face-to-face several times, but somehow I never could. In a way, I guess I was selfish. I was afraid if I told you it would change our friendship. Anyway, remember that night when we went to the hospital to visit Easy Earl, and I was worried that if he woke up from his coma he might talk? I made sure he didn't wake up. Later that night, I killed Easy with a pillow, or at least I think I did. It was dark, so I'm not absolutely sure he was still breathing when I entered his room, but I know he wasn't when I left. Now, I'm so sorry that I did it, J.T., and I am very worried about my mortal soul. I hope I don't burn in hell.

Your friend forever,

Mick

Jack dropped the note as if it was the business end of a hot branding iron. What the hell was this? Mick had killed Easy? No, this had to be Mick's last ditch effort at a practical joke. Jack's head was spinning. He stumbled to a ditch bank and sat down. Was this why Mick had suddenly found religion? Was this why he had been reading the *Book of Mormon*? Why he kept asking about repentance and if some sins were not forgivable? Why he insisted that Jack did not know everything?

What if the teachings of the church were true? That there was no forgiveness for blasphemy against the Holy Ghost or murder. Where did that leave Mick? Certainly not in the Celestial Kingdom. Did this mean that for time and eternity he would never see Mick again? Was he a Son of Perdition? But Mick had said, "I'll see you in a few years?" Was this a joke? Did dying men joke? Did Mick really think he was going to heaven?

Bitterly, Jack wondered if he still loved Mick. Could he love a murderer? How the hell could Mick do this? Why hadn't he told him sooner? If he had known sooner, Jack had to admit, it would have changed their relationship.

He should report this to the authorities, to Chief Callahan. But what purpose would that serve? It would just create more agony for two families who were still suffering from the losses of their loved ones. And certainly, the state could not punish a murderer who was already dead. In this instance, justice belonged to God. If indeed there was a God. If not, then Mick just got off scot-free with murder.

Shaking, Jack returned to the car and drove through the gate, then re-latched it. There were just too many hard questions with no easy answers. It might take him years to sort it all out.

Still consumed by the enormity of it all, Jack strapped on the canvas picker and started down the first row of tomatoes. Staked up with cedar posts tied with twine and free of weeds, the tomato rows looked like long columns of manicured hedges, but to Jack they just looked like death. With their leaves already turning brown, they too would be dead in a few weeks.

Mechanically, he brushed aside the leaves and parted the vines, looking for the red or pink ones. He'd have to pick everything with a hint of color if he was going to get five lugs. The vines were just not producing as well as his father thought. After all, it was mid-September and there was a drought.

Jack plucked a tomato from the vine and stared at it for a few moments. Was this the meaning of life? Work your ass off for a few years, make enough money to pay your bills, then you die. After death, then what? For Mick, if you believe the church, an eternity of hell. For the non-believers, an eternity of oblivion. Which was better? In despair, Jack heaved the tomato. It sailed over the patch and landed in the Loren Webber piece. Right now he just could not do this. He took off the picker, dropped it in the tomato row and briskly walked to the car.

For a brief moment, Jack had the fleeting thought that he'd better hurry so he could get over to see Mick before it got too late for Mrs. Graff's visiting hours, then reality came crashing home. There was no hurry. He'd never see Mick again. Nor would he see Greg or Easy. In one summer, three out of six, fifty percent, of them were dead. And, what about what Mick did to Easy? How could Mick do that to Easy? My God, murder! What he really needed right now was a drink.

Jack headed for Saint George and bought a six-pack of Colt 45 at the State Liquor Store, then drove slowly back to Santa Clara ending up at Hafen Lane. For a minute he rested his head on the steering wheel, then he grabbed his six-pack and got out of the car.

Picking his way through the tenacious squaw bushes, Jack finally arrived at Boy's Pond. It seemed like more than a mere twenty-four hours since he and Mick had floated and splashed in these waters, reliving old times. It felt like an eternity. Jack kicked off his shoes and slumped down on the bank.

After a minute, he fished in his pocket for a beer opener, then punched two holes in the can. In the darkness he finished the six-pack as he listened to the sounds of frogs and crickets. He could hear the soft sound of the water rippling in the canal. To the rest of the world, nothing had changed.

As he listened to the symphony of the pond, tears began to flow. "Goddamn you, Mick," was all he could say, over and over again.

21

Jack awoke the next morning with a hellish headache and a sour stomach. Yesterday's events dawned on him heavily like the gloom of winter. For a moment he wondered if they had really happened. He looked around his bedroom. His clothes were in a heap on the floor and sunlight was pouring in through the east window. On the surface, nothing had changed.

He was just staggering out of the house to do morning chores when the phone rang.

"Jack," Mrs. Graff said. "Thank you for all you did."

"I'm sorry, Mrs. Graff. Sorry, I couldn't do more."

"We did all we could. I wanted to let you know Mick's funeral will be at the chapel day after tomorrow at four in the afternoon."

"I'll be there," Jack said tiredly, as he rubbed the pain from his temples.

"He wanted you to speak at the funeral. That was one of his requests. I haven't worked out the entire program yet, but for the speakers, I think it appropriate that Bishop Heinke talk, then you."

"I don't know, Mrs. Graff," Jack replied, not sure how he felt after having read Mick's note. "I'm not sure I'm the right one. How about his Priests Quorum President, or his Sunday School Teacher?"

"You were his best friend, Jack. You two were like brothers. He requested you. It's the least you can do."

"You're right, Mrs. Graff," Jack said, feeling ashamed. "I owe him that."

"And Jack," Mrs. Graff said. "I want you to know, I don't hold you responsible for all that's happened to Mick. I realize that part of it was Mick's doing. Even that trip to Boy's Pond."

For a moment Jack was silent. He wondered which part of Mick's life she did not hold him responsible for. Perhaps, the part about murder. That was all Mick. "I appreciate knowing that, Mrs. Graff," he said, as he ground his teeth.

Jack hung up and drove to the orchard. He still had to finish picking the apples and tomatoes. Also, the cattle had pretty much grazed alfalfa stubble to bare ground. Today, he would have to start feeding them hay. The work occupied his hands, but left his mind to consider everything that had happened.

With mixed emotions, Jack had accepted Mrs. Graff's invitation. It would really be hard to speak at the funeral, almost impossible for him to rein in his emotions. What would he say? It would be impossible to find words that would genuinely convey his feelings, Jack thought. And, right now, he was not sure what his feelings were. Was Mick a true friend or a murderer? Was it possible to eulogize a murderer? At least he had a couple of days to think about it.

The day of the funeral dawned with a few maverick clouds floating in the sky, looking out of place in the immaculate, azure-blue. Though it was still warm, the oppressive heat had pretty much abated, replaced by the milder air of fall. By noon, the clouds had condensed and darkened and at 4:00 p.m. the sky had become dull, overcast and dreary. This weather, Jack thought, was appropriate for the occasion, and it reflected his own gloomy disposition.

Jack had trudged the two short blocks from his house to the chapel trying to organize his thoughts for the eulogy on the way.

As he approached the church, Jack considered not going in at all. He thought about how nice it would be to just keep walking. In his frame of mind, he shouldn't be giving Mick's eulogy anyway. He paused at the sidewalk that led to the front door. Longingly, he gazed down Highway 91, then with hands in his pockets and head downcast, he turned toward the chapel.

Once inside, Jack immediately spotted Witless Walt Hafen. Jack had not seen Witless since the fight at the old airport hanger, and he certainly was not in the mood for any of his shit today. Abruptly turning, Jack tried to duck into the chapel.

"Hey, Jack! Hold up.I want to talk to you," Walt shouted across the foyer.

Braced for the worst, Jack doubled his fists. Even the new and reformed Mick, Jack thought, would not object if he were to belt Walt right here in church. "Yeah, Walt. What do you want?"

Jack flinched as Walt offered his hand. "Jack, I just want to tell you how sorry I am about Mick. I know you must miss him as much as I miss Greg. Anyway, I just wanted to tell you how sad I am at Mick's passing." Walt squeezed Jack's hand one last time before walking away.

Jack was stunned. He was not entirely sure that he could believe what had just happened. Walt Hafen expressing his sorrow in complete, sincere and articulate sentences, then extending a hand in friendship. This was unbelievable.

Shaking his head in disbelief, Jack turned and entered the chapel. Jack looked around the congregation, his pulse quickening when he spotted Emily sitting next to Brenda in the back row. She appeared to be engaged in quiet conversation with Brenda. For a brief second, Jack though he caught her eye. Maybe not. She either didn't notice him, or ignored him.

He looked around again. Not surprising, his father was not there, but there was Smoky Grayman sitting by himself on the fifth row next to the aisle. Even though the chapel was filled to capacity and the overflow room had been opened, there was still enough space next to Smoky for three more people. His long gray-black hair was combed and he was wearing a pressed, white cotton long-sleeved shirt with brown slacks, and no reservation hat. This was the first time Jack had seen Smoky look, well, almost respectable.

Heads turned as Jack moved slowly down the aisle. Everyone knew he and Mick had been like brothers. Jack stopped at the fifth row, and tapped Smoky on the shoulder.

"*Yaa' eh t'eeh*, Smoky."

"*Yaa' eh t'eeh*, Jack," he replied. His usually immutable black eyes appeared more soft and readable today.

Jack paused a minute, his hand resting on Smoky's shoulder, then continued down the aisle toward the speakers' platform.

With his emotions barely under his skin, Jack made his way to the raised platform behind the podium. As a speaker, he would sit with priesthood officials, and the other people participating in the funeral. Jack glanced at Bishop Heinke as he made his way on to the platform. The bishop nodded to Jack.

"I'm sorry about Mick. I know how tough this is for you."

"You have no idea," Jack mumbled.

"I know you've had a lot to deal with." The bishop stood up and placed a hand on Jack's shoulder. "But do you have your speech ready?"

"Not completely. I just don't know what to say."

"Put your trust in God and it will come to you," Bishop Heinke said, smiling as he patted Jack's shoulder. "This is good training for your mission."

Jack sat down, and picked up the mimeographed program that had been placed on every seat. It was about what he had expected. The opening prayer would be given by an uncle, Adolf Graff. Next, the congregation would sing, "Nearer My God to Thee." Then, Bishop Heinke would speak. Following the bishop's remarks, the Relief Society sisters would sing, "God Be With You, Til We Meet Again," and the next speaker would be Brother Jack Kunz. Finally, the congregation would sing "Tis Eventide" and the benediction would be given by Chief Wade Callahan. Following the service, internment would be at the Santa Clara Cemetery. Bishop Heinke would dedicate the grave.

Jack's mind was awash during the opening prayer and first hymn. He was frantically searching for the right things to say. But when Bishop Heinke got up to speak, Jack found himself concentrating on the Bishop's speech.

"My brothers and sisters, I wish I didn't have to be here today. Certainly, I would rather be picking my apples or pears than con-ducting another funeral. Nevertheless, we are here. Here to honor the life and times of our brother Michael Graff, and to try to make some sense of this tragedy. Why should someone so young, so vibrant, be snatched away from us in the prime of his life? Especially when he has done nothing to deserve this fate. He wasn't racing a car at high speeds, nor was he drinking and driving, or acting foolishly. So why does Michael Graff deserve this fate?"

Why indeed, Jack thought.

"Perhaps we're looking at this all wrong, approaching it from an improper point of view. Have you considered the possibility that this is not a tragedy at all, but a blessing in disguise? It is conceivable that Mick Graff is in a far better place."

And, it's conceivable that he's not, Jack speculated in his mind.

"Through the years, there is one thing I have learned. There is a purpose and season for everything. There is no question in my mind that God had a reason for calling Mick back. Undoubtedly, he needed Mick for some glorious work waiting to be done in heaven, a mission."

A mission indeed, Jack thought bitterly. Yes, I'm sure God has a lot of celestial work and a number of missions for murderers.

"Just because we don't understand it, does not make it any less true. Here on earth, we must have faith, but someday all this marvelous plan of God's will be revealed to us. Right before his death, I visited with Mick in his home. He was convinced that God had a mission for him to perform. And, I might add, Mick's testimony was strong before he died. He was an amazing and wonderful young man."

Amazing, yes. I am still amazed at what he was capable of doing. Wonderful, I'm not so sure, Jack thought, staring at the ceiling.

"We will miss him. But take consolation in the fact that right now he is with God and in a few short years, we all will be reunited with him in the bosom of God."

That's a laugh, Jack though almost out loud, unless we all meet in the bosom of Lucifer.

"Brothers and sisters, let me tell you once again that I know this is the true church, that Jesus is the Christ, and that Joseph Smith is a prophet of God. I say these things humbly and sincerely in the name of Jesus Christ, Amen." Bishop Heinke then slowly sat down, wiping the tears from his gnarled face.

Suddenly, Jack's mind went blank and the blood rushed from his head. He tried desperately to recall the few words he had managed to come up with as the Relief Society sisters sang.

With growing panic, Jack slowly approached the podium. The congregation hushed and even the babies stopped crying. Tears streamed down his cheeks and he gripped the podium feeling faint, his tongue thick and dry. He stared out at the congregation, his kin, his neighbors and friends in painful, awkward silence. With his right hand he brushed away the tears and swallowed hard.

Struggling to choke back the tears, he blurted in a husky voice, "This may sound strange to you, but I think I can now tell you with some certainty that I loved Michael Graff. Other than that, regardless of what Bishop Heinke says, none of the rest of this makes any sense at all to me!"

With that, Jack stumbled back to his seat unaware of the stunned congregation and the look of disdain hurled by Mrs. Graff or the look of disappointment on Bishop Heinke's face. But there was a smile of satisfaction, almost pride, on Smoky's leathery face.

Jack was almost oblivious to the rest of the service. He did not notice the fervor as the congregation sang the closing hymn nor did he hear Chief Callahan when he asked God to shed some of his glorious light on his obviously troubled son, Jack Kunz, in his benediction.

Then the pallbearers, including Jack, Curley and Alan, lugged the casket to the waiting black hearse, and the funeral party departed for the melancholic red sands of the Santa Clara cemetery.

Jack hurried home to get his car and drove the two miles in silence and sick at heart. Dispassionately, he noted the sky had blackened and a mammoth bank of clouds seemed to hang over the cemetery, throttling the sunlight.

Jack stood slightly apart from the other mourners and listened in anguish as Bishop Heinke dedicated the grave for the housing of Mick's mortal body, charging God with the safe keeping of his eternal soul.

Then, the Elders positioned themselves on each side of the casket. As they slowly lowered Mick into the ground, Jack felt water drops on his face. Soon they were fiercely pounding on the casket, creating a hollow, lonely sound.

Unbelievable, after all these months, it had started to rain.

Through bitter tears, Jack watched as the elders shoveled the red sand on top of his friend.

Thud—thud—thud.

Suddenly, Jack felt a slim arm around his waist. Slowly, he raised his eyes from the grave.

" Emily," he whispered.

AFTERWORD

From October 22, 1951 to January 1, 1963, the Atomic Energy Commission, under the auspices of the United States Government, detonated one hundred and twenty-six nuclear devices at the Nevada Test Site in Yucca Flats, Nevada. At that time, the only other major nuclear test facilities were located at the various atolls and islands of the Marshall Islands. One hundred and five shots were tested above ground in the Pacific. In 1963 the tests were moved underground in accordance with a newly-signed agreement with the Russians to ban atmospheric testing.

As was their protocol, the AEC would only detonate the "shots" when the winds were favorable. This meant a dependable, and strictly easterly flow. With a west wind, there were not any immediate densely populated areas and certainly no cities of any magnitude at risk. To the northeast of Yucca Flats was Salt Lake City; to the south, Las Vegas; and to the west was Los Angeles. At the time, it was inconceivable that the AEC would conduct any test under conditions other than a strict easterly wind, and indeed, many tests were canceled when the winds were not right. People living in the path of this easterly flow became known as the downwinders.

During those twelve years, and for decades after the tests went underground, the rate of leukemia deaths more than doubled in southern Utah, as did deaths from solid tumors such as thyroid cancer, lymphoma, breast cancer, pancreatic cancer, lung cancer and gastric cancer.

On August 30, 1979, the Irene Allen vs. United States suit was filed in the U.S. District Court by twenty-four of the downwinder plaintiffs. This case was heard by Federal Judge Bruce Jenkins who eventually ruled in favor of ten of the twenty-four plaintiffs. In his written opinion of May 10, 1984, Judge Jenkins concluded:

1. The AEC programs at the NTS (Nevada Test Site), public safety and monitoring fallout were badly flawed.

2. The information given to the downwinders was deficient.

3. There was a failure to inform.

4. There was a failure to monitor adequately.

5. There was a failure to explain the increased risks to children.

6. There was a failure to advise people who were at risk about simple things they could do to minimize danger.

7. There was a general failure to inform the public of the nature and extent of the hazards and of the precautions they could take to minimize the danger to themselves and their children.

Finally, Judge Jenkins concluded that the AEC operatives "negligently and wrongfully breached their duty of care to the plaintiffs as off-site residents placed at risk."

The U.S. government appealed the decision and managed to successfully tie up the adjudication. Two years later, the 10th Circuit Court of Appeals in Denver reversed Judge Jenkins' judgement. The case was then appealed to the Supreme Court of the United States. In January of 1988, the Supreme Court refused to hear the case, thus ending the legal challenges.

Two years prior to the Allen suit, the 1977 Congress had passed the Marshall Islands Compensatory Act which offered monetary redress to the islanders. But, it was not until 1990 that Congress enacted the Radiation Exposure Act that included compensation for the downwind victims of southern Utah. This was a baffling thirty-nine years after the testing began at Yucca Flats, and thirteen years after the Marshall Islanders were compensated. In the year 2000, the Radiation Exposure Act was amended to include a few more classes of solid cancers.

Presently, hundreds of cancer victims, or their families, have been compensated and many more were filing for compensation as this book was written. However, we are constantly reminded this is an ongoing tragedy, as new cancers are diagnosed almost daily in many of the heretofore unscathed, downwinder veterans.